Eight for Losing, One for Loving

Wicked Sons Book 9

By Emma V. Leech

Published by Emma V. Leech.

Copyright (c) Emma V. Leech 20

Editing Services Magpie Literary Services

Cover Art: Victoria Cooper

ISBN No: 978-2-487015-45-6

About Me!

I started this incredible journey way back in 2010 with The Key to Erebus but didn't summon the courage to hit publish until October 2012. For anyone who's done it, you'll know publishing your first title is a terribly scary thing! I still get butterflies on the morning a new title releases, but the terror has subsided at least. Now I just live in dread of the day my daughters are old enough to read them.

The horror! (On both sides I suspect.)

2017 marked the year that I made my first foray into Historical Romance and the world of the Regency Romance, and my word what a year! I was delighted by the response to this series and can't wait to add more titles. Paranormal Romance readers need not despair, however, as there is much more to come there too. Writing has become an addiction and as soon as one book is over, I'm hugely excited to start the next so you can expect plenty more in the future.

As many of my works reflect, I am greatly influenced by the beautiful French countryside in which I live. I've been here in the Southwest since 1998, though I was born and raised in England.

My three gorgeous girls are all bilingual and my husband Pat, myself, and our four cats consider ourselves very fortunate to have made such a lovely place our home.

KEEP READING TO DISCOVER MY OTHER BOOKS!

Other Works by Emma V. Leech

Wicked Sons

Wicked Sons Series

Daring Daughters

Daring Daughters Series

Girls Who Dare

Girls Who Dare Series

Rogues & Gentlemen

Rogues & Gentlemen Series

The Regency Romance Mysteries

The Regency Romance Mysteries Series

The French Vampire Legend

The French Vampire Legend Series

The French Fae Legend

The French Fae Legend Series

Stand Alone
The Book Lover (a paranormal novella)
The Girl is Not for Christmas (Regency Romance)

Audio Books

Don't have time to read but still need your romance fix? The wait is over…

By popular demand, get many of your favourite Emma V Leech Regency Romance books on audio as performed by the incomparable Philip Battley and Gerard Marzilli. Several titles available and more added each month!

Find them at your favourite audiobook retailer!

Acknowledgements

Thanks, of course, to my wonderful editor Kezia Cole with Magpie Literary Services

To Victoria Cooper for all your hard work, amazing artwork and above all your unending patience!!! Thank you so much. You are amazing!

To my BFF, PA, personal cheerleader and bringer of chocolate, Varsi Appel, for moral support, confidence boosting and for reading my work more times than I have. I love you loads!

A huge thank you to all of my beta readers and cheering section! You guys are the best!

I'm always so happy to hear from you so do email or message me :)

emmavleech@orange.fr

To my husband Pat and my family ... For always being proud of me.

Table of Contents

Family Trees

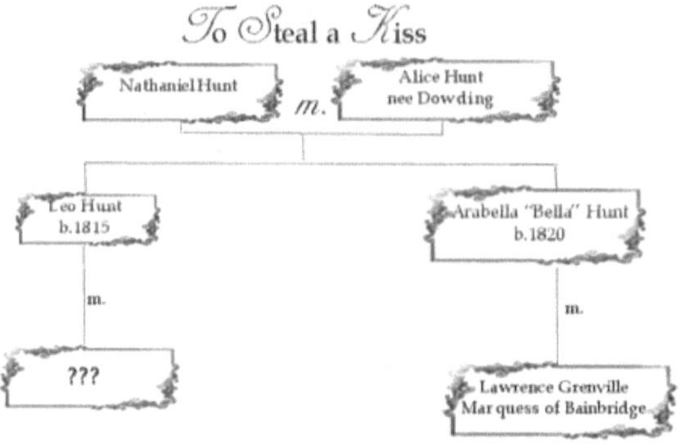

HOUSE OF BEDWIN
To Dare a Duke

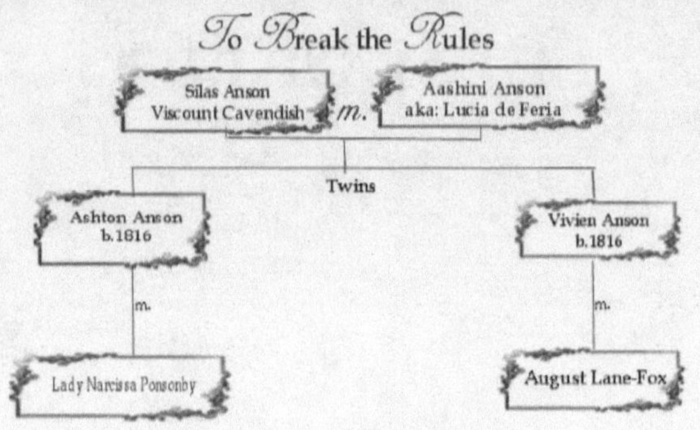
HOUSE OF CAVENDISH
To Break the Rules
Silas Anson
Viscount Cavendish
m.
Aashini Anson
aka: Lucia de Feria
Twins
Ashton Anson
b.1816
Vivien Anson
b.1816
m.
m.
Lady Narcissa Ponsonby
August Lane-Fox

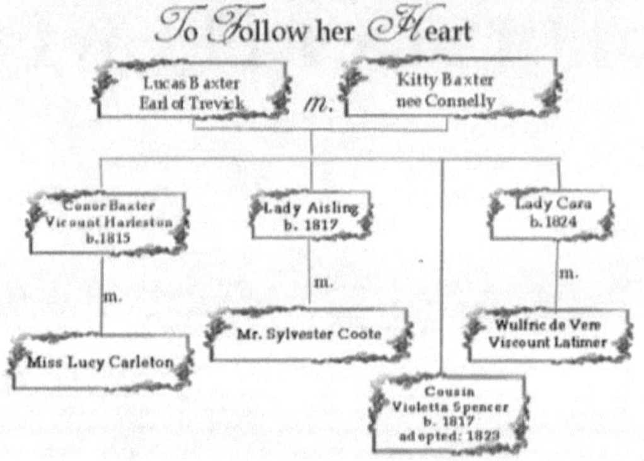
HOUSE OF TREVICK
To Follow her Heart
Lucas Baxter
Earl of Trevick
m.
Kitty Baxter
nee Connelly
Conor Baxter
Viscount Harleston
b.1815
Lady Aisling
b. 1817
Lady Cara
b. 1824
m.
m.
m.
Miss Lucy Carleton
Mr. Sylvester Coote
Wulfric de Vere
Viscount Latimer
Cousin
Violetta Spencer
b. 1817
adopted: 1823

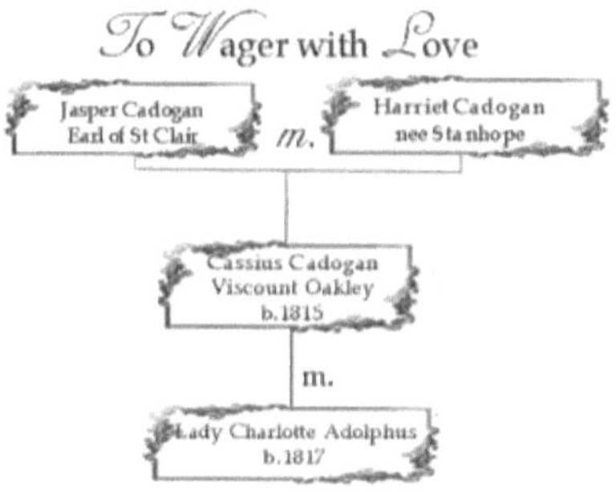

HOUSE OF ST CLAIR
To Wager with Love
Jasper Cadogan
Earl of St Clair
m.
Harriet Cadogan
nee Stanhope
Cassius Cadogan
Viscount Oakley
b.1815
m.
Lady Charlotte Adolphus
b.1817

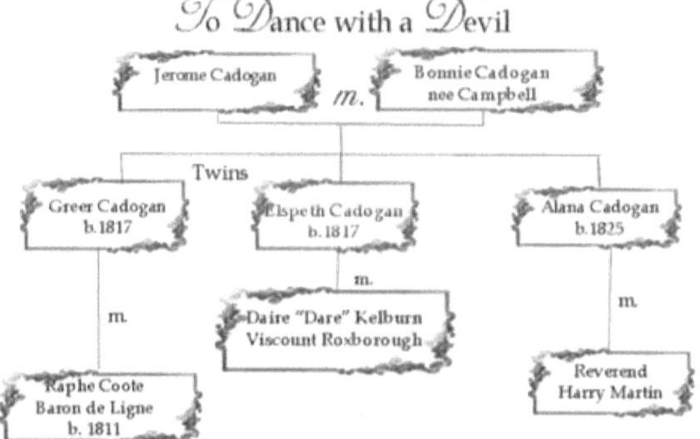

HOUSE OF CADOGAN
To Dance with a Devil
Jerome Cadogan
m.
Bonnie Cadogan
nee Campbell
Twins
Greer Cadogan
b.1817
Elspeth Cadogan
b.1817
Alana Cadogan
b.1825
m.
Daire "Dare" Kelburn
Viscount Roxborough
m.
m.
Raphe Coote
Baron de Ligne
b. 1811
Reverend
Harry Martin

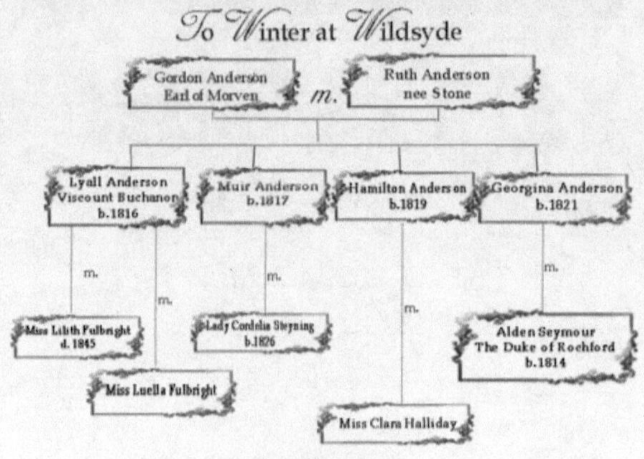
HOUSE OF MORVEN
To Winter at Wildsyde
Gordon Anderson
Earl of Morven
m.
Ruth Anderson
nee Stone
Lyall Anderson
Viscount Buchanon
b.1816
Muir Anderson
b.1817
Hamilton Anderson
b.1819
Georgina Anderson
b.1821
m.
m.
m.
m.
Miss Lilith Fulbright
d.1845
Lady Cordelia Steyning
b.1826
Alden Seymour
The Duke of Rochford
b.1814
Miss Luella Fulbright
Miss Clara Halliday

HOUSE OF DE BEAUVOIR
To Experiment with Desire
Inigo de Beauvoir
m.
Minerva de Beauvoir
nee Butler
Hartley de Beauvoir
(adopted at Age 6)
b.1809
Kathleen de Beauvoir
(adopted at birth)
b.1824
m.
m.
Lady Fidelia Ponsonby
Maxwell Drake
The Earl of Vane

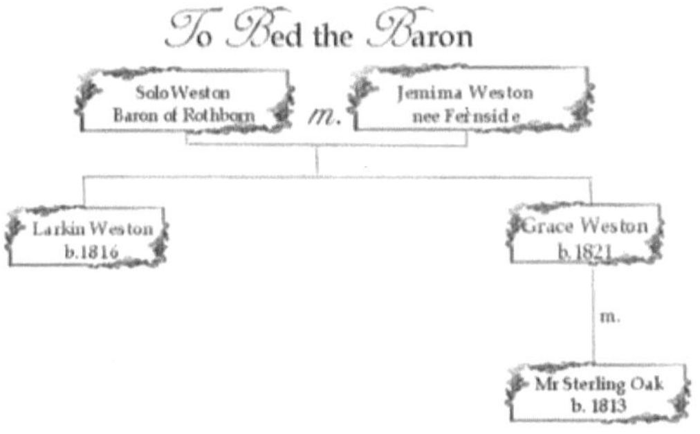

HOUSE OF ROTHBORN
To Bed the Baron
Solo Weston
Baron of Rothborn
m.
Jemima Weston
nee Fernside
Larkin Weston
b.1816
Grace Weston
b.1821
m.
Mr Sterling Oak
b. 1813

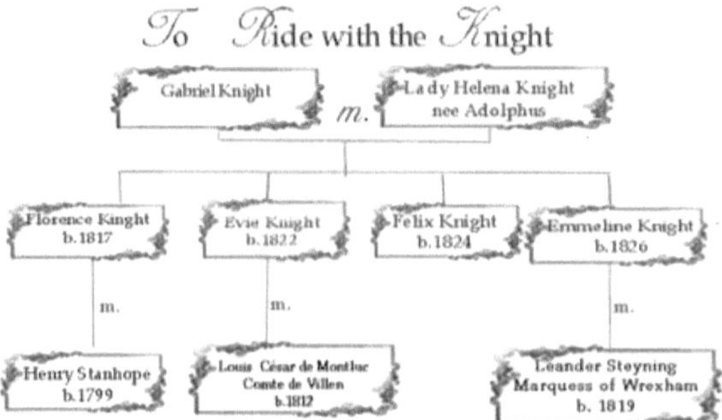

HOUSE OF KNIGHT
To Ride with the Knight
Gabriel Knight
m.
Lady Helena Knight
nee Adolphus
Florence Knight
b.1817
Evie Knight
b.1822
Felix Knight
b.1824
Emmeline Knight
b.1826
m.
m.
m.
Henry Stanhope
b.1799
Louis César de Montluc
Comte de Villon
b.1812
Leander Steyning
Marquess of Wrexham
b. 1819

HOUSE OF MONTAGU
To Hunt the Hunter

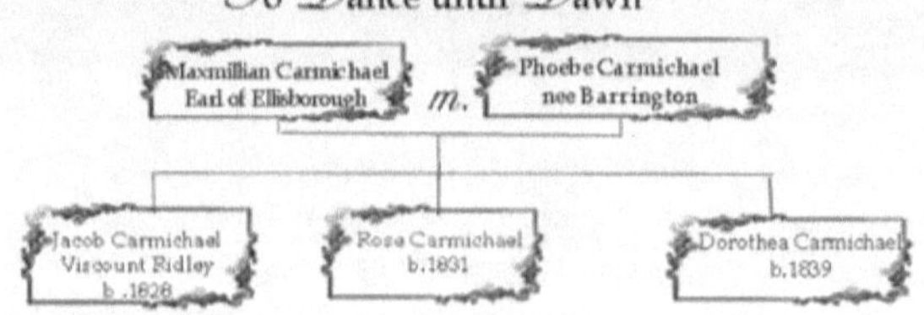

HOUSE OF ELLISBOROUGH
To Dance until Dawn

Chapter 1

Leo

I'm getting married. To a vicar's daughter, if you can believe that. I am undoubtedly a lucky dog, and so you shall see if you can bestir yourself all the way to such a heathenish place as Scotland.

I shan't expect to see you but figured you might like to know you're invited.

—Excerpt of a letter from The Hon'ble Hamilton Anderson (son of The right Hon'ble Gordon and Ruth Anderson, The Earl and Countess of Morven) to Mr Leo Hunt (son of Mr Nathanial and Mrs Alice Hunt).

21st June 1850, Albany, Piccadilly, London.

Violetta stared out of the parlour window that faced onto the street and scanned the road in both directions. So far, so good. The embroidery in her lap lay untouched. Her adopted mama, Lady Trevick, had gone to see Lord Trevick off on a visit to his club, so there was no need for pretending she was doing anything but keeping a lookout. She only hoped her mama had since gone upstairs for a little nap to gather her energy for the ball tonight. Not that Mama seemed ever to have anything less than boundless energy. Unlike Vi. Of late, she'd felt lethargic and out of spirits and Leo blasted Hunt was not helping matters.

She gave an anxious look up and down the street, tentatively hoping that he would not come today. He'd come three times every week for the last three months, however, and today was Friday, so…

Vi started as she glimpsed sunlight glinting on hair the colour of ripe barley. Heads turned as the fashionable tilbury drawn by a beautiful grey horse trotted smartly past. Two young ladies on the pavement almost walked headlong into a lamppost as they stared. She couldn't blame them. God—or more likely the devil—had excelled himself when he created Leo Hunt. Blond and blue-eyed, he had the looks of an angel combined with the body of an athlete, and a smile that could make females from toddlers to aged dowagers giggle like complete ninnies.

Giving an exclamation of frustration, Vi shot to her feet, letting her embroidery fall to the floor and disregarding it as she hurried out of the room.

"Button!" she shouted, startling their poor butler so thoroughly he almost leapt from his skin.

"Miss Spencer?" he said, gazing at her as though he expected an announcement of a flood or a plague of locusts at the very least. A smart rap on the front door had him looking away from her and Vi cried out desperately.

"Don't answer it!" she said, though she knew at once that was entirely ridiculous. The knocker was up, and everyone knew they were in town. "That is to say… I am not at home," she added, putting up her chin and trying belatedly for dignity.

The butler sighed. "Mr Hunt is a… a rather forceful young man, Miss Spencer," he said hesitantly.

"He is a thorn in my side, Button, a stone in my shoe. I. Am. *Not*. At. Home."

"Very good, miss," Button said gloomily, squaring his shoulders as he headed for the door.

Vi scurried back to the parlour and closed the door, and then opened it an inch and peered out, knowing she had completely lost her mind. This, then, was what the dreadful man had reduced her to.

She could not see the door from here, but she could eavesdrop on the conversation at least.

"Good afternoon, Button, how do?" Leo's cheerfully irreverent voice reached her, making her idiotic heart give a little leap in her chest. "You're looking fine as fivepence, old man. New cravat?"

"No, Mr Hunt."

"You've cut your hair, then?"

"No, Mr Hunt."

There was the sound of fingers snapping. "I've got it, you've found a new recipe for shoe polish. I can see my face in those. Must give me the recipe."

"Certainly, Mr Hunt. I'm afraid Miss Spencer is—"

"Well, don't keep me on the doorstep, Button. Vi's expecting me. Is she ready?"

"No, Mr Hunt, I was just about to explain that Miss—"

"Don't worry about showing me in, I know the way."

Vi gave a squeak of alarm and leapt away from the door, hurrying to stand by the fireplace and trying her best to adopt her best ice maiden demeanour.

"But Mr Hunt, Miss Spencer is not at home today," Button said frantically, just as Leo pushed the door open. Leo grinned at Vi and then turned to the beleaguered Button. "Sorry to contradict you, old man, but she's right there. Plain as a pikestaff, I should say, though a good deal prettier."

"Miss Spencer," Button exclaimed in despair.

Vi let out a sigh of resignation. "Never mind, Button. Not your fault. He's dreadful and there's nothing either of us can do about it." Button glanced between them and fled before things got difficult, as they generally did when the two of them were in the same room.

"Oh, come now, Vi," Leo said, shaking his head at her. "I've been positively angelic for months now and all you do is tell poor Button you're not at home. I've called three times a week for months and have successfully escorted you out on precisely four occasions."

"You took tea on five others," she pointed out.

"Only because Lady Trevick was here and wouldn't let you throw me out."

"One would think under those circumstances that you would give up and go away," she replied tartly, turning to the mirror over the mantelpiece and studying her hair with more interest than she was feeling.

"Faint heart, Vi," he said, meeting her eyes in the mirror and returning a rueful smile. "Come on, love. It's a beautiful day. Come for a turn about the park with me. We won't be gone above an hour. You can stand me for that long, can't you?"

"Oh, Leo, why are you doing this?" Vi demanded impatiently, turning back to face him. "I wish I knew."

Leo shrugged. "I think I've made that obvious enough, Vi. I can't help it if you don't believe I'm sincere."

"Really?" she said sceptically. "When you've never been sincere about anything in your life before?"

"Harsh, Vi," he said, frowning over her words. "I was a young man with money and the good fortune to know how to enjoy it. But I've grown up. I know what's important and—"

"Leo!"

Vi groaned inwardly as her mama came into the room. She was still a lovely woman with a naughty twinkle in her eye and never failed to say things that made Vi blush. She adored the woman, though, who had taken her in when her own parents had tragically died and loved her like her own daughter, and with such generosity of spirit that Vi could never say no to her. Sadly, her mama adored Leo and was determined they were a match made in heaven.

"Kitty, you wicked creature. What have you been up to now?" Leo asked her, hugging her as if she were his own mama.

"Why, what can you be meaning?" Kitty said with a laugh, patting his cheek fondly, her Irish accent giving the playful words a lovely lilt.

"You look divine, love, which tells me you've been up to no good. You don't sparkle like that unless you've been naughty," Leo told her, setting Kitty off into whoops as he always did.

"Well, you are perfectly right, of course," she said confidentially. "But I can't breathe a word."

"Of course you can't," Leo said with a grin. "I've come to take Vi for a turn about the park, but she won't come," he told Kitty with a sigh.

"I never said I wouldn't come," Vi said in a rush, which was blatantly untrue, but she did not want Mama to scold her for her rudeness.

Leo lifted an eyebrow, and she blushed a little.

"Well, of course she will go! Vi, hurry along and get ready. I shall talk to Leo in the meantime, but where is Mau?" Kitty asked, looking about the room for the huge cat that Leo took everywhere with him. He had caused rather a stir during his last visit, frightening Mama's ancient spaniel, who had barked wildly until a footman came and rescued her from the corner under the stairs that Mau had stalked her into. The footman, a new fellow by the name of Pembury, had been badly scratched for his trouble. She did not think he had forgiven Mau for it either, or Leo, judging on the icy glare he'd given on his next visit.

"He's asleep on the seat of the tilbury, the lazy creature," he said, smirking as Vi shot him a look of pure exasperation and hurried out.

Resigned to her fate, Vi made quick work of changing her gown and readying herself for a drive. She may as well get it over with, she told herself. Yet she could not deny the little thrill of anticipation as she made her way back down the stairs. Leo was a marvellous whip and much admired. He was, in fact, one of the few people she found she could relax with. Her parents had died in a terrible carriage accident and if the driver did not pay complete attention, she found herself increasingly afraid, twitching with the desire to take the reins herself. Driving with Leo was different. He might risk his own neck, but with her he drove with the utmost precision, aware of her anxiety. With him she could relax and driving out became a pleasure. Too much of a pleasure. It would be so easy to let herself believe he was in earnest, that he really wished to marry her, but it would be a terrible thing to allow herself to hope for something which she had always known was out of her reach.

"Well, here I am," she said curtly, pulling on her gloves as she walked back into the parlour.

"So you are," Leo said, his gaze running over her in a way that made her skin feel hot and most peculiar. "That's a lovely outfit, pet. Most becoming."

"Thank you. Shall we go?" she replied, refusing to allow his words to please her, for he said such things all the time and such flattery came far too easily to his lips.

"Yes, do run along and have a lovely time," Kitty urged them.

Leo got to his feet and then frowned. Vi followed his gaze and cursed inwardly as she saw her embroidery still in a heap by the window. Leo strode over and picked it up, smoothing out the fabric and deftly putting the needle through it to keep it safe. He walked back to the settee and placed it on the coffee table before following Vi out of the house to his waiting carriage.

"Anyone would think you'd been watching for me," he murmured as he helped her up into the tilbury.

Vi ignored the comment and refused to look at him, fighting a blush.

"There's someone in my seat," she said, gazing down at Mau, who blinked sleepily up at her.

He was an enormous creature, far bigger than most cats, and solidly built. A handsome fellow, his torn ear did little to detract from his rather aristocratic profile and sleek coat of brown and black. Leo had become something of an eccentric figure among the *ton*, but everyone had grown used to him taking Mau almost everywhere with him.

"Mau, up you get lazy bones. Let the lady sit down," Leo said, shaking his head as the cat got up and stretched, stalking across the seat and pushing his head against Leo's. "Thank you," Leo told him. Once Vi had sat down, he got up beside her and Mau lay across both their laps, making himself comfortable. Vi laughed despite herself, stroking the cat's silky head.

"You are as dreadful as he is," she told Mau frankly, but he simply began purring, a deep, sonorous sound that vibrated through her.

"Let him go," Leo instructed his tiger, who had been holding the sleek gelding's head. The man ran around and leapt onto the back of the tilbury as they moved off. Happily, the hood of the tilbury and the sound of the wheels on the road gave them privacy, and he did not overlook them. Vi watched with pleasure as his beautiful grey trotted, taking them down the road and into the busy city traffic.

They didn't speak until they had reached Hyde Park, for the roads were overburdened with carts and carriages and people and Vi did not wish to distract Leo from his horse. He drove to an inch and Vi relaxed, knowing she was in the safest of hands. She turned her face to the sun, enjoying the warm breeze as he found a faster moving flow of traffic and gave the horse leave to move faster. They trotted along, moving beautifully, and she wished there were no traffic so he could let them go, for though she did not enjoy riding, she was not afraid of speed in Leo's capable hands, and secretly rather delighted in the opportunity to go fast. Back at Trevick Castle, she had her own little gig and pony and often galloped along the paths when no one was about to see her. To experience any of Leo's fine horses do such a thing, however, that would be quite something.

Once inside the park, Leo let the horse walk and turned his attention to Vi.

"That's a charming bonnet," he said appreciatively.

Vi let out a sigh of frustration. "Why are we doing this? Why aren't you here with Miss Fellowes or Miss Saunders? They're much more in your line."

"Are they?" Leo replied with apparent interest. "How so?"

"They're very beautiful, for one thing. They come from good families, but not so good they would frown on a connection with Hunter's—"

"Ah, yes, mustn't forget Papa's dreadful gambling den, or The Sons of Hades," he said, naming the club he part owned with his friends. "Quite shocking."

Vi rolled her eyes and carried on. "They are nice, intelligent girls, and they are young," she added, savagely repressing the stab of regret that hit her square in the chest.

"You mean, they're not an old maid like you are?" he said with interest.

Vi stiffened. She knew very well that was what she was, but she had not expected him to tell her so. "Indeed," she said coolly. "I've been on the shelf so long I'm gathering dust. It only astonishes me you've failed to notice until this moment."

Leo snorted and shook his head. "Vi, you accuse me of being dreadful, but you're a wicked creature."

"Me?" she exclaimed, turning to stare at him in outrage.

"Yes, you," he said, though there was amusement in his voice. "You know very well I do not think you are an old maid. Only you think that, so don't keep on. You're just fishing for compliments and then you'll scold me and accuse me of turning you up sweet if I voice them."

"I *am* an old maid," Vi said stubbornly. "And I do not want your compliments or flattery when there's no substance to them."

"No substance!" Leo said, and Vi's heart skipped at the obvious anger in his voice. "Why must you insist on believing me to be a frivolous boy? I'm no boy, Violetta. I'm a man who knows his own mind. I'm courting you with the intention of making you my wife."

"You're mad," she said flatly, crossing her arms as if that might stop her heart from escaping her ribcage, for it was beating far too hard and too fast. "We'd kill each other before the honeymoon was over."

"But what a way to go," Leo remarked.

Vi slanted a glance at him, seeing a mixture of irritation and devilry in his blue eyes that made her feel rather nervous.

"Out of the two, I think Miss Saunders would suit you best," she continued, as if the conversation had not been diverted at all. "She's a delightful girl, friendly but not bold, and she has a lively sense of humour. She loves animals too," she added, stroking

Mau's head and feeling rather wistful that such a girl might have both these ridiculous creatures in her life.

"I see," Leo said, as he took them past the Serpentine, which sparkled invitingly in the sunshine. There were boats out on the water and many people taking advantage of the lovely summer day. "Will she be at the ball tonight?"

"I expect so," Vi said cautiously.

"Very well. I shall dance with her and see what I think."

"Good," Vi replied, though there was a leaden feeling in her chest that made her feel every bit the old maid she told herself she was.

"Good," Leo agreed, and they trotted on in silence.

Leo gritted his teeth and counted. It was something he'd had to do remarkably often over the past few months and, not for the first time, he wondered why he was bothering. Once the surge of annoyance had diminished a little, he glanced sideways at the impossible girl by his side. She *was* a girl too, he thought as his irritation vanished at the sight of her. No matter her insistence that she was too old and on the shelf, she looked no more than two and twenty. Her skin was the finest porcelain, her eyes a pale crystalline blue that never failed to capture his attention. Lord, but she was beautiful. He'd always known it, but in an abstract fashion, like the fine painting that you saw every day and knew was lovely but did not stop to appreciate. But one day he had stopped, and he had appreciated, and he had cursed himself for a fool at having wasted so much time.

Mau shifted on his lap, digging his claws in, and Leo winced. He glanced at the cat whose head was pillowed in Vi's lap—lucky devil—and large yellow eyes regarded him with something that looked like pity. Leo sighed inwardly. He felt like he was running out of time with Vi. Not because she was too old—curse her for getting that idiotic thought in her head—but because she would bolt, eventually, and keep him away from her with whatever means she could manage. He knew he was on thin ice. If he put a foot wrong, she'd use it as an excuse never to see him again. Not that he intended to put a foot wrong, but his life had always been adventurous, one where he took chances and went where the wind took him rather than following any plan. Having made a plan to court Vi and win her heart, he was finding it harder than he imagined to stick to it.

At this moment, for example, instead of taking her for a sedate little jaunt about Hyde Park, he wanted to whisk her away to a hidden corner of London she would never have seen in her life before. He wanted to show her shops that sold wonderful silks from India in the most marvellous patterns and colours; he wanted to take her to the river and get her to try jellied eels and show her a dozen other things that would shock and delight her, but you couldn't do that with a proper young lady.

If only he had nine lives like a cat, perhaps then he'd be able to figure out how to get it right before his luck ran out.

He'd used one up this morning, he knew. What a fool, for he should never have said he'd dance with Miss Saunders. He'd wanted to bite his tongue off the moment the words had left his mouth, but Vi made him do and say things he'd had no intention of doing or saying just seconds earlier. It was true they drove each other distracted, just as she said they did, but in a good way—or at least Leo thought so. He loved her sharp wit and the way she challenged him, and never tired of crossing swords with her, but he wished she would soften towards him, just a little. He felt certain she cared for him. He had seen fleeting evidence of it: a glance in his direction when she'd thought he wasn't looking, a smile of such warmth when he'd finally done something she approved of, and… and a million tiny things between two people who had known each other their entire lives that could mean everything or nothing.

"Would you like to go to Gunter's? I'll buy you an ice," he offered, knowing that Vi adored sweet things, especially strawberry ice cream.

He watched her face, amused despite himself as he saw her wage an internal battle between getting out of his company as quickly as possible and her favourite treat.

"Very well," she said grudgingly.

Leo let out a sigh of relief. He'd not been sure even ice cream was enough to keep her beside him for a minute longer.

"I won't dance with Miss Saunders," he told her, wondering if he was being a fool for trying so hard and finding he didn't care if he was.

If he hadn't been looking at her as he said the words, he knew he would have missed the look of sheer relief that flickered in her eyes, there and gone in an instant, but not before he'd noticed. Relief flooded him too. She hadn't wanted him to dance with Miss Saunders; she didn't want him to give up on her. Vi had her own battle to fight, one that must allow her to believe that Leo could love her and her alone for her own sake, and not for any foolish reason she'd convinced herself of. For that, though, she needed time. She needed to see that he could be sensible and well-behaved, and Leo was going to give her that if it killed him.

Chapter 2

Hamilton,

Congratulations, Lord, but we're falling like flies. I'm happy for you and wish you and your bride good fortune – not that you need any more good fortune. Indeed, if you could send some of your golden touch my way, I'd appreciate it.

I would have loved to come to the back end of beyond to celebrate with you – truly I would – but I am on a quest, an honourable one, and doing my best to be a Sir Galahad, or Lancelot. Wait, no, he was the one who had an affair with the king's wife, wasn't he? Not him. Galahad then. Anyway, it's not going terribly well. Pray for me.

—Excerpt of a letter from Mr Leo Hunt (son of Mr Nathanial and Mrs Alice Hunt) to The Hon'ble Hamilton Anderson (son of The right Hon'ble Gordon and Ruth Anderson, The Earl and Countess of Morven).

21st June 1850, Piccadilly, London.

"Leo!"

Leo turned to see Ashton Anson waving at him and pulled the tilbury over to let the man jump in. Ash took a moment to negotiate a space with Mau and sat himself down.

"Well met, Ash. Lord, where did you get that dreadful waistcoat?" Leo asked, grimacing and tearing his gaze away from the appalling apparition while he manoeuvred himself back into the throng.

"My wife bought it for me," Ash replied dryly.

Leo choked, not having expected that for Ash was famous for his extravagant waistcoats. "Ah," he said remorsefully. "Beg pardon."

"Stow it," Ash said amiably. "Where've you been?"

"Taking Violetta out for a turn about Hyde Park," Leo admitted, glancing at Ash to see the same pitying expression Mau had given him earlier.

"The eternal battle," Ash replied with amusement. "How goes the war for Miss Spencer's heart?"

"I'm not dead yet," Leo said resolutely. "Only wounded."

Ash chuckled and patted Leo's shoulder. "Courage, my friend."

Leo harrumphed and changed the subject, not wanting to speak of his woeful love life any longer. "Where've you been then, and where is the lovely Narcissa? I didn't think you let her out of your sight."

"I've been visiting Larkin, and that's not somewhere I'd take my wife these days. One never knows what one will find."

"Ah. Yes, I went last week and tripped over a naked girl. Modelling for a painting apparently, but all the same, not something one wishes to explain to one's wife, I suppose."

"Quite," Ash said with a laugh, and then shook his head sadly. "Was he drunk?"

"Not drunk," Leo allowed. "Hungover. In good spirits, though, I thought."

"He's burning the candle at both ends."

Leo nodded. "Yes, but he's not drinking like he was. I thought he was in real trouble for a while there, but it's more a lot of partying than drinking alone, which was what really worried me."

"True. But he's working all hours and out with that artistic set he hangs about with the rest. I don't think he sleeps. At all," Ash replied, shaking his head.

"Well, at least a lot of artists and poets are not likely to murder him. Some of the dodgy types he was hanging about with before made me fear he'd end up in the river with his throat cut. Still, whatever he's up to now, it all might be about to change," Leo said, falling silent as he negotiated a tight turn.

Ash waited until they were back on the straight and turned to Leo enquiringly.

"His father is coming and intends to shake him up."

Ash winced, and Leo nodded. They both had a healthy respect for Larkin's father: a war hero and a man not to be trifled with.

"Your mama told you, I suppose?"

"She did," Leo agreed. "Lady Rothborn is one of her intimates, but I was sworn to secrecy, so for God's sake, don't warn him or I shall be in the basket."

"He needs a shake. A bloody good one," Ash said, frowning. "I only hope it does some good."

"Can't hurt, at least," Leo said as Ash gestured for him to stop.

"Drop me here, there's a good fellow. Are you going to the Marchams' ball tonight?"

"I don't know. I suppose so," Leo said, not much caring for the idea. Vi wasn't going because Kitty was giving a dinner party.

"Well, if you go, I'll see you there," Ash replied, jumping down and disappearing into the crowd.

Leo drew his team back into the traffic, not feeling the slightest interest in the ball that evening, and far more concerned with his strategy for winning Vi over. He turned to Mau, who was sitting up now, watching the passing scenery with the dismissive eye of a creature who'd seen it all before.

"What should I do, Mau?" he asked the great cat, as he often did. Large yellow eyes turned in his direction and stared placidly back at him. "Don't give up? Yes, that's what I thought. If at first you don't succeed, eh? Good advice, old man," Leo replied, stroking the cat's silken head.

Mau closed his eyes and purred and the two went home in perfect accord.

♡♧◇♤

24th June 1850, Piccadilly, London.

It was with a sense of déjà vu that Vi saw the tilbury coming down the street towards her home the following Monday. Having decided on another tactic, Vi strode out of the parlour to the front door. Pembury handed her gloves to her, standing as stiff as a ramrod. He was extremely tall, and she had to look up a good way to nod her thanks. His expression was one even the queen's butler would find impressive. She must tell Mama to get the poor fellow to relax, for he looked like he'd swallowed a wasp. Button opened the door for her and Vi strode out, surprised when Pembury followed her. She walked down the front steps and stood on the pavement waiting as Leo brought the tilbury to a halt in front of her.

For a moment, he stood staring at her in bemusement.

"You're keen," he observed, his lips twitching.

"The sooner we go, the sooner it will be over," she told him candidly. "Are you just going to sit there, or are you thinking of helping me up?"

"Of course, love," he said, grinning at her as he leapt down and offered her his hand. He glanced at Pembury and waved the fellow away. "I can look after the lady."

Pembury cast Leo a dark look and glared at Mau but stayed where he was. Leo shook his head and turned back to her. "I say, I like that rig, Vi."

Vi gently pushed Mau to one side as the cat sighed and rearranged himself, and then sat down, smoothing out the lovely shot silk of her gown

"Shove up, Mau," Leo said, giving the cat a little push.

Mau protested, miaowing volubly, and Vi stifled a laugh as Pembury stared at Leo and the cat with an expression that might have been horror.

Leo touched the ribbon of her bonnet, giving it a little tweak. "Fabulous colour."

The ribbons matched the rest of her ensemble. It was a pretty outfit, and she was secretly delighted by it. A soft dusty pink shot silk, it had a green aspect when the light hit it, and the flounces on her skirts fluttered and ruffled in the light summer breeze. Her high brim bonnet was lined with the same fabric with little clusters of silk roses that framed her face. The effect was charming, though Vi had worried that perhaps it was too young and frivolous an outfit for a woman on the shady side of thirty years. The trouble was she had fallen in love with both the design and the fabric and Kitty had persuaded her to buy it.

Vi glanced at Leo as he climbed in, for she had to admit his taste was exceptionally good and, whilst she would have bitten off her tongue rather than admit it, his approval mattered.

"You like it?"

"I do," he said, waiting for Mau to settle himself down again before turning in his seat to give her a critical once over.

Vi blushed under his scrutiny, wondering if the tiny lines she feared she had detected around her eyes that morning were very noticeable in the bright sunshine.

"Dashing," he pronounced after a long moment. "But with elegance enough to carry it off."

"Yes!" Vi exclaimed, before she remembered she was not supposed to encourage him. "That's just what I thought. I fretted it was too young a style, but I think the dusty pink elevates it. If it had been a rose pink, it would not have been at all the thing."

Leo rolled his eyes at her. "Yes, you'd have looked a shocking sight, and everyone would have stared," he said, deadpan.

Vi ignored the sarcasm. "I don't think everyone would have stared, but I do believe many would have thought me foolish for trying to pretend I am still a girl."

"Lord, Vi, I swore I would not vex you today, but you try my patience when you spout such blasted nonsense," he said. "In the first place, I'm not interested in silly young girls who do not have a thought in their heads worth listening to. In the second, you talk as though you are in your dotage, when every fellow with eyes turns to stare at you wherever you go."

"Indeed, they do not!" Vi exclaimed, not about to accept this piece of flummery, for it was pure fantasy.

"They do," Leo insisted, his expression somewhat mulish. "You just don't notice them, drat you."

"Fiddlesticks," she retorted. "Now for heaven's sake, drive on. Or do you wish to sit and quarrel on the doorstep all afternoon? I believe we have given our new footman enough of a show," she added in an undertone, aware that Pembury was watching them. No, not them – *Leo.* She frowned but Leo's voice caught her attention.

"No, I want to go on a romantic drive with a beautiful woman who is doing her best to send me to Bedlam," he replied, before giving his tiger the instruction to let the horse go.

Vi sighed, wishing such words didn't have the effect of making her feel happy and tearful at the same time. Turning her head resolutely away from Leo, she watched the world around her as he took them through the busy street. It was impossible to ignore him, though, and she felt herself drawn back into the aura that surrounded him. Being close to Leo was like being bathed in sunshine. Whilst his attention was upon you, it was as if you were the best and most special person in the world and, when it was gone, you were left feeling chilled and alone. As a girl, she had adored him, and drank in every scrap of attention he would give her, but she had become used to the fact she could not hold it for long. There was always a boxing match, a race, a party or some event that would see him careering away from her at breakneck speed to whatever bit of fun was on offer that day. He was an energetic man, one who loved to ride and drive, and he found it hard to sit still. People gravitated towards him because of the energy and enthusiasm that radiated from him. It was magnetic and irresistible, but it was also fleeting, for his attention waned rapidly and then he would look for the next source of interest, the next bit of fun. Dangerous fun, usually.

Perhaps if the things that took him away had not been so reckless she could have been braver, could have taken that chance on him, but there had been too many times when she had feared he would wind up dead in a ditch, thrown from a horse or carriage, or beaten to a pulp by some adversary he had underestimated. She only knew a small fraction about his hare-brained adventures, but there had been enough to give her sleepless nights. How would that feel if he was no longer just a childhood friend, she was far too fond of for her own peace of mind, but her husband, father to her children?

Vi could not live that life with him. She liked peace and quiet. A morning sitting in the sunshine with her embroidery was one of her favourite things. She loved the serenity it gave her and the time to just be, without having to think or to please anyone but herself. There was no chance of her life being turned upside down by grief if she sat still and concentrated on her beautiful designs. She knew what it was to lose everything, for the people she loved to be torn from her and leave her all alone. Losing her parents had felt like the end of her world, and even Kitty and Luke's generosity and boundless love had struggled to mend the damage. She feared losing Leo might actually destroy her if she allowed herself to love him. But even if he did not kill himself doing something reckless, life with Leo would be a series of arguments punctuated by goodbyes as she waved him off to one event after another, leaving her to worry over him and to wonder what he was up to and whom with. Leo was a beautiful man, and women wanted him, women far prettier and younger and more exciting than Vi. She'd seen one of his mistresses once and marvelled at her extravagant beauty. She had quite cast Vi in the shade… and there would always be women like that wanting his attention. No matter his intentions, temptation would beckon on all sides, and Vi did not rate her own assets highly enough to believe she could hold him.

"Penny for them?" Leo asked, his voice soft.

Vi blushed as she realised he was watching her and shook her head. "They're not worth that much, I assure you."

"I'd give a king's ransom to know what they were all the same," he told her. "Perhaps then I could understand you better."

"You understand me well enough," she replied, darting him a swift smile. "I'm an argumentative, contrary creature who would say black was white just to vex you."

He laughed at that, and her stupid heart leapt at the sound. "At least you admit it, you dreadful girl."

To Violetta's surprise, Leo stopped the tilbury once they were alongside the Serpentine and the tiger came around to take hold of the horse.

"Find some shade, Norton. Miss Spencer and I are going to take a little stroll. If that's all right, Vi?"

"Certainly," she replied, accepting his hand and climbing down from the carriage.

"Come along, Mau, you too. You're getting fat," Leo told the cat, who stood and stretched languidly before leaping to the ground. He wound himself back and forth around Leo's shiny boots, purring.

"Don't you ever worry he'll run away?" Vi asked, as Leo offered her his arm and they walked along the lakeside. Mau trotted beside them, occasionally running off to investigate something scurrying in the undergrowth.

"No," Leo said, shaking his head. "He's had plenty of opportunity to do so. I think he was a dog in a previous existence. Either that or a king."

Vi laughed. "There's a rather large discrepancy between the two states."

Leo shrugged. "All the same." He looked around at Mau, who had stopped to take a drink. When he was done, Leo whistled and Mau bounded after them and then stalked on ahead, tail aloft. "He's the most marvellous companion. I adore the great brute."

"I know you do," Vi said, glancing up at him and feeling the usual stab of melancholy as she looked at the handsome face she knew and loved so well. The affection he held for Mau, and for all animals, was one of the most endearing things about Leo. She knew he thought nothing of staying up all night and sleeping in the stables if one of his horses was hurt or unwell. He'd had dogs as a boy and had always taken them everywhere, and even when they were old, he'd carried them in and out of rooms and carriages if he thought they needed the help. She'd seen his devastation when each of them finally went to sleep for the last time, and knew he was capable of great compassion and kindness. A wife, however, was a different kettle of fish, and she did not trust him quite far enough to give him her heart entirely. He had too much of it already, more than was comfortable. She'd be a fool to hand him the rest.

As they walked, people stopped and exclaimed at the sight of Leo and Vi and the large black and brown cat trotting beside them. People they knew greeted them, and Mau too, as they meandered along the paths.

"Mau!"

Vi turned to look and saw a girl running towards Mau, skirts and plaits flying as she flew towards him. For a moment Mau froze, bristling all over like a bottle brush, but then the girl drew closer, and he trotted happily to meet her.

"Good afternoon, Miss Tilly," Leo said, grinning at the child as she tried and failed to hoist Mau into her arms. The poor cat sent Leo a plaintive look but endured patiently. "He's too heavy for that, I'm afraid."

"Good afternoon, Cousin Leo," Tilly said, giving up on picking the cat up and falling to her knees on the dusty path to hug him instead.

"Tilly, don't sit in the dirt!" remonstrated a female voice.

Vi looked around to see her governess, Mrs Harris, hurrying after her charge. Behind her strolled the Marquess and Marchioness of Montagu.

"Afternoon, Auntie," Leo said, raising his hat to Lady Montagu. "My lord," he added deferentially to Montagu.

"Leo, Violetta, how lovely to see you both. I see you are enjoying the lovely sunshine as we are," his Aunt Matilda said, smiling at them.

"We could be enjoying it even better at Dern," Montagu murmured dryly, earning himself a look from his wife.

"We will return once the season is over. Isn't that right, Tilly?" Lady Montagu said to her granddaughter.

"I'd rather go now," the child said gloomily. "But I'm not leaving Papa with all these marriage-minded ninnies chasing him about."

"Tilly!" Mrs Harris said in exasperation. "Good heavens, child, are you trying to put me to the blush?"

"Don't fret, Mrs Harris," Leo said with a grin. "We all know Tilly is a dreadful girl."

Tilly shot him a grin and got to her feet, unsuccessfully brushing dust from her skirts as Mau had got bored and strolled off. "Dreadful girls are the best sort, aren't they, Pops?"

Lord Montagu looked from his wife to Mrs Harris and back to Tilly. "Not content with embarrassing Mrs Harris, now you wish to get me a scolding, I see," he said reproachfully, making Vi choke with laughter.

"But you did say so, Pops!" Tilly insisted.

"Quite dreadful," Vi murmured with a chuckle, so only Leo could hear.

"Yes, but it was not supposed to be repeated in company, you wicked child," he said with a sigh. "And they are only the best sort if they know how to behave when they must," he added firmly.

Tilly pouted at this but went and took her grandfather's hand and tried her best to look the picture of innocence.

"Tilly Barrington, you are just like your Auntie Cat, and I thought no one could ever be worse than that," Leo said, laughing, a comment which appeared to make Tilly very happy indeed.

Bidding the Montagus and Mrs Harris a pleasant afternoon, Vi and Leo strolled on for a while longer before turning and retracing their steps, heading back to the carriage.

"If you had the choice, would you like to return to town for the season each year, or would you prefer to stay in the country?" Leo asked.

Vi shrugged. "I have no great liking for too much society, but I should miss visiting friends now and then, and the theatre and concerts, and I enjoy a bit of shopping. But the season is tedious if one must stay for the whole."

"Quite so," Leo agreed easily. "Just what I was thinking. We'll live mostly in the countryside but come to town now and again for a bit of culture and shopping."

Vi shot a glance at him. "Don't do that," she said crossly.

"Do what?" he regarded her with wide celestial blue eyes, the exact colour of the sky above them.

"Make believe that I will change my mind if you just keep nagging me."

"I have to believe that, or I shall be sunk into gloom," he replied, looking away from her and watching Mau as he stalked a sparrow.

"For a day or two until something new catches your attention," Vi remarked. Rather to her surprise, she felt him stiffen and realised the remark had been too harsh. She forgot sometimes that she could hurt Leo's feelings, for he hurt her so every day without even realising it. "I beg your pardon. Please forget I said that," she told him contritely.

They walked on in silence for a while until he spoke again. "Do you really think me so shallow, love?"

Vi sighed, shaking her head. "Not shallow, no. Just… Just full of energy and easily distracted, eager for the next interesting thing to divert you."

He frowned, considering this. "I like the unexpected," he admitted. "There's nothing better to me than going out intending to do one thing and finding two or three other things along the way. I like discovering new places, new people, new experiences. Is that wrong?"

"Not in the least, but I like sitting quietly with my embroidery and enjoying the birds singing in the garden."

"I could like that too. Well, not the embroidery. But I could enjoy being quiet with you."

Vi shot him a sceptical glance. "You would last precisely five minutes."

Leo shook his head. "You're wrong. If we had our own home, if I could wake each morning and know I had that, that bit of peace to begin the day with. I think I should like that."

Vi blushed at the idea of them waking each morning together, never having heard him say such a thing before. She stared at him in shock, hearing the sincerity in his voice. *Don't believe it, don't believe him, that way leads to heartbreak*, said a panicky voice in her head. Her heart was beating too hard, too fast.

"I wouldn't say such things if—" he began, and then his head whipped around as a feline shriek of indignity reached his ears. "Mau?"

Vi looked around them, realising she couldn't see the big cat who rarely strayed far from them. "Mau?" she called.

A muttered oath and more howling, yowling, and furious noises came from the small thicket of trees beside them.

"Mau!" Leo called, hurrying into the undergrowth as Vi followed, heedless of her skirts catching on brambles or branches, or the impropriety of dashing headlong into a secluded woodland with Leo Hunt.

Leo crashed through the assorted bracken and bushes in the direction the noises had come from, with Vi hurrying to catch him up. He stopped as he exited the small copse, so suddenly that Vi ploughed into the back of him.

"Where is he?" she demanded, rubbing her nose and readjusting her bonnet.

"I don't know," Leo said, and she could hear the worry in his voice. "I can't see—"

"There!" Vi cried, suddenly spotting a stocky fellow in an ill-fitting suit carrying a heavy sack. He was holding it at arm's length and the sack was writhing and occasionally emitting hissing noises. "Oh, Leo, look there, that man—"

But Leo was already moving, running flat out. The man must have heard the heavy footfalls and turned, the colour draining from his face as he saw Leo thundering towards him.

"Edgar! Edgar!" he shouted, as a hackney carriage pulled up beside him. With surprising speed for such a stocky fellow, he threw the sack inside and leapt in after it, slamming the door closed as it careered away, back through the park.

Leo was a second too late, his hand pounding on the side of the carriage as it took off. He reached out, trying to grab hold of something, but clutched only air.

"Oh, Leo! They've got Mau!" Vi cried, so appalled her voice trembled.

"Not for long," Leo said savagely.

He turned, stuck his fingers in his mouth and gave a shrill whistle, gesturing madly at the stand of trees beside the Serpentine, some yards away where the tilbury and tiger were waiting for them. Norton leapt into the driver's seat and got the horses moving, cantering them over to where Leo was waiting.

"Some bastard took Mau," he told his tiger.

Norton's face contorted. "No, sir! Oh, surely not?"

"No mistake," Leo said grimly. "Get down and see Miss Spencer safely home, would you?"

"Certainly," Norton said at once, but Vi was already climbing up beside Leo.

"Don't be ridiculous and don't argue. Get after them, Leo, before you lose them."

"Vi, I don't know where this is going to lead or—"

Vi gave him an aggravated shove, bouncing on the seat with impatience. "Go! Go! Go!" she shouted.

Leo muttered an oath as Norton hurried to the back. He took up the reins, and the horses leapt forward at his command, so fast they might have been fired from a pistol. Vi swallowed a shriek of alarm, clutching at the tilbury with one hand and her bonnet with the other. People stopped and stared, some shouting in annoyance at their breakneck speed as they galloped in pursuit of the villains.

"Why would anyone take Mau?" Vi cried over the din as they flew through the park.

"Ransom," Leo said. His face was expressionless, but she could well imagine his feelings. "It's not the first time," he added grimly.

"It's not?" Vi asked in shock.

Leo shook his head. "I've stopped putting a collar on him. The first time, someone just took the collar because it had a gold tag with his name on, but left Mau."

"I remember that. It was reported in the scandal sheets," Vi said, clutching again at the carriage as they hit a pothole.

"Unfortunately, yes, which gave other people ideas, I think. I've stopped taking him into the city with me, but I never imagined the park in broad daylight would be a problem, damn me for a fool."

He fell silent, his face impassive as he concentrated on keeping the hackney in view.

"Well, he'll be well cared for, then, if they mean to extort money from you," Vi said, hoping to calm him, for the unreadable look on his face frightened her more than any show of anger and told her he was beyond being reasonable.

"I'll murder them with my bare hands before they get the chance," he growled.

"I'll help you," Vi offered, earning herself a brief, if grateful, smile before he fell silent again. They reached the exit to the path and stared up and down the highway.

"Where are they?" Vi cried, terrified they had lost the villains already.

"There, sir, towards Marble Arch," Norton shouted, hanging around the side of the tilbury.

"Hold on, Norton," Leo said, which turned out to be good advice.

Vi had always considered herself an excellent passenger. Being a reasonable whipster herself, she knew when she was in the hands of someone with skill and never so much as twitched when Leo was driving. Today, it was all she could do to keep a still tongue in her head as he weaved in and out of traffic and took corners with such speed, she could only close her eyes and pray. From Marble Arch they flew down Tottenham Court Road, and she did not know whether to thank God or curse for the fact the traffic was lighter than usual. For as much as it helped them to follow, it left the path clear for the villains to make their escape.

"All right, Vi?" Leo asked her in concern, noticing her white knuckle hold on the side of the tilbury.

"Quite all right," Vi replied firmly, determined not to halt his pursuit. Nothing was going to happen. Leo was an excellent driver she told herself over and over. They would *not* crash. Her stomach churned all the same.

"They're heading for the Great North Road," Leo said furiously. "Damn them, where are they taking him?"

"I think perhaps their plans have changed as they're being pursued. They probably expected to deliver a ransom note to you this evening," she said, closing her eyes as he passed a heavily loaded cart with barely the width of her finger between them.

"They're not getting away from me," Leo said, in a tone that left Vi in no doubt that he would follow them to John o'Groats and back if he had to. "But Vi, love, I'm going to have to drop you off. I can't be haring all over the countryside with you in tow. I know you're scared to death, too."

"No."

In some dim part of her mind, Vi knew that her choice was one that would change things, change her life, perhaps even herself, forever. The voice of reason shrieked at her, telling her Leo was quite right and the sensible thing to do was to get down and leave him to his pursuit. She was scared, terrified in fact, but Leo would get Mau back without her. She did not doubt that, not for a moment. He would go off on his adventure and tell her all about it when he got back.

She didn't want that, she realised. Much as she loved her peaceful life and felt sure she did not wish to live at the frantic pace Leo set, she was tired of hearing of his adventures, second, third or even fourth hand. She had read about them in the papers, seen print shop caricatures, and overheard people gossiping. Never had she been a part of them. Now, unexpectedly, was her chance. If she wanted to take it. If she were brave enough, just this once.

He turned to stare at her. "Vi, I might be in Brighton, or halfway across the country in a few hours. Then you'll be in the basket."

"I'll get a train back. One advantage of being an old maid is that my reputation isn't quite so easily ruined. I'm sure no one will notice," she said, waving this away.

"Not notice!" Leo said in astonishment. "Vi, love—"

"Oh, do stop Vi-loving me," she said impatiently. "Oh, Leo, Leo, look out!"

Leo cursed as he saw the drunkard weaving from the pavement and into the traffic and his attention was entirely focused for the next few moments as he negotiated the near disaster. By the time the crisis had passed, the hackney had made the turn.

"Hurry, Leo, hurry, you'll lose them," Vi urged.

"Vi, for the love of—"

"Don't you dare think of putting me down," she shouted at him. "Oh, heavens, Leo, look!"

Leo did as she told him, momentarily diverted as he saw what she did, hackney carriages as far as the eye could see.

"Curse it," he muttered.

Vi grabbed his arm. "Which one? Which one is it?"

Leo shook his head. "It had faded red paint on the doors. It might have said Reed, or Reeves, something of the kind."

"We'll find it," Vi said resolutely. "Hurry now."

Leo gave her a long, searching look, and made the turn onto the Great North Road.

Chapter 3

It has been remarked that Lord A has been seen in company with the lovely Miss S on several notable occasions during the past weeks. The observant may have noticed that he danced with her twice at the Marchams' ball on Friday night. This author wonders if the elusive lord, arguably the biggest prize on the marriage mart, has finally found his lady. Lord K will be disappointed indeed, having thrust his lovely daughter Lady B under the nose of said Lord A most publicly of late.

—Excerpt of an article in the society pages of The Morning Star.

24th June 1850, The Great North Road, London.

An anxious quarter hour passed as they overtook hackney after hackney, none of which was the one they were after. As they got farther out of town, however, the traffic thinned, but in the far distance, they saw an old hackney ahead of them.

"That's it," Leo said.

Vi glanced at him. "How can you tell?"

"The axle is lower on the left side than the right. I think it's held together with string."

Vi stared at him, rather impressed he'd noticed such a thing. "Well done," she said.

To her surprise, he coloured a little. "I'm not a complete fool, Vi."

"I never thought it!" she exclaimed, stung by the remark. She might think him a lot of things, but a fool was not one of them. "How did they get so far ahead of us?" she asked in dismay as it disappeared over the brow of the hill.

"They've not had to check each hackney carriage on the Great North Road before passing it," he said in frustration.

"I wonder where they're going?"

"I think you're right, Vi. I think they've had to change their plans. What that means, however, I don't know. We just need to stick behind them. Those nags won't last forever. They can't stop and change horses, for we'll catch them then, and Persius there is fine fettle. We'll get them, providing we can keep them in sight."

Vi nodded her agreement to this, finding with a little surprise that she had complete confidence in Leo. So, she sat back and left him to the business of driving. Islington, North Finchley, and Barnet came and went before Leo turned back to her.

"All right, Vi?" he asked, concern in his eyes.

"Perfectly," she replied, hoping she sounded calmer than she felt as she patted his arm. "Don't you fret about me, Leo. Just concentrate on getting Mau back."

"You're a great gun, do you know that? A real Trojan," he said with admiration. "I've always known it, but… but I ought to have told you before now. Long, long before now."

Vi blinked, a little taken aback by what truly was high praise from Leo and meant far more to her than any flattery about her looks. "Thank you," she replied cautiously, finding herself glowing with happiness at words which some women would have little appreciated. After all, women were supposed to aspire to be fragile creatures who would swoon at the least breath of chill wind, never mind a breakneck race to recover a kidnapped cat. Ought that to be catnapped? She wondered absently, before scolding herself for clearly losing her mind.

"Where are they?" Leo demanded as they reached Potter's Bar.

They had been gaining steadily upon the hackney, but it had turned a corner and had been out of sight for a few minutes. Now, it had simply vanished.

"I can't see them," Vi exclaimed, turning in her seat as they flew down the High Street. "They must have turned off."

"Hell and damnation!" Leo muttered, which Vi thought a most appropriate response and only wished she'd been brave enough to say it herself.

"Ask this lady," she suggested, pointing to the side of the road where a woman was walking with a basket on her arm.

Leo nodded and did as she suggested.

"Good afternoon, madam. I beg your pardon, but might you have seen a hackney cab come this way in the past few minutes?"

The elderly woman, who appeared to be returning from the shops with a full basket, gazed up at Leo with blatant admiration and returned a surprisingly coquettish smile. "No, pet, sorry. Did someone run off with your sweetheart? More fool them, if they did," she remarked with a chuckle. "I'd let you catch me, right enough."

Leo shook his head, too worried to banter with the lady, as Vi suspected he would have otherwise done. "Not my sweetheart, but they are running away, the villains."

"Perhaps they're catching the train. Blasted noisy, dirty things," she added in disgust. "They opened that new line this year. Horrid thing. My hens won't lay since those great rattling engines started coming through."

"Oh, Leo," Vi said in concern. "You don't think…?"

"I don't know," he said grimly. "But we had best find out. Thank you, madam, for your help."

"You'd best hurry," she called after them as the distant but shrill whistle of a steam engine pierced the air.

Cursing, Leo sped the horse and Vi just held on, praying, as he negotiated the streets towards the train station. They had just turned a corner when Leo was forced to pull Persius to a swift halt as a hay-laden cart filled the road before them as the owner negotiated a tight turn into a small farmstead.

"Sorry, sir, won't be above a moment," the farmer called out cheerfully, but they could not afford to wait, so Leo backed the tilbury up and with such skill, Vi exclaimed in admiration.

"Oh, well done, Leo!"

He was in no mood to comment now, however, and the moment he could he urged the horse on once more, cantering down the road until they found the next turning. They could hear the train, and Vi's heart sank as she realised it was moving. They arrived beside the still unfinished station to see the train leaving.

"There's the hackney!" Vi exclaimed, praying that they had given up on the idea of taking Mau and left him behind. Leo thrust the reins into Vi's hands, leapt from the tilbury and ran over to the abandoned hackney cab. Vi watched, praying silently as Leo wrenched the door open and looked inside. She knew at once that Mau was not there.

Leo's shoulders sagged for a moment before he gathered himself and ran back to the tilbury.

"We'll have to follow the line and ask at each station if anyone has got off carrying a sack," he said, his tone even as he climbed back in beside her. "Vi—"

"We're following the trainline, Leo. I can hop on a train back at any time," she told him firmly, determined not to give him the opportunity to send her home. She could see how worried he was now, and he would need her support. Norton was a good man, she knew, but it was not the same as having a friend with you when things were going wrong.

"Alone?" he said in disgust. "You know that's not possible, Vi. Anything could happen."

"I'm sure it could not," she countered, but the set of his jaw suggested she would not persuade him otherwise.

"Very well, I can send a telegram then, and get someone to meet me," she suggested. "All the train stations have them these days. I'll send word to Mama, and she'll sort something out, for she'll worry when we don't come home."

"Not all the stations have telegraph offices," he warned her sternly. "Only the larger ones."

"Well, we shall find one that does, I'm sure," Vi replied firmly.

"Don't blame me when your reputation lies in shreds," he grumbled, though she knew very well he did not mean the harsh words.

"I shan't do so, don't fret," she said comfortably, earning herself a look of sheer incredulity from Leo.

"I must change horses. Persius can't keep this pace up forever," he said, returning them to the high street.

"Do I have your approval to ask Norton to go in and arrange a basket of food?" Vi asked him. "It's dreadfully hot and I think it may be a long afternoon. We shall need to keep our strength up and have a good supply of drinks."

Leo nodded, absently reaching over and patting her knee. "Good idea, love, thank you."

Vi blinked, the feel of his gloved hand on her knee burning through her skirts. It just showed the depths of his worry, she supposed, that he had taken to treating her like one of his light o' loves. More worryingly, she discovered she didn't mind in the least.

They were back on the road again in good time, and Leo was relieved to discover the new horse was a good goer. Not anywhere near so good as a train, however. The fear that they might not catch up with the villain nagged at him. He wondered if he had done the right thing in setting out after them. Perhaps if he'd gone home, a ransom would have arrived that night and he could have had Mau back beside him before morning. Yet he knew he could not have done such a thing, sensible as it might have been. Mau was his friend, and you did not abandon friends under any circumstances. Leo would find him, no matter what. The worry that the great cat might make the villain's journey so difficult they disposed of him rather than continue with their plan was something of which he was horribly aware. If they just let him go, perhaps Mau could make his way home. He had heard such stories of animals undertaking vast journeys, but he knew such a trip would be fraught with danger and would take time and, during all that time, he would not know if Mau was dead or alive. His stomach clenched, and he shook off the maudlin sensation. Mau was the cleverest animal he'd ever known, and Leo was determined to find him. Between them they would make it work.

With Vi's help, of course.

Leo darted a look at her, guilt sitting heavily in his guts. He knew very well he ought to have forced her from the carriage and told Norton to escort her home, but he hadn't wanted to. He needed Vi beside him, wanted her there. She was far bolder and more courageous than she gave herself credit for. He knew that; it was only Vi herself who had forgotten. As a girl, she'd flung herself into whatever madcap adventure he'd suggested and loved every moment of it, but something had changed. She had grown up, he supposed, into a proper young lady and not a hoyden. Sometimes, however, he felt certain she longed to do something she ought not, something wild and reckless, like joining him in a mad dash across town and country in pursuit of Mau.

After Hatfield and Welwyn Garden City, they stopped at Woolmer Green, where they also changed horse again, all with no luck. By the time they'd arrived at the bustling market town of Biggleswade, it was approaching seven in the evening and Leo knew he must force Vi to be sensible. He knew the stubborn creature well enough to believe her ruination would not be enough to make her agree to marry him. If it were, he'd play his part in it happily enough. But Vi could be ruined ten times over and would endure everything that went with it, rather than be forced into doing something she did not wish to do. He had to admit he admired her principles and her fortitude. He only wished she wasn't so wilful on this particular subject.

"I'm going to send a telegram to Mama. I think Biggleswade is a big enough station to have one," she said, as Leo threw the reins to Norton. Leo nodded, beyond relieved he would not have to persuade her to do so, though he wished he could keep her with him more than he dared admit. He'd leave Norton to look after her until her family arrived, whilst he carried on his pursuit alone. A dismal thought.

"That's the ticket," he said as he leapt down from the carriage, knowing it was for the best. It was almost five hours since he'd collected her in Piccadilly for a jaunt in the park and she must be worn to a thread. Her family must be fretting by now, too. He looked up at her as he offered her his hand and she stepped neatly down.

"Thank you," she said, smiling at him.

Damn him, but he wished she didn't have to go, selfish devil that he was. "Here," he said, taking a handful of coins from his pocket. "Dashed expensive things, telegrams, and you'll have not come prepared for such an outlay when you were expecting a quiet turn around Hyde Park."

"No, indeed," she agreed ruefully, accepting the coins with a smile.

"Well, I'll leave Norton to accompany you and make enquiries about our villains," he said. "Perhaps you could also send a telegram to my father, ask him to keep an eye on my place and see if anyone arrives with a ransom note for Mau. If we can telegram, one must assume the blackguards who have him could. Perhaps they have an associate in town awaiting them."

Vi reached out and squeezed his fingers. "I shall, of course. That is a wise idea. Good luck," she said softly. "I'm sure there will be news this time."

Though she would probably scold him for it, Leo grabbed her hand and pressed it firmly to his lips, kissing her knuckles.

"Thanks, love," he said, and turned and hurried away before she could do so.

♡♧◇♤

Vi stood for a moment, staring stupidly after Leo. *Don't be a ninny*, she warned herself sternly. Shaking off the desire to run after him and not let him out of her sight ever again, she set off with Norton to send the telegrams.

Once her task was completed, and she had finished exclaiming over the exorbitant sum of seven shillings and sixpence for each telegram, she returned to the tilbury. Norton hurried to look over both carriage and horse, having paid a boy to look after them. Finding all in order, he paid the lad and helped Vi back into her seat.

"He won't like it," he warned her. "And likely he'll be mad as fire with me for allowing it."

"Piffle," Vi said succinctly. "In the first place, you did not allow me. You have no authority over me, as Leo knows very well. If he can't make me do as he wishes, he cannot expect you to do so."

"All the same, Miss Spencer, don't you think—"

"No, I do not," she replied, glaring at him. "I believe I have made my feelings clear."

"Yes, miss, but—"

"No buts!" she said firmly, holding up her hand. "You have made a compelling argument, Norton, of which I am in perfect agreement. However, I will not abandon my friend when Mau is missing. Once he is safely returned, I shall go meekly home, my word upon it."

Norton groaned and muttered predictions of chaos and destruction under his breath until Leo reappeared. Vi sat up straight, immediately noticing the renewed sense of energy about him.

"They were here!" he said triumphantly. "The station master distinctly remembered a stocky fellow and a tall, rangy man with him, carrying a sack. Said it was howling and hissing, and they were getting hassled by the other passengers who thought him cruel to transport a cat under such conditions."

"Oh, Leo! That's marvellous news but poor Mau, he must be so frightened," Vi exclaimed. "Where did they go?"

His expression faltered a little. "That's where the good news ends. It seems they cadged a lift with a farmer, but no one knows who, and one witness said they went off northeast in the direction of Tadlow, the other swears blind they went south on the Langford road."

"So, what shall we do?" she asked.

"Well, I shall carry on to the northeast," he said decisively. "I don't like the idea of retracing my steps and if I'm wrong, having to do it all again."

"That makes sense," Vi agreed, patting the seat beside her. "Hop up, then. There's no time to waste. We might have Mau back before nightfall yet."

"We?" Leo said, still standing beside the carriage. He stared at her intently and Vi felt the tiny hairs on the back of her neck stand on end. Determined, she sat a little straighter.

"Yes, Leo, *we*. Do hurry, now. There's not a moment to lose."

"Hold up, Vi," he said, shaking his head. "I thought you were sending a telegram to your mama?"

"I did do so," she said, but before she could carry on, Norton cut in.

"She told 'em Mau had been taken, and that she was helping you get him back and not to worry. She didn't say nothing about coming to fetch her."

"Norton," Vi said reproachfully. "That was not helpful."

"Vi!" Leo exclaimed, snatching the hat from his head. "You wicked girl! You said you were going to send word to your mama to collect you."

"I never did," Vi protested. "I merely said I was sending a telegram."

"Before," Leo gritted out through clenched teeth. "At Potters Bar, you said—"

"Oh, then," she said, waving this off dismissively. "That was before. I changed my mind."

Leo made a sound of frustration and leapt up into the tilbury. His thigh pressed hard against Vi's, and she shifted nervously, suddenly vibratingly aware of the size of him, and the fact that he was quite furious with her. She had never seen Leo truly angry before and it was an interesting experience.

"I could shake you," he said, glaring at her.

Vi swallowed. "I can see that."

"Norton," Leo said, not taking his eyes from her.

"Yes, sir."

"Take your place, please."

"Yes, sir." Norton fled to the back of the tilbury. Vi rather envied him.

"What are you going to do tonight, Violetta?" Leo asked, his voice low. "If I don't find Mau, I'll have to stop for a few hours at least or I'll not be able to keep going tomorrow. I'll get a room in one of the inns here. What then, love?"

Vi tried to swallow again but her mouth was dry. "I-I thought of that," she said unsteadily. "I shall put my shawl over my head and pretend to be your maiden aunt."

"Ha!" The crack of laughter was so sudden and so loud she jumped, glaring at him with indignation. "In that outfit? I think not, pet. Oh no," he said, in a tone that made her skin prickle with foreboding. He leaned in, putting his mouth close to her ear, so close his warm breath fluttered against her neck, making her shiver.

"Leo—" she protested, but his next words chased anything she might have said clear from her mind.

"No, love. If you're staying, I shall take a room for us both. *One* room, and I shall sign you in as my wife. Unless you prefer to be my mistress?"

"Leo!" Vi said in outrage.

"Want to go home now?" he demanded, his eyes narrowing.

Vi's stubborn streak leapt to the fore, suppressing the immediate desire she'd just had to do exactly that. "Certainly not," she retorted, putting up her chin.

"Fine," Leo said through his teeth.

"Fine," she shot back, crossing her arms.

"Unbelievable," he muttered furiously, taking up the reins.

Vi pressed herself against the side of the tilbury as the horse walked on, wanting to be as far from Leo and his obvious displeasure as possible. His anger scalded her, a prickling sensation against her skin. As the minutes ticked past, Vi sighed, telling herself not to be such a ninny. This was Leo – *Leo*, not some man who might take advantage of her and the situation. Now that the worst was over, she allowed herself to relax a little. Leo might rant and rage and threaten, but the truth was, he would never lay a finger on her or do anything to risk her reputation. She knew it as she knew the sun would rise again in the morning. She trusted him. Still, while the daylight dimmed by degrees and the roads became quieter as they left the town behind, the realisation of what she'd just done sank in.

Oh, lud, she thought desperately, and wondered if she really had lost her mind.

Chapter 4

Dearest Matilda,

I think it's finally happened. Violetta did not come home after her outing with Leo. I think that nephew of yours has finally come to his senses and run off with her! How he persuaded her into it, I cannot imagine. Well, I can, obviously, but that Vi agreed is something else. Still, he's such a handsome fellow she was never going to hold out forever. I confess I would have capitulated to his advances the first time he flashed that wicked smile my way. Oh, I'm so excited. Also, I had the most peculiar message from Vi by telegraph this evening. Some story about Mau being kidnapped, as if I should believe such a thing. Why she thought she needed to make up a bizarre story, I do not know, but I suppose one does not wish to announce an elopement over a telegram. The news would be all over the city by morning. I wonder if they shall go to Greta Green. How romantic it would be. Of course there will be a dreadful scandal, not that I care a button for that, though Luke will not be pleased. I confess I have not told him the whole... I shall be in a deal of trouble, no doubt, when he discovers it.

Never mind. I must give Leo the chance he needs without his soon to be father-in-law barging in and spoiling things.

Keep fingers and toes crossed for me, Tilda. I shall keep you posted.

—Excerpt of a letter from The Right Hon'ble Kitty Baxter, The Countess of Trevick, to her friend The Most Hon'ble Matilda Barrington, The Marchioness of Montagu.

24th June 1850, somewhere northeast of Biggleswade.

Tadlow was a tiny village on the river and Leo's spirits sank as they arrived in the centre by the parish church, for they were no nearer to finding Mau. There had been a magnificent sunset that had lightened both their hearts while it endured, for it had been a thing of great beauty, streaking the sky with great swathes of vibrant pink and startling orange. It would be full dark in little more than half an hour, however, though there was a bright waxing moon that promised not to leave them entirely plunged into gloom. No one he'd asked had seen a farmer carrying two men, one tall, one short, in his cart, and now anyone with a grain of sense had gone indoors for dinner. This was utterly pointless. He could hardly stop at every house and cottage after dark and demand if anyone had his cat. Worse, he had likely ruined Violetta and, whilst he was all for marrying her to get her out of a fix, he very much doubted his luck was about to improve.

"Look there," Vi said, and Leo turned towards her, seeing her white-gloved hand as a ghostly shape in the rapidly dimming light. "There's the vicar. Perhaps he might know if there were any such desperate fellows in the neighbourhood, the kind that might ransom a cat."

"Well, it's worth a try," Leo admitted. "Though I don't know how I'm going to explain you away."

"Tell him I'm your wife," Vi said with a shrug.

"You want me to lie to a man of God?" Leo said, raising his eyebrows.

"Well, you were ready enough to do it to an innkeeper," she replied, tart as ever. "Don't tell me you're coming over all principled now."

"Are you suggesting I'm unprincipled?" he demanded indignantly.

"I don't know," she said, putting a finger to her lips and affecting an innocently quizzical expression. "What might have put such a thought in my head?"

Despite himself and the dire nature of their predicament, Leo gave a bark of laughter. "And you had the nerve to say Tilly was a dreadful girl. You are the queen of dreadful girls, Vi. No, the empress. You are far too regal to be a mere queen."

"Ridiculous man," Vi said, but without heat.

Leo thought she looked quite pleased by his words. "Come, then, lady wife. Let us tell the poor vicar a tissue of lies that will likely come back to bite us at some point soon."

"Yes, let's," Vi said placidly, accepting Leo's hand and stepping down from the tilbury.

She took his arm and Leo felt a sudden, urgent desire for the ruse to be true. He was worried sick about Mau but comforted himself that any kidnapper with an ounce of sense knew it was in their interest to keep their victim hale and hearty if they wanted their money. The only thing that truly distracted him from his anxiety, however, was Vi's calm and no-nonsense presence on the seat beside him. Not that he felt calm. Not in the least. Between desperation to have his friend back with him and the tantalising idea that he might really share a bedroom with Vi tonight, he was all on edge. That his plans might be best served by not being entirely a gentleman was one that he was having a good deal of trouble putting to one side.

"Excuse me! I beg your pardon, Reverend?"

Leo brought his unruly musings to a halt and returned his attention to Vi, who was hailing the vicar.

"Good evening, sir, madam. How might I be of service to you?" the vicar asked. He was standing by the door to the church, clearly about to close it and make his way home.

"We're sorry to trouble you, sir," Leo said politely. "And I'm afraid you will think it a very odd thing, but we need to ask your advice."

"Well, I'm rather fond of odd things," the vicar said with a crooked smile that showed large tombstone teeth in the front. He was a largish man, a little on the portly side, with thinning white hair and glasses and an air of bonhomie that immediately made Leo feel more relaxed. "Not that asking a vicar for advice is such an odd thing," he added with a chuckle before looking between them with sudden concern.

"Oh, of course, it is a sensible thing indeed to ask your advice," Vi said hurriedly, clearly anxious about what the man was thinking. "It's more the nature of the advice that is a little… out of the ordinary."

The vicar looked intrigued. "Well, how thrilling. Might I invite you to come to the vicarage and take a little sherry with me? I usually have one at this hour. It's just a few steps away, over the road there."

"That would be most kind of you," Leo agreed, wanting nothing more than to find Mau, but the man seemed a good sort and it wouldn't do to offend him. Moreover, the idea of sitting on a seat that didn't move for a short while was more than appealing. It had been a warm day, and the night was muggy still. He was hot, sweaty and dusty, and in dire need of a bath and his dinner. Not so long ago, he'd have thought nothing about a race from one end of one county to the other end of another, lasting several days over terrible roads. The idea of such a thing now was in no way tempting.

"Must be getting old," he muttered to himself, shaking his head as they followed the vicar.

"Sorry?" Vi asked, looking up at him.

"Nothing," he said with a sigh.

"He seems like a very nice man, I'm sure he'll help us," Vi said, squeezing his arm.

Leo nodded. "He does, and I'm sure he will. *If* he can."

They were let inside a small, thatched cottage with many beams that Leo had to duck low to navigate. Vi looked around the cosy vicarage with approval. Whoever the reverend's housekeeper was, assuming he wasn't married, she did a splendid job.

"I'm afraid Mrs Chalmers, my housekeeper, has taken herself off for the night," the vicar said, answering her question for her. "Or you'd be pressed to eat a 'little something' that more closely resembled a four-course meal. As it's just me, would sherry and a plate of sugar biscuits suffice? Or I could run to a hot cup of tea?" he added, though Vi thought he looked a little uncertain about this last.

"Sherry would be splendid," she agreed at once. "And sugar biscuits are just the thing. We've had a rather long day, I'm afraid."

"Excellent," he said, with obvious relief. "Oh, and do sit down. Where are my manners? What a shocking fellow I am, to be sure."

"Indeed, you are most kind to be so hospitable at this hour of the evening," Vi said soothingly, as the reverend poured the sherry.

He handed her the first glass. "There you are, Mrs—good heavens! I forgot the introductions. Dear me. Mrs Chalmers would be most disappointed in me. Don't tell her," he added in an anxious whisper.

"We shan't, and we are to blame, I'm sure," Vi told him.

He beamed at her and held out his hand. "The Reverend Harbottle at your service, madam."

Vi opened her mouth and then closed it again, suddenly aware she would need to lie. She looked desperately at Leo, who raised one eyebrow.

Devil take him!

"Mrs Hunt-*ington,*" she said, adding the extra syllables in a rush as she belatedly realised she couldn't possibly use his real name.

"Charmed," the reverend Harbottle said, offering his hand to Leo, who shook it warmly. "And your drink, Mr Huntington."

"Thank you."

Having settled himself down with his own sherry, the reverend looked between them with an air of great expectation. "Now then, about this very odd thing you wished to ask me about."

"My cat has been abducted," Leo said baldly.

Vi glared at him, not thinking this was the best way to introduce the topic but it was too late now. The reverend stared at him, obviously reassessing his opinion of them as sensible people and wondering where they'd escaped from.

"Forgive my husband," Vi said quickly, before Leo could make things worse. "It's a rather silly story, I know, but the thing is, Mau is a rather… unusual cat. That is to say… he's rare," she added.

"Rare?" the vicar said with interest. "As in, valuable?"

"Indeed," Vi said, glad he'd caught on so quickly. For they could not explain how well-known Mau was among the *ton*—and apparently with anyone who read the scandal sheets. She only hoped the vicar did not keep up with fashionable gossip. "He's very rare, and extremely valuable."

"Mau?" the vicar mused, tugging at his ear thoughtfully. "Sounds Egyptian."

"It is!" Vi cut in. "He's an Egyptian… err… Water…" She floundered, the only word coming to mind being *spaniel* which clearly wouldn't do.

"An Egyptian Water Sphinx," Leo said, and with such utter confidence that it was all Vi could do to keep her countenance. As it was, she could not look at him.

"You don't say," the vicar said, clearly fascinated. "I've never heard of such a thing."

"Well, you wouldn't have," Vi said with a touch of hysteria.

"Because he's terribly rare," Leo added. "We don't care in the least about his value, however, for he is a much beloved pet, and we are desperate to get him back. The thing is, we were out walking him in Hyde Park—"

"Walking him… the cat… in Hyde Park," the vicar said doubtfully. For whilst he was prepared to believe in an Egyptian Water Sphinx, this part of the story seemed a little dubious.

Leo nodded. "He's more like a dog than a cat, you see. Follows me everywhere. Of course, the villains who took him must have known this. They swiped him from under my very nose— something I shall never forgive myself for," he added, and Vi knew every word he spoke this time was entirely true. "We gave chase but lost them at Potters Bar, where they caught a train. We've been stopping at every station since and finally discovered they got off at Biggleswade. I spoke to witnesses who suggested they headed this way, but it's late and the few people about had seen nothing of them."

"So we wondered," Vi carried on hopefully. "If perhaps you might know of anyone in your parish who—"

"—who might abduct an Egyptian Water Sphinx," the vicar finished.

"Quite so." Vi gave him an encouraging smile, and the vicar sat back in his seat, contemplating the question.

"Well," he said thoughtfully. "The kind of people who would be involved in such a despicable act are not often the sort who come to church, but…" he said, leaving the one word hanging there as he helped himself to another biscuit and chewed with a pensive expression.

"But?" Leo pressed, too anxious to let the fellow cogitate for long.

"Might I request you leave the question with me and return in the morning?" the vicar asked them with an apologetic smile. "The thing is, I do have a suspect or two in mind, but I should like to do a little, er… investigating before I go throwing accusations of kidnapping about or should that be catnapping?" he added reflectively.

Leo opened his mouth to protest, and Vi poked him. He closed it again, glaring at her, and Vi felt a sudden thrill of something she refused to name at the prospect of spending a night in the same bedroom as Leo. A blush crept up the back of her neck and into her cheeks and she feigned fascination with the tiny glass that held what remained of her sherry rather than look at him any longer.

"Of course, Reverend," Leo said politely, resignation in his voice. "I am grateful indeed for your help. I confess I had hoped to have Mau back before nightfall, but I cannot expect miracles, I suppose."

"Don't lose heart, young man," the vicar said cheerfully. "If they have taken the poor creature for ransom, one supposes they will keep him fed and watered. If there's anything I can do to help you in your quest, I shall do it."

"You are most kind, and if your help leads to the return of my cat, I can promise you a generous donation to your church fund," Leo said with his most charming smile.

The vicar beamed at him. "Oh! Bless you! We desperately need a new roof so such a thing would indeed be miraculous from my point of view. I confess, I've been worrying about it, for Tadlow is such a small place and the people don't have funds enough for such donations. There's talk of moving me on," he added sadly. "I shall retire if they suggest it. I'm too old to start over."

"Then perhaps we can help each other," Vi said hopefully. She knew Leo was a generous man and, if Mau was returned to him and Reverend Harbottle was instrumental in that happening, she did not doubt he would pay for the church's new roof.

"God truly does work in mysterious ways," the vicar mused as he bade them goodnight and escorted them to the door.

"Let's hope so," Leo muttered under his breath.

"If you need lodgings for the night, might I suggest the Queen's Head in Wrestlingworth? My sister is the landlady there, so if you say Archibald sent you, I'm sure you'll be well looked after. She's a fine cook and keeps a clean, orderly place."

"Thank you for the recommendation," Leo replied, shaking the man's hand. "Shall we come here in the morning?"

"No, no. Sit tight and wait for me at the Queen's Head, for I don't know how long it will take me to stick my nose about the place and see if anything smells off," the vicar said confidentially.

He waved them goodbye with a cheerful smile and Vi turned to Leo as Norton climbed back onto his seat and they trotted away.

"I think he's looking forward to playing detective," she said ruefully.

Leo said nothing, and once again the prickling sense of unease crept over her skin.

"Are you still cross with me?" she ventured, after another five minutes passed in uncomfortable silence.

"Mad as fire," he replied succinctly.

Vi swallowed. "Really, Leo. We're grown up. So long as no one finds out, I really don't see why you must be so missish about it."

He shot her a volcanic look that made her wish she'd held her tongue.

"Missish?" he repeated, a hard note to his voice that boded ill. "I'm worrying about ruining you, Vi, for I know damned well you'll still not accept me as a husband, no matter if the entire world thought you were my mistress."

"We're in the back end of beyond. A tiny village. Who is likely to see us?" she protested. "And I trust you to behave like a gentleman."

"Oh, you do, do you? You've forced me to do the complete opposite of that by allowing you along on this farcical jaunt and refusing to be sensible and go home. I've treated you like I would a mistress by allowing you to remain at my side, not like a young lady in need of my protection. Why stop now?"

"Why indeed?" Vi retorted, her temper flaring as it always did when Leo vexed her. "Perhaps you treat your mistresses like sensible, intelligent women who know their own mind instead of like a silly child who needs constant chaperoning and watching over in case she does something foolish. That being the case, please continue."

Leo's eyes glittered, his handsome features silvered in the moonlight. He looked away from her, his jaw set, his profile the kind that ought to be stamped on a coin, for he looked like a prince or a monarch, all stiff pride and arrogance. "If you want me to treat you as my mistress, I shall be sure to do so, Vi," he said, a dangerous note to his voice that set all the hairs on the back of her neck prickling, her blood thrumming in her veins.

Vi opened her mouth to demand exactly what he meant by that but thought better of it. Instead, she considered what it might like to be Leo's mistress. The glamorous creature she had once seen had certainly seemed pleased with herself. The phrase 'cat that got the cream' had lingered in Vi's mind for days afterwards whenever she had recalled the chance encounter. She *had* recalled it too, though she had refused to acknowledge why the woman had bothered her so. Leo was a grown man, and even a sheltered young woman knew that men had needs which they were entitled to indulge so long as they were discreet about it.

Vi was not exactly sheltered, an impossible state when brought up by the indomitable Kitty. Her adopted mama was a woman who loved life, and loved her husband passionately, and had no qualms in discussing subjects which other ladies of her station would have thought quite beyond the pale. Vi knew very well what happened in the bedroom, and she knew too that there was pleasure for a woman as well as a man, if the man was a skilled and generous lover. If she were being honest, she was dreadfully curious about what such pleasures felt like and admitted to more than an occasional pang of longing that she would never know the touch of a man's hand, a passionate embrace, or kisses that made one giddy with longing. Mama had been enthusiastic about the raptures of a happy marriage, but then one only had to see Mama and Papa in the same room to know that they were still head over ears in love with each other.

Vi did not believe she could have that with Leo. He cared for her, that was true, she could even believe he loved her, in his own haphazard way, but it wasn't the kind of love she could put her trust in. She had too much evidence to suggest his attention span was short, and he bored easily. At best, she believed she would see little of him. At worst, she feared jealousy and misery would plague her whenever she discovered he had taken a new mistress. She could not live like that. But perhaps if Leo really could be brought to treat her as his mistress, just for one night, she might know what physical love felt like. So long as he knew it was just for one night, that they would never be more than friends, she could not be accused of using him or leading him on, could she? Leo would be kind and generous, she knew, and she had no doubt of his skills in the bedroom. Sadly, she had heard gossip enough to suggest he was not lacking in that department, another event which had given her weeks of sleepless nights and unwelcome, unsettling dreams. Of course, he would be impossible afterwards. He would feel it his 'duty' to marry her after he had ruined her so entirely, but she would simply have to refuse him. He could not bully her into accepting him, after all, and Vi knew she was every bit as stubborn as he was.

There was the question of a child. It was a risk indeed, but Mama had assured her there were ways of mitigating the risk. Vi was aware of some, and felt certain Leo would know them all intimately. She glanced sideways at him, heat burning in her cheeks at the idea she might really take him into her bed tonight. For a moment, she wondered what it might feel like to touch what lay beneath the exquisitely cut clothes he wore, wondered what that hard, athletic body might feel like against her own.

She must have made a small sound, for he turned, his eyes narrowing as he stared at her.

"Have you come to your senses?" he asked curiously. "Ready to admit you've been foolish and ought to have gone home like I told you?"

Vi swallowed, forcing herself to hold his gaze. "Not precisely," she replied, licking her lips nervously. His gaze shot to the movement and lingered on her mouth, giving her an odd, hot sensation low in her belly. Interesting. His gaze returned to hers and his eyes narrowed.

"Don't look at me like that," he said crossly.

Smiling a little to herself, Vi bit her lip and wondered if her courage would hold out when they got to the inn.

Chapter 5

Dear Larkin,

I'm not sure you'll get this in time, but I'm in a bit of a fix. Actually, Vi and I are in a good deal of trouble. Mau has been taken and we are in pursuit of the kidnappers. Now we're stuck overnight in the backend of beyond and I'm terrified someone will see Vi with me. She'll be ruined and then she'll never marry me, stubborn creature that she is, because she'll think everyone will believe she must. I never knew a woman more contrary. I know I can count on your discretion, old man. For the love of God, get down here with her maid, and if you can manage it, her mama too. I know it will be devilish awkward for you, but Kitty is a no-nonsense sort, so if you explain things carefully, it will all be fine. Kitty will know how to deal with things before the entire world thinks I'm the sort of fellow who goes about ruining ladies of quality.

We're staying at the Queen's Head in Tadlow. The Vicar, the Reverend Harbottle, is helping us search for Mau, though he believes we are married. His sister owns the inn, and we are signed in as Mr and Mrs Huntington.

I'm paying a young man an exorbitant fee to ride through the night and get this to you by morning. I pray you are sober enough to do as I request. Please, Larkin, Vi is depending on you, little does she know it, and so am I.

—Excerpt of a letter from Mr Leo Hunt (Son of Alice and Nathanial Hunt) to The Hon'ble Larkin Weston (Son of The Right Hon'ble Solomon 'Solo' and Jemima Weston, Baron and Baroness Rothborn).

24th June 1850, The Queen's Head, Wrestlingworth, the Bedfordshire, Cambridgeshire border.

The Queen's Head was a handsome, red brick building and Leo felt a surge of relief at finding it was everything the vicar had suggested. Window boxes adorned the façade, planted up with bright flowers and moonlight reflected off the gleaming glass behind them. Inside, they were greeted politely by the reverend's sister, who looked askance at their lack of baggage until Leo explained that her brother had sent them.

"We've had a bit of a mishap," Leo explained, in no mood to get into a long-winded tale about Egyptian Water Sphinxes at this time of night. He was tired and hungry and horribly aware he would need his wits about him for the coming night. "Your brother is helping us, but thought we would do well to come here for the night. He is to meet us here in the morning."

The landlady, a Mrs Caruthers, relaxed in the light of this information. She was a pleasantly plump woman in her late fifties with the ruddy complexion of a woman who spent long hours in the kitchen. "Oh, well, if Archie thinks it's all right, then of course

I shall welcome you," she said with a sigh. "Only one must be so careful. We're a respectable house, we are, but you'd be surprised at the sorts who try to book a room. Pretending to be married," she added confidentially, mouthing the words behind her hand to Leo so she did not shock Vi.

"Indeed," Leo said gravely, praying the woman never discovered the truth. "Shocking."

"Well, it is," she said, shaking her head. "I don't know what the world is coming to with such goings on, but not in my inn! Now then, Mr Caruthers would normally greet you and show you up, but he's indisposed tonight—his gout is playing him up—but as you've no baggage to carry, perhaps I might just give you your key, for I'm run off my feet, truth be told."

"Certainly," Leo said, giving her his most winning smile as she handed the key over.

"It's our best room," she told him, responding to his smile with a warm expression that crinkled her eyes. "A nice big comfy bed and there's a lovely view, though you'll only appreciate that in the morning."

"Thank you kindly," Leo said, aware that Vi had turned a startling shade of scarlet at the mention of the 'nice big comfy bed,' and was eager to get her away from the woman before Mrs Caruthers noticed and got suspicious.

"There's a lamb stew for dinner, and apple pie," she added, looking enquiringly at them.

"Yes, perfect. In our rooms, if you don't mind. And perhaps a hot bath?" Leo added, placing a generous pile of coins on the counter between them.

"Oh! Yes, sir. Certainly, sir, I'll see to it at once," the woman replied, beaming at his generosity, calling for the attention of a passing serving maid in the light of such munificence. "Jenny, leave that a moment. Run up to the rose chamber and light the candles and turn the bed down, there's a good girl. If you'd like to follow Jenny, sir, she'll show you the way."

Leo nodded but went to speak to Norton first. "Arrange your dinner and a room, but then I want you to leave at first light and return to town. Explain everything to Lady Trevick," he said, handing Norton enough coin to cover the expense of such a journey. "I shall send a messenger to Mr Weston which will arrive before you do, but just in case he is in no fit state to help me, I should like a backup."

"Yes, sir," Norton said, understanding at once. "I'll bring a change of clothes and the like for you too, sir."

"Good man," Leo said in approval before turning and guiding Vi away and towards the stairs as Jenny darted quickly ahead of them. "Come, lady wife," he murmured. "Let us investigate that nice, big, comfy bed."

It was wicked of him, but he could not help but feel she deserved a little retribution for landing him in this fix. He had no doubt who it was would shoulder the blame should they be discovered. He *would* bear it too, and gladly, if only she would marry him.

Fat chance.

He glanced at Vi to see how this sally had been swallowed, expecting a frosty glare of indignation, and was startled to see something else entirely in her gaze. Speculation, or was that curiosity, glinted in her eyes and a little sliver of apprehension slid down his spine.

Following in Jenny's wake, they were guided to the rose chamber, which was aptly named. The door opened on well-oiled hinges and showed them a clean, spacious room with whitewashed walls upon which a deft hand had painted simple but recognisable pink roses. The roses climbed extravagantly over beams and around an enormous four-poster bed, over which was a counterpane likewise embellished with embroidered pink cabbage roses and hung with bed curtains in a printed rose fabric. A vase of fresh roses in varying shades from pale blush to shocking fuchsia sat on a small table by the window, their sweet scent perfuming the room. Leo blanched, a little overwhelmed by the excessive amounts of pink, but Vi seemed utterly charmed so he relaxed, pleased that she was content with the room at least.

Jenny hurried to light the lamps, draw the curtains and turn down the bed. "Will you be wanting a fire, sir?"

It was a warm night, but Leo looked to Vi, who shook her head, much to his relief. He had no desire to sleep in a sauna, which the room would surely become with a fire *and* a bath.

"No, thank you, but a cold bottle of your best white wine would be appreciated," he told her, giving her a generous tip as she grinned at him and bobbed a curtsey. "Yes, sir."

Jenny went out, closing the door behind her and Leo turned back to Vi, who was regarding the huge bed with an arrested expression.

"Second thoughts, pet?" he asked her casually, setting his hat and gloves down on top of the chest of drawers beside him.

"Not in the least," she said briskly. "There's room for an army in that thing," she added, nodding at the bed.

"Well, certainly fifty dozen roses, at least," he remarked.

She laughed at that and glanced back at him. "Do you hate it? I find the effect quite charming."

"It's not to my taste, but if it pleases you, I am in alt, sweet," he said, wondering how far he could push his luck with the pet names. He had promised to treat her as he would his mistress, after all. She had apparently decided to ignore such endearments, for she made no remark, only untying her bonnet.

"I wonder if the excellent Mrs Caruthers could do something with my frock?" she asked, looking at the dust and creases upon the fetching gown with dismay.

"Why don't you take it off and I'll have Jenny see to it when she comes back with the wine?" Leo said, a challenging glint in his eyes. Now, surely that would get a reaction, he thought, bracing himself for the fallout. None came.

"Very well," she said, casting her discarded bonnet down on the bed with her gloves. "You'll have to help me, though, for the buttons are all in the back."

Leo froze, certain he must have misunderstood as she undid the short jacket and laid it over the back of a chair. She stood waiting, her hands on her hips. Leo stared at her. She couldn't be serious. Could she?

She glanced over her shoulder at him a moment later, her expression one of impatience. "Well? What's wrong? Have you forgotten how to undo buttons? From what I hear, you've had practise enough."

"No," Leo said carefully, his heart beating too fast, and what exactly had she heard? "Have you forgotten I'm not your maid?"

She looked back at him again, giving him a swift look up and down. "No. I've not forgotten. Rachel is much smaller than you, but at least twice as wide. I'm simply not *that* forgetful."

"Really?" he demanded incredulously, temper rising now. What was she thinking? "For you seem to have forgotten who you are. Have you taken leave of your senses? You are alone in a bedroom with a *man.*"

"No, I'm alone in a bedroom with *you*, Leo. That's quite different," she said coolly, not looking at him.

Leo reared back as if she'd slapped him. "I beg your pardon? What the devil is that supposed to mean?"

She let out a long-suffering sigh and shook her head. "Oh, good heavens, I meant no insult to your manly pride. I only meant that I trust you. I know you would do nothing I did not wish for you to do, and we are to be here all night, and you did order a bath. Did you suppose I would get into it fully dressed?"

"No," he said, somewhat mollified. "I supposed I would get Jenny to help you undress and make myself scarce while you bathed."

"Ah. Then you only offered to give her my gown when she returns to rile me," she suggested with the lift of one eyebrow.

Leo shrugged, feeling like a boy caught with his fingers in a biscuit tin.

"And when *you* bathed?" she asked with interest, for they both knew she could not go downstairs unescorted. "What was your plan for that eventuality?"

"I assumed you would look the other way," he said irritably, though if he were entirely honest, he'd rather hoped she might peek.

"I see. Well, Jenny and Mrs Caruthers are clearly run off their feet, so you may help me," she said, turning away from him once more. He wondered if he detected a tremor in her voice, but she looked entirely cool and poised. He, on the other hand, was not. The idea of laying his hands on Vi and undressing her was doing terrible things to his composure. Before he could decide how or what to do with the vexing woman, there was a knock at the door.

He opened it to find Jenny bearing a tray. "Your wine, sir. Mrs Caruthers said it's Mr Caruthers' best. An excellent Portuguese hock, medium dry, from Bucelas," she recited, obviously having been told just what to say.

"Thank you, Jenny. How long until dinner?" Leo asked.

"Missus said it will be up directly, so I reckon about ten minutes."

Leo nodded. "My wife needs her gown freshened up. Can you…?"

Jenny, who he had noticed regarding Vi's stylish outfit with obvious interest, nodded at once. "Yes, sir. I can see to it. Should the lady like me to assist her?"

"She would," Leo said at once and with relief. "And is it possible you have something suitable to lend her? We did not expect to be away overnight, you see."

"Oh," Jenny said, this apparently not so simple a request. "I have something I can lend her, I suppose, but it's not very fine, I'm afraid. Not what she'll be used to."

"It will be perfect," Leo assured her, opening the door. "Come in and I shall leave you ladies to your tasks. Call me when all is in order," he said with a wink, making the girl blush.

"Yes, sir," she said with a giggle, carrying the wine inside as Leo made himself scarce.

♡♧◇♤

"Coward," Vi muttered crossly as Leo closed the door behind him.

"Beg pardon, madam?" Jenny said, looking at her in confusion.

"Nothing, Jenny. Might I have some of that wine, please?"

Jenny nodded and poured her a glass before hurrying out again to fetch whatever item of clothing she had in mind for Vi to borrow.

Vi sat on the bed, sipping the wine and considering what to do next. She wondered if Leo was right and she had taken leave of her senses, but as she went through her options again, she decided it was an entirely sensible decision. She had known in the back of her mind that she would never marry, though she had not allowed herself to face the prospect head on until recently. It had been Leo who had made her face it too, by demanding to know why she rejected every man who showed an interest in her. He had accused her of refusing them because she only wanted him, which Vi had denied strenuously. Of course she had. But once alone, with his words ringing in her ears, she'd had to consider them seriously and discovered he was right, damn him. She wanted Leo or no one, and as Leo was out of reach—if she did not want to spend the rest of her days in a state of constant anxiety and likely misery too—then no one it was.

She'd thought she'd made peace with her decision, though the idea of having no children of her own was a sharp stab of regret in her heart. Even if she married now, she was likely too old to produce any babies, though, another reason she must not marry Leo, for he ought to be a father. He'd be a fine one once he grew up himself. She discovered there were other aspects of her spinsterhood which she was less sanguine about than she'd perhaps realised before, though, and now, through no fault of her own, she could do something about it. Fate had given her a once in a lifetime chance to take something for herself before she settled down to a respectable existence as an old maid. Supposing Leo could be persuaded to go along with her plan.

Vi looked down at the empty glass, rather surprised to discover she had drunk the contents. Well, that might be the best idea. Another glass might give her courage, though she must take care not to appear foxed, or else Leo would accuse her of not being in her right mind. So, she poured herself another glass and sipped at it until Jenny returned.

"Here we go, miss," she said, holding up a clean but rather worn cotton nightgown. It's not what you'll be used to, I'm afraid," she said apologetically.

"It's perfect, Jenny," Vi assured her, though privately she lamented the lack of lace or ribbons. She could have done with something a bit more seductive to help her entice Leo, for she did not have the greatest confidence her own attractions were enough to tempt him. Still, she had heard it said that men were not precisely choosy if a woman was free with her charms, so perhaps he would overlook such an unflattering item of bedwear.

Jenny helped Vi out of her travel-worn garments with deft hands and hurried away with the billowing pile of fabric, leaving Vi to regard herself in the mirror on the dressing table.

"Oh dear," she murmured, for she ought to have considered that Jenny was not of the same shape as she, the girl being rather less well-endowed in the bust and hips. Still, there was no help for it now, as there was a knock and Leo entered the room.

"Dinner is on the way up," he said cheerfully. "Did Jenny find—"

He broke off as Vi turned, staring at her with an expression she could not read.

Reminding herself forcefully of what her aim was tonight, Vi unlocked her hands from over her bust and watched dubiously as Leo's gaze roamed over her. Colour crested his high cheekbones, and she saw his Adam's apple bob as he swallowed.

"Christ," he muttered, his voice hoarse.

Vi felt her own colour rise as she considered what she had seen in the looking glass, for the cotton was soft and thin from age and washing and was nigh on sheer. Clinging against her breasts and hips, it left little to the imagination, the darker shapes of her nipples clearly defined.

A knock at the door broke the strange, prickling atmosphere and Leo almost jumped out of his skin, tearing his gaze from her. Before Vi could ask what he was doing, he pulled the counterpane from the bed and wrapped it tightly around her, guiding her to the chair and sitting her down in it.

"Don't move," he told her, his blue eyes strangely electric in the lamplight as he gazed down at her.

Vi almost demanded how he expected her to do so as she was sat upon the outer fold with her arms trapped inside the layers. She felt like a large caterpillar. Leo turned away before she had the chance, however, and stalked to the door, pulling it open.

"Dinner, sir."

"Bring it in," Leo said, nodding at Jenny and another maid, an older woman this time, perhaps in her early thirties. She stared at Leo with unashamed interest as they came into the room and arranged the plates and dishes on the round table by the window. Her gaze also took in Vi, biting her lip against a giggle as she saw her looking like an overstuffed mummy. Vi did not doubt she was wondering how or why such a handsome fellow had caught himself such a homely wife and blushed harder than ever. Well, at least it illustrated very nicely why marrying Leo would be fraught with anxiety and never give her a moment's peace.

Leo tipped the girls, apparently oblivious to the older woman's flirtatious glance, which made Vi feel somewhat better. He closed the door after them and turned back, gazing abstractedly at the dishes on the table in silence.

"Are you proposing to feed me?" Vi asked, remembering too late she was intending to seduce him and regretting her caustic tone. "Perhaps I'll turn into a butterfly."

"Eh?" he said, turning to her. "Oh, beg pardon." He moved towards her and then stopped, staring down at her with an odd look in his eyes.

"Leo," Vi said, striving for a softer tone than she was feeling. "I can't move. Please help me up and unwrap me."

"Unwrap you," he repeated, an unsteady note to his voice.

"Yes, my arms are trapped and—," she complained and then remembered she couldn't seduce him and berate him at the same time and tried for a winning smile that felt stiff and odd.

The expression seemed to disturb him, for he took a step back. "Maybe that's for the best."

Good lord, he was thinking of leaving her this way.

"Of course it isn't for the best!" she retorted, before reminding herself once more that starting a row and vexing him was not the best start to a seduction. "Please, Leo," she said sweetly.

Leo narrowed his eyes at her. "Why are you being nice?"

"I am nice," she said, aggrieved.

"No," he shook his head. "You are only sweet and docile on the surface, underneath you are temperamental, demanding, and full of fire."

"I am not!" she said indignantly.

He only returned a smug smile.

"Fine!" she snapped. Odious man. She would simply have to free herself. Vi tried to stand, only to sit heavily down again. Avoiding Leo's eye, for she did not doubt he was smirking at her expense, she tried again, throwing her weight forward to keep herself upright. Sadly, she overdid it. The quilted fabric bunched about her feet, and she stumbled forwards, crashing into Leo. He staggered but caught her and might have righted them both if he'd grasped the bedpost and not the curtain beside it. As it was, there was the curtain broke free of its hooks, and they both fell in a heap on the floor. Leo landed heavily, cursing as they went. Padded on all sides as she was, Vi took no harm and simply unravelled, rolling off Leo as the counterpane released her. She lay beside him, gasping.

"Well," she said. "That will teach you."

The situation struck her then as being the most ridiculous she had ever encountered, and she laughed.

"Have you been drinking?" Leo's terse voice muttered from the floor beside her. He sat up, rubbing his right elbow, which must have struck the floor first.

"N-Not enough," Vi remarked, and dissolved. She laughed heartily, sitting up with an effort, and then her laughter died as Leo turned and their eyes met. The counterpane had released her, and her nightgown had ridden up, exposing her legs. Leo's face hardened, and he looked away.

"Cover yourself up," he said coldly, and got to his feet, stalking away to the bottle of wine and pouring himself a drink.

Vi swallowed, any urge to laugh vanishing. Though she told herself not to be such an imbecile, tears pricked at her eyes all the same. She had never understood why Leo had wanted to marry her, having few illusions about her charms. Yes, she was well enough, but already past her best and her looks had faded. What benefit he would gain from marrying her when he could have any beautiful young woman he wanted, she could not fathom. They weren't even proper friends, not really, not when she vexed him so often. They had been once though, when they were children, and she could only believe it was some strange sense of nostalgia that made him persist in believing they could be happy together. Perhaps he was just being kind, for Leo *was* kind. Erratic, too, but terribly generous if he discovered someone needed something… anything. Yet any faint hopes she'd harboured that he really wanted her, desired her in the same way he had desired his lovely mistress shrivelled and died in the light of that indifferent look, those cold words. She felt a fool for believing she could tempt him into bedding her.

The ungainly struggle to get to her feet as she found the counterpane had not entirely given up the fight did not help her composure. Finally upright, she clutched it tightly around her and went to sit on the bed, keeping her back to Leo.

"We'd best eat before it gets cold," Leo said, and she heard him moving to the table but did not dare look in his direction. It was ridiculous to get herself in such a silly state, she told herself severely. The idea of crying in front of him was mortifying, but she didn't seem able to stop. Fighting to steady her voice, she replied, trying her best to sound cheerful.

"Y-You start. I'm not terribly hungry," she managed, though her voice wobbled a little.

"Vi?"

Vi didn't answer, praying he would just leave her be and get on with his dinner.

Naturally, the wretched man had to decide at that moment to pay attention.

"What's wrong?"

"Nothing," she said brightly. "Quite all right. Do eat before it g-gets—" Vi cursed as her voice quavered, and she closed her mouth on a sob.

"Vi! Love, what's wrong?" Leo rushed over, crouching before her and taking her hands. "You're crying!" he said, shock and accusation in his voice, as though she were doing it on purpose.

"I'm not," Vi retorted crossly, which was an obvious and pointless lie as tears streamed down her face, but she was not feeling entirely rational.

"Then your face is leaking," he said, deadpan, making her give an unladylike squawk of unwilling laughter. He returned an anxious smile and shoved a large and mercifully clean handkerchief at her. She took it, wiping her eyes and giving her nose a good blow, which was likely the least seductive thing she could have done, but she supposed that hardly mattered now.

"I'm all right," she said thickly, trying to smile at him. Apparently, the effort was a poor one, for he looked more worried than ever.

Getting up, he sat on the bed beside her. "Did you hurt yourself when you fell?"

"Not in the least," she said impatiently, wishing he would go and eat his dinner and give her a moment to compose herself.

It was too humiliating for words, sobbing in front of him because he didn't want her. Of all the embarrassing situations to get herself into, this had to be the worst imaginable. At least before she'd had her pride.

"Then why—"

"Oh, just leave it be, Leo," she cried, pushing to her feet. She crossed to the fireplace and stared down into the empty grate.

"How can I?" he demanded, following her. "One moment you're laughing and looking like… well, never mind what, and then this! I know I'm only a man, so incapable of understanding the workings of the female mind, but give me a clue, love."

"Looking like what?" Vi asked suspiciously.

"What?"

"You said, laughing and looking like—looking like what?" Vi repeated, narrowing her eyes at him.

Leo swallowed. "Never mind."

"Like a frightful old maid?" she suggested tartly. "Did you come to your senses, Leo, and realise you ought never to have been so foolish as to show an interest in me?"

Leo's mouth fell open, and he made a strangled sound of pure outrage so Vi swallowed the rest of the accusation she had ready to throw at him. There was a look of such fury in his eyes that she feared what he might say or do next. Indeed, he looked really—

Before Vi could think of *how* he looked, other than quite unhinged, he grabbed her roughly, hauled her into his arms, and kissed her.

Chapter 6

Dearest Kitty,

Good heavens! Are you quite certain? I thought he was courting her. From what I understood, he was determined to make her see that he was serious, not the reckless fellow he's been in the past. It seems a somewhat desperate change in plans.

Are you quite certain the story about Mau is a fabrication? It's a rather odd story to concoct. Did someone not try something of the sort before?

Do please keep me posted, for I am sat upon thorns now wondering what to do? Should I tell Alice do you think?

I am in no better state of worry over Pip, however, and not half so happy. If only I could find a suitable woman for him. He's driving me distracted. All these years I have been nagging him to marry, and now he's doing exactly as I asked and all in his power to find a wife. I ought to be happy, but he's treating it as a military operation, writing notes of pros and cons, for heaven's sake! What am I to do with him? His father refuses to get involved any farther than he has done and suggests I leave him to it, but I'm afraid he's going to make the most dreadful mistake.

—Excerpt of a letter from The Most Hon'ble Matilda Barrington, The Marchioness of Montagu to her friend The Right Hon'ble Kitty Baxter, The Countess of Trevick.

24th June 1850, The Queen's Head, Wrestlingworth, the Bedfordshire, Cambridgeshire border.

"Like a frightful old maid?" Vi suggested, her voice brittle. "Did you come to your senses, Leo, and realise you ought never to have been so foolish as to show an interest in me?"

Leo stared at her. He felt sure his mouth was hanging open, but he didn't seem able to do anything about it. From the moment he'd set foot back in the room, he'd been in deep trouble, and it was getting worse by the second. It had taken every ounce of willpower to get to his feet and leave Vi in that delectable pile on the floor. His pulse had been thrumming in his ears so loudly he could not think, his hand unsteady as he'd poured the wine, swallowed an entire glass in two mouthfuls, before pouring another. And then... *then* she'd been weeping.

Really, it was too much. His nerves were not equipped for such... such...

Vi stood there, glaring at him furiously, yet there was something else in her eyes too, something that looked vulnerable and hurt and that blasted nightgown was giving him far too much information about things he'd dreamed of and imagined far too many times. His willpower frayed, vibrating under the strain, and finally snapped.

Leo lunged for her, hauling her into his arms, his mouth crashing down upon hers like... well, like a madman. He was mad, he decided, concluding that he didn't much care. Vi gave a startled squeak, which he assumed was the prelude to a slap or a knee in his privates and found himself a little stunned when she simply clung to his coat as if her life depended on it and kissed him back. As kisses went, it was inexpert to say the least. She simply pressed her mouth hard against his. Leo opened his eyes to discover hers screwed shut, an expression of intense concentration on her face, and was struck with a wave of such tenderness he felt quite winded by it.

He pulled back, breaking the kiss, seeing something that might have been panic flare in her eyes.

"Like this," he told her softly, stroking her cheek as he returned his lips to hers, brushing them gently back and forth and pressing dozens of tiny kisses to her lips. She sighed then, her body softening against his and he felt certain his brain melted in response. Certainly, his next action was foolish in the extreme as he licked her bottom lip and then teased his way inside the crease of her mouth. She opened, uncertain what he wanted, and then gasped as his tongue swept in and he illustrated what it was he needed from her.

She was stiff in his embrace once more for a few tense seconds, and then her arms coiled around his neck and she pressed herself closer, devouring him eagerly and with such enthusiasm Leo's entire body throbbed with desire. Good God. What had he done? This was Vi. *Vi!* Violetta Spencer. She wasn't his mistress, was certainly not a light skirt, and… and…

"Vi—" he rasped, managing that much as her lips left his for a bare second, but they returned again, her tongue questing, sliding against his and her lovely body clung to him. Leo groaned, his arms going around her, hands sliding down her back to grasp her splendid behind and— "No!" He let go of her so abruptly she staggered, and he was forced to reach out a hand and steady her.

She blinked at him, her eyes glassy with desire, her cheeks flushed, mouth reddened and lush and… Leo turned his back, putting distance between them and running an unsteady hand through his hair.

"No?" she repeated, sounding somewhat dazed.

Leo shook his head, not yet ready to trust his voice.

There was a taut silence that stretched on so long he found he had to turn and look at her. He immediately wished he had not, as he regarded Vi, shivering and clutching her arms about herself. She looked smaller somehow, fragile and uncertain, not the magnificent, sensual creature who had just kissed him so passionately.

"Vi," he began, but she just held up her hand, shaking her head.

"No explanations required," she said, her voice faint. "I—I beg your pardon, Leo."

What? What the devil was she apologising for? He was the one who ought to be on his knees begging for forgiveness for his appalling behaviour.

"Whatever for?" he asked, bewildered.

"For... For vexing you so that you... and then... taking advantage of the situation," she said, her cheeks blazing with shame.

"Taking advantage," he repeated uncertainly, wondering if the events of the day had been too much for her too. Perhaps she was going down with something. It had been rather hot. Heat stroke?

She nodded sadly. "It... It was not well done of me."

"It wasn't?" he asked, frowning in confusion. "But I kissed you, Vi."

"I know, but I was driving you distracted. You just wanted to teach me a lesson, I suppose, but I... I wanted... and so..."

Leo digested this somewhat disjointed explanation with interest, managing to extract the most salient point. *She wanted.* Well, he wasn't a complete moron, that much had been obvious. He rarely needed any help in understanding when a woman fancied him, but Vi wasn't just any woman. She was complex. Interesting. Fascinating. A challenge.

"What did you want, Vi?" he asked her, noting another flush of colour as it swept up her neck in a wave.

She shook her head, turning away from him and Leo crossed the room again, daring to take her arm and force her back to look at him. It was dangerous being this close to her, but he had to know.

"You owe me an apology for taking advantage of me," he reminded her, which was outrageous of him, but she believed it, and he needed all the help he could get. "The least you can do is explain."

She glared at him, the flash of fury in her eyes reassuring him he had done no serious damage during his dreadful lapse in self-control. "Oh, really," she said indignantly, but then the fight went out of her and her shoulders sagged. "Very well."

Leo opened his mouth to take the words back—he could not bear to see her so defeated—but then he would never know. So, he forced himself to hold his tongue, watching as she gathered up the counterpane, wrapped it around herself and went back to the bed. She climbed awkwardly onto the mattress, sitting in a rather ungainly heap beneath the quilt, resting her back against the headboard.

"I shan't ever marry, Leo," she began, holding up her hand to silence him when he protested. "No. Listen to me. I shan't, and don't ask me for reasons, I don't have the will to discuss it tonight. But I shan't marry, and so I shan't ever… well, *you know,"* she said uncomfortably.

Though he wanted very much to demand why she would not marry, he let that go for now, and felt his lips curve a little at her discomfort, but he nodded. "I do know," he agreed amicably.

She huffed, aware of his amusement. "Well, I don't know, Leo, and if I don't marry, I never shall, but… but we're here, in this room, alone and…"

She shrugged and Leo suddenly understood. She thought to get him to bed her, so she would not live the rest of her days as an old maid.

Confusion tangled his thoughts together, desire and the need to give her just what she wanted, right there and then, fought with what he believed to be right. He wished to court her, to treat her with all the care and respect a woman ought to expect from the man she intended to marry. Except she didn't intend to marry him. *Why not, dammit?* Indignation followed, hot on the heels of desire. So, she thought she could just use him, did she? Take what she wanted and then throw him aside. He rubbed a hand over his face, wondering if he was becoming overwrought.

Leo turned his back on her, needing to think. His body still ached with baulked lust; bedding her would be no hardship. There again, he could give her pleasure without removing her virginal status. He knew many ways they could please each other with no risks of getting a child on her or claiming her maidenhead. So why not? *Because she won't marry you, bloody halfwit,* he told himself irritably. Except maybe she would. Maybe, if he showed her what there could be between them, he could tempt her into wanting more, into wanting him so much she could do nothing but say yes to him. He knew he had the power to do it if he wished. Though he was by no means vain, he was not so blind to his own powers that he did not know women wanted him, wanted him badly. Vi was female, after all, and though she was the most contrary woman he'd ever known, he now knew she was not as immune to his charms as he'd believed. But was that an honourable thing to do? He wasn't certain he cared overly much in the circumstances. If Vi accepted him, he'd have the rest of their lives together to prove she'd not made an error in judgement.

"Come and eat your dinner," he said, moving to the table and holding out a chair for her.

"What?" she asked, incredulous. "Did you hear what I just said?"

"Of course I heard. Not deaf. I'm considering," he told her, treated then to a glare of such exasperation it was all he could do to keep his face impassive.

"Well, please don't go to any trouble on my account, Leo," she said tartly, stalking over to the table, counterpane trailing behind her. "It's not as if I don't know you find the prospect less than appealing."

She sat down with a muffled thud as the quilted fabric softened her heavy descent. Lord, but she was in a temper now, he realised with interest.

"Less than appealing," he repeated, wondering if she had taken leave of her senses.

"Just forget it," she snapped, swiping the cover off the chafing dish that held their meal. She ladled two generous servings onto their plates and Leo's stomach growled at the sight of the lamb stew with dumplings.

Forget it? Ha! Leo knew he would not forget a single thing about this night until the day he died, but he sat down all the same, eyeing Vi with curiosity.

She took a bite of the lamb, chewing vigorously, though Leo discovered it was so tender it fell apart. Temper again, he realised, wondering what to do about the intriguing woman opposite him. Yet much of this temper seemed to stem from hurt feelings, from a sense of vulnerability. Leo considered this, considered how she had thought to use him for her own ends, and found his own emotions veering dramatically back and forth. They had too much history together to make this easy though, too many years of friendship, aggravation and pretending there was no spark of attraction between them to let them love each other with complete trust and understanding.

They ate in silence and Leo watched her surreptitiously, aware of her anger dissipating as the meal progressed. Little by little her shoulders slumped, and he watched the indignant goddess he adored fade by degrees, replaced by the uncertain young woman he'd glimpsed for the first time earlier this evening. By now, she was just picking at her meal lethargically.

"Vi, you're off your head, you do know that?"

As he'd hoped, her head came up, a warning glint in her eyes. "Oh? How so?"

"If you think I, or any man, could see you in that… that indecent bit of nothing you're wearing under that quilt and find the prospect of bedding you less than appealing, you are not in your right mind."

As he'd hoped, she perked up at this information, regarding him with interest. "Oh?"

That she wanted to hear more was obvious and Leo counselled himself to have a care. He was in dangerous territory here.

"Vi, how many men have told you how beautiful you are?" he asked her gently.

She shrugged. "I don't know, but they don't know me. It's not like they meant it. They wanted my dowry or the connection to Trevick more than they wanted me, I'm afraid."

"That is not true," he said, shaking his head in frustration. "And if they did not know you, whose fault is that? Did you allow them to know you? I have that privilege because we grew up together, but you don't let anyone else near, pet. You're friendly and sweet-natured, right up until the point they get seriously interested, then the ice maiden appears."

"That's not—"

"That is entirely true, and I'm glad of it," Leo said frankly, before she could contradict him. "For otherwise some other lucky devil would have snapped you up before I came to my senses, and then where should I be?"

She gave him a sideways glance, clearly still disbelieving him but he thought perhaps there was a sliver of doubt there now and… and she *wanted* to believe him. The revelation hit him square in the chest. He'd been right. Damn him, he was a blasted fool, but despite that, he'd been right all those weeks ago when he'd accused her of not wanting to marry anyone else but him. She didn't want anyone else; she wanted him. She *wanted* him, he amended, repeating the words with more emphasis as he recalled that heated kiss. His body stirred, heat simmering beneath his skin, and he told his libido to back off and let him think. He would not mess this up.

She might want him, might even be foolish enough to wish to marry him, but she wasn't fool enough to go through with it. Vi didn't trust him, and if he went bedding her now, taking that which could never be replaced, she never would. Yet ought he to trust that she knew her own mind? She was a grown woman, after all, not a child. If Vi had come to this decision, ought he to respect that? His thoughts circled in ever decreasing circles until his head hurt.

"Pie?"

"Huh?"

He looked up to see Vi had cleared the plates and chafing dish and set the apple pie in its place.

"Oh, yes, thank you."

"Do you have a headache?" she asked him, a small frown tugging at her brows.

He looked up in surprise, wondering how she knew.

"You get a sort of pinched look when you have a headache," she said with a shrug. "Shall I send for some willow bark tea?"

Leo shook his head. "No, thank you."

"Is it me?" she asked, candid as ever.

"Is what you?"

"It is me giving you a headache?"

He laughed at that and nodded. "Yes, pet. If you must know. I'm tying myself in knots, trying to decide what to do about you."

"Thought as much," she said, taking up the cream pot and putting a large dollop on his pie, and then the same on hers.

He watched with approval, discovering he liked that she enjoyed her food. Watching a young woman pick at her meal when she was clearly dying to devour the lot was never comfortable when you were enjoying your own dinner.

"Why don't we discuss it, then?" she suggested.

Leo watched as she took a spoonful of pie and ate it with obvious relish. He lifted his glass and took a drink, wondering if that were a good idea. Well, what the hell? It was not like he had any answers.

"Very well. I am trying to decide what to do, as I said."

"Whether or not to take me to bed?" she said, shocking him a little, for that was certainly to the point.

Gathering his nerves as he reminded himself Vi was not someone to cross wits with lightly, he nodded. "I want you to marry me, Vi," he said, holding up a hand before she could tell him such a thing would never happen. "Hear me out."

She sighed, rolling her eyes. "Very well."

"I want to marry you. If I bed you, I'm not sure if that will get me farther from that eventuality or closer to it."

"Neither," she said with such confidence that he felt a little surge of annoyance.

"You do not know of what you speak," he told her firmly.

"I know my own mind," she said with a shrug, and took another bite of pie.

"You do at this moment, sitting at a table eating dinner. You may not feel so sure of yourself, my love, lying naked in my arms once I have brought you more pleasure than you ever dreamed of."

To his satisfaction, she froze, the spoon bearing her next mouthful suspended before her. Colour rose in her cheeks, pink as a new dawn.

Leo quirked one eyebrow. "Quite," he said, holding her gaze.

Vi set down the spoon, avoiding his gaze and staring at her pie thoughtfully. She looked up then, curiosity in her expression. "Would… Would the experience really…"

"Yes," he said firmly.

"Oh." She nodded, biting her lip, and this time it was Leo who looked away as desire surged through his veins, making his skin ache with the need for her to touch him. Please God, let me get through this, he murmured inwardly. "Mama did give me the impression that it was… well, rather lovely, but then she and Papa are so very much in love and… and I wondered if perhaps they were unusual."

"They are, in some respects. You know as well as I many marriages are based on breeding, or finance, or any other reason than that the two parties care a fig about each other. But my parents are much the same. It's embarrassing sometimes," he added with a smile. "And as for my sister, good lord, Vi. Have you ever been in a room with Bella and Bainbridge? It's appalling."

Vi, who had, smothered a laugh and nodded. "I take your point. But we're not in love," she added sadly.

Leo's heart jolted, but he told himself not to react, instead he forced himself to look at her, really look. "Aren't we, Vi?" he asked her softly.

As he had hoped, colour flooded her cheeks once more, and she got to her feet, turning her back on him. This, he decided, was the most encouraging development he'd had on that front, for she clearly did not wish for him to read her expression. Instead, she took the bowl and spoon and stalked back to the bed, sitting on it and finishing her pie in silence.

"You didn't answer me, love," he said, suddenly not the least bit interested in his own dessert, good as it was. He got up, following her to the bed and sitting beside her, but Vi refused to look up at him, her attention focused on her bowl.

"Because you are talking nonsense," she said firmly, avoiding his eyes. "And there is no point in talking to you when you are in such a mood."

"I'm not the one in a mood, or the one sounding so defensive," he countered, his heart lifting as his confidence rose.

"I am not defensive," she snapped, opening her mouth to rail at him once again and then realising what she sounded like. Her eyes flashed with frustration as she returned her attention to her bowl. Giving an irritated huff, she scraped the last of the dessert from the sides of the bowl, taking a good deal of time over ensuring she scooped up every crumb and smear of cream.

"Do you want mine too?" he asked her, unable to keep the amusement from his voice.

"No, thank you. I'm not greedy," she said, still staring at the bowl, her posture stiff.

"No, but it was giving you a reason not to look at me. If you want to avoid doing so for a few more minutes, you are welcome to it, but you'll have to look at me eventually, Vi. Do you think you can hide your feelings forever? I know I can't."

She made another sound of frustration but then she looked up and his breath caught at the fear in her eyes. "Your feelings are unreliable, Leo. Your attention span is limited, and I do not believe I have charms enough to hold it for long. What then? We bicker and vex each other badly enough now."

For a moment, resentment burned inside him at her accusations, but when he looked back upon his life, he knew she was justified. She could not see inside his heart, his mind, could not know how tired he was of all that, how ready he was for what came next. Not that he wanted a dull life, which was why he wanted Vi. Today she had proved to him what he'd always known, how brave and capable she was, and he wanted to bring that adventurous spirit out in her, to show her she could be bold and brave because he was there to keep her safe. What she was so afraid of, he did not know, but that she was frightened was something he had instinctively believed for some time. Why, though?

"I'll turn into a shrew, and you will want to get away from me and—"

Leo realised she was still talking, still finding reasons they would not work, and he could not have that, could not have her work herself up by imagining how it would go wrong. Instead, he would give her the very best reason it would be perfect.

Leaning in, he grasped her chin, holding her still as he pressed his mouth to hers. She froze, the list of reasons silenced by his kiss. Leo's heart thudded hard when she did not put up even a token resistance but reached for him. It was an awkward position, with her empty bowl still between them on the bed, but he did not dare break the kiss for fear she would start up again. Instead, he stroked her cheek, pleased when she opened her mouth to him, tasting the sweet, tart flavour of apples and cream. God, but she was delicious. Desire rose like an incoming tide, and he reached for the bowl, putting it aside on the bed as he pressed Vi back against the pillows, following her down. The blasted counterpane was between them, keeping the feel of her body from his but for the moment it was enough that she kissed him with such enthusiasm, her hands grasping his shoulders.

"Vi, you are going to drive me distracted," he murmured in her ear as he finally dragged his mouth from hers long enough to press kisses along jawline, down her neck.

She sighed, not saying anything at all, which was a first, but he'd take it. He looked at her then, her lovely blonde hair a tumble of messy curls about her face, her cheeks flushed pink, and her eyes… her clear blue eyes were dark with desire. The need to show her just what it was she wanted from him was a rush of liquid fire in his blood.

"Vi," he said, his voice low.

"Mr Huntington, your bath is ready, sir. May we come in?"

Leo jolted, cursing roundly as he realised he'd not even heard them knock.

"Damn and blast."

Vi bit her lip, and he saw amusement glinting there. "I would like a bath first if… if we're to…"

Leo nodded, he had not yet decided just what they were doing, but he was sweaty and dusty, and he was damned if he would let Vi any closer to him smelling as he did.

"Stay there," he told her, forcing himself to relax enough to give her a smile. "I'll get rid of them as quick as I can."

She nodded as he pulled the curtains on the bed closed, tugging hard to cover the gap from the one they had accidentally torn down, and went to the door so they could bring in the bath and the following cans of hot water.

Chapter 7

Dear Cara,

I have done the most ridiculous thing…

—Excerpt of a letter from the Hon'ble Miss Violetta Spencer (cousin and adopted sister to Lady Aisling, Lady Cara and Conor Baxter – Viscount Harleston) to The Right Hon'ble Cara De Vere, Viscountess Latimer.

24th June 1850, The Queen's Head, Wrestlingworth, the Bedfordshire, Cambridgeshire border.

I have done the most ridiculous thing, and yet I don't regret it. Not in the least. How shocked you will be when you hear, assuming I am ever brave enough to reveal all. There is a good chance I will take it all to my grave…

Vi considered that as she mentally began a letter to her sister, one she would write tomorrow if she got the chance.

My lonely grave, she corrected morosely, though she knew she would not write such a maudlin sentiment in black and white. Foolish beyond permission, she scolded herself, shaking her head. Outside the curtains she could hear the servants coming in and out, the slosh of the water as they filled the bath. Though she had deeply regretted the interruption to their kiss, she was relieved, too.

It seemed as if she might have persuaded Leo to take her to bed, and that being the case, she could not bear to be anything less than clean and sweet smelling for him. Like a bride on her wedding night, she thought wistfully, before scolding herself all over again.

She would never be his bride. That way lay a lifetime of worry and stress and dispute between them. For if she curbed his wild behaviour, he would grow to resent her for it, and she would hate that. If she did not curb it, then she would be sat upon thorns for the rest of her life, waiting to hear the news that he had been killed during some ridiculous race or wager. She remembered hearing via her brother that Leo had once leapt from a cliff over seventy feet high into the sea, just for a lark. Even thinking about it now, years and years later and knowing he was perfectly safe and well, made her feel both sick and so furious with him she could wring his blasted neck.

Don't think about it, she told herself sternly. It was a familiar refrain. Don't think about it, or don't think about *him*, words she had repeated to herself more times than she cared to remember over the past years.

She heard the door close, and then the bed curtain was pulled open. Leo smiled at her.

"Your bath is all ready, Vi. There's even soap," he said. His gaze fell to her mouth, and he cleared his throat, looking hurriedly away. "Well, I'll leave you to it then and—"

"No."

Vi's heart was thudding very hard as he turned back to her, an arrested expression in his eyes.

"No?" he repeated.

She shook her head. "If… If we're going to… well, it's silly, isn't it? For you to go, and I should feel happier bathing in a strange place, with… with you here," she said firmly.

"You would?"

Vi nodded. "You hear terrible stories about people being walked in on or getting robbed when in their baths in places like this, or—"

"You want me to stay?" he repeated, apparently not interested in all the reasons it was a good idea he stay past that she wanted him to.

Vi nodded again, deciding it might be safer to keep her mouth shut. Less chance of vexing him that way.

"Very well," he said. "I'll sit on the bed and close the curtains."

"Oh," Vi said with a sigh, for having him watch her bathe was something she had been uncertain she was brave enough to endure. "Yes, please."

His lips quirked at her obvious relief. "Don't worry, love. I won't peek. You're quite safe."

"Well, there's no need to sound so certain about it," she said, suddenly indignant, which was unfair and ridiculous, but there it was. Did he not *wish* to peek?

Leo gave her a sharp look of interest and then came forward, taking her hands and drawing her off the bed and to her feet. "I shall be listening to every sound you make, imagining the scene beyond the curtains, and driving myself wild with frustration and the desire to peek, but I am a gentleman, so I shall not do so." He reached for a loose curl, tucking it behind her ear. "Does that help?"

"It does rather," Vi admitted ruefully. "You must think me terribly foolish."

Leo shook his head. "No. I think you woefully out of touch with reality. How can you be so accomplished, and so sensible, and not know that any man would give his right arm to be where I am? How can you not know how lovely you are, how special? You are beautiful, and intelligent, and very, very alluring. Don't you forget that."

Vi gazed up at him, searching his eyes and finding nothing but sincerity there. He really meant it.

"Yes, I really mean it," he said, his lips quirking as he correctly interpreted her intent gaze. "Do you really think every word I say is nonsense? It's not very flattering, love."

"Of course I don't," she said at once. "It's just… some things are far harder to believe than others. I… I saw your mistress once, you see, and she was so very lovely and it's hard to believe—"

"Who did you see?" he demanded, frowning at that.

"I'm afraid I don't know her name, we were not introduced," she said dryly.

"Where and when?" he asked, ignoring her sarcasm.

"At the theatre, the year before last. Really, Leo, have there been so many that—"

"Ah. Mrs James," he said, nodding. "A rather buxom brunette."

"Quite so," Vi said tartly, the warm feeling she'd had upon his lovely words dissipating. Her own fault, of course, she ought never to have mentioned his mistress.

"Yes, she was a handsome woman, but we did not last long."

"Why not?" Vi asked before cursing her own stupid curiosity. She really did not wish to know. "No, don't tell me, I—"

"Because she bored me silly," he said frankly. "No conversation past whatever piece of jewellery she wanted me to buy her or where she wanted to go to be seen wearing it. Very tedious. You, however, are never dull. I never know what you are going to say, and your opinions are always your own, not recited from overhearing something someone else said. You think about things, Vi, and if you think I'm wrong, you'll explain why, not just tell me I'm wrong and sulk about it if I disagree."

"Oh," Vi said, mollified, though she felt abruptly bad for Mrs James. Had he broken her heart?

"Have your bath, Vi," Leo said, smiling at her. She watched as he tugged off his boots and tossed them to the floor before stretching out on the bed and pulling the curtains around him.

Vi shook her head and sighed, picking the boots up and setting them neatly in the corner of the room before investigating the bath. Steam rose from it, fogging the mirror. She dipped her fingers in, pleased to discover it was the perfect temperature.

Stripping off the worn nightgown, she stepped into the bath. The water lapped against the sides. Leo would hear that too, and know she was getting in. The idea he might be imagining her just as she was, naked and standing in the bath, brought a rush of heat to her skin that had nothing to do with the temperature of the water.

Slowly, she sat, unable to repress a sigh as she lay her head back and the water eased away the aches from too many hours sat in the tilbury.

"The water is not too hot?" Leo's voice came from behind the curtains.

"No. It's wonderful," she said, wondering why she was not more scandalised by the situation, but it was surprisingly natural to speak to Leo whilst she bathed.

"There's soap, on the little table beside you. Did you find it?"

Vi looked around and saw a small wrought-iron table had been set beside the tub, holding a clean flannel and what looked like a homemade cake of soap. There were bits stuck in it that looked like petals.

"Guess what it smells of?" Leo asked her, his amusement obvious.

Vi lifted it to her nose and laughed. "Roses!" she said. "Of course."

She lathered it between her hands, luxuriating in the delicate scene.

"What are you doing, Vi?"

Vi froze, her hand upon her forearm. "Er… washing."

Leo made a muffled sound that she thought might have been a snort.

"Give a fellow a bit more information, love. My imagination needs a little extra help."

Though he could not see her, Vi blushed scarlet. She couldn't possibly… could she? Steeling her nerves, she told herself to be brave, just this once. Tonight was a night out of time and place, a once in a lifetime, never to be repeated time, and the person she was here and now could do that.

"I… I've lathered the soap between my hands. It's lovely, though the scent isn't very strong. Now I'm st-stroking the lather up my arms," she said, fitting action to words. "My shoulders now, and my neck."

She was silent for a moment, not thinking he needed to hear about her washing her armpits.

"What now, love?" he asked, his voice a low rumble in the quiet room.

Vi swallowed, knowing what she would do next if she were alone, but discovering she wasn't *that* brave. "My feet," she called out cheerfully, ignoring the little chuckle of amusement. "And my ankles, now my calves, behind my knees and—drat, I dropped it."

"Don't leave out all the good bits," he called out to her.

Vi huffed at him, amused. "I am not going to annotate *everything*."

"Spoilsport," he replied, still laughing softly.

Vi rediscovered the soap and spent the next few moments attending to the private places she was not about to tell Leo about.

"Shall I come and wash your back?"

The question hung in the air, somehow having far more weight and substance that the steam coiling around her.

"Vi?"

One night out of time, she reminded herself. *Be brave, Vi.*

"Yes, p-please," she stammered, squeezing her eyes shut and wincing. The desire to change her mind was in every heavy thud of her heart as it pounded behind her ribs, but then she heard the curtains pull back and Leo was standing before her.

Vi shivered in the bath water, though she wasn't cold. She had wrapped her arms about her legs and now pressed her face against her knees, avoiding his gaze.

"That was a yes?" he asked her, his tone careful.

Vi nodded, feeling the heat in her cheeks against her bare legs.

Leo sat down on the floor beside the tub and reached for the soap she had set back on the table.

"A lovely scent, delicate," he said, dipping his hands in the water behind her. She felt the movement ripple the water, but he did not touch her. The sound of the soap, slick between his hands made her pulse leap, however, knowing he would do so any moment.

"Vi? Is this all right?"

She breathed steadily for a long moment before she nodded. "Yes, Leo."

He shifted behind her and then she felt his warm hands, slick with soap, gliding over her shoulders and upper back.

"How lovely you are," he murmured. "Your skin is so beautiful, like silk. You have the loveliest back."

A sarcastic comment about it being her best side leapt to Vi's tongue, but she swallowed it. Why not believe him? She had offered him everything, with no strings. If he was the kind of man to say such things merely to get her into bed, she had done the hard work for him, and she did not believe Leo to be such a man. Though his reasons for wanting to marry a woman past her prime who would only nag him dreadfully still eluded her, perhaps she ought to believe that he at least found her attractive, desirable. It was true men had told her she was beautiful before, just as he'd said, and it wasn't as though she believed she was unattractive, just that their words had been gilded by the promise of a connection to Lord Trevick and her rather hefty dowry. Leo would not say it for those reasons.

His hand slid down her spine, smoothing the soap over her skin and she gasped as he got to her waist, jumping a little.

"Ticklish?" he asked, and she could hear the grin in his words without looking at him. "Beg pardon. I'll be careful."

He was too, though her breath hitched again as his hand drifted lower.

"Th-That's not my back," she said in a rush.

"No, but it's the next part on the list," he said with amusement.

"I did that bit," she told him, turning to look at him over her shoulder, his warm gaze meeting hers.

"Without telling me? How cruel you are, to leave out all the interesting places."

She rolled her eyes at him but felt a smile tug at her lips. "Heartless, I know," she agreed.

He chuckled and got to his feet, drying his hands before unfolding the large towel that had arrived with the bath. He stood beside the bath, holding the towel out before closing his eyes and turning his head away.

"Up you come, then. I'm not looking."

Vi smiled and got to her feet, feeling strangely cosseted and cared for as he wrapped the towel around her. He kept his arms in place about her, holding her for a moment as he cracked one eye open.

"All covered up?"

"All covered up," she agreed, though the idea of being uncovered before him was suddenly not as daunting as it had been. His hands rubbed over her arms and legs briskly, drying her so she wouldn't feel chilled.

"I suppose I'd best let you do the rest," Leo said with obvious regret. He stared at her for a long moment, his gaze full of warmth and… and something tender she did not dare name for fear of being unspeakably foolish. "Well, my little love. You're all clean. So, now it's my turn."

Vi nodded and stepped out of the tub with his help to steady her.

"I'll sit on the bed, I shan't peek."

"No. Sit there," he nodded at the chair by the empty grate.

Vi's expression must have been a picture, for he gave a choked laugh. "You can look away while I get in if you prefer, but I'd rather talk with you beside me, not hidden away behind a curtain. Is that terribly shocking?"

Vi shook her head. It was a bit late to shriek about indecency after all.

"If you prefer," she said, pleased with herself for sounding so calm when she was a very long way from it. Taking a moment to extricate her arms from the wrappings, she padded over to the chair and sat down, keeping her eyes cast down as Leo made quick work of stripping off his clothes.

"We ought to have asked Jenny to see to your coat and trousers too," she said, investigating her fingernails with apparent interest. "I'll be all neat and tidy in the morning and you will look thoroughly disreputable."

"Well, the truth is hard to disguise," he said amiably. "I'm a shocking villain, after all."

"Indeed, you are not," she said, a little surprised by her own vehemence.

She heard the water sloshing and dared a glance up to find he had settled back in the tub. Vi glanced hurriedly away again, though the desire to look more closely was hard to deny.

"I'm not? Are you quite certain? In the circumstances," he added, and she could hear the smile in his voice.

"Quite certain," she told him, finding she meant it. Leo was a good man, not perfect by any means, but kind and honourable. If he gave his word, he would keep it. She considered this more carefully. Would that extend to marriage vows? She had never believed so before, but had that been unfair to him?

"What are you looking so intent about?" Leo's voice broke into her thoughts, and she looked up, shaking her head.

"Just woolgathering," she replied, and then swallowed as she watched him soaping his arms and chest. Powerful shoulders filled her gaze and arms far more muscular than she had appreciated beneath his exquisitely tailored coats. The soap lathered up in the golden hair on his chest and Vi suppressed the sudden and urgent desire to wash him herself. She imagined his shock if she ran over and wrested the soap from his hands, and blushed, tearing her gaze away once more. Surely, she had scandalised the poor man enough for one night. What must he think of her for kissing him so… so enthusiastically? Vi pressed her hands to her cheeks, which were now scalding.

"What on earth are you thinking about? You're red as a beet, Vi, my pet."

"I'm not your pet," she said automatically, grasping at the silly endearment rather than answering the question.

"Oh, but you are, and you're not diverting me that easily. What made you blush so hard? Are you thinking naughty thoughts, Vi? If you are, for heaven's sake, tell me," he added, grinning.

Vi huffed and covered her face with her hands. "Stop it!"

"Want to wash my back?" he asked, a note of challenge in his voice. "Is that what you were thinking about?"

Vi peered at him from between her fingers, her heart thudding. "M-Maybe," she admitted.

He looked so thoroughly pleased by this confession that she dropped her hands into her lap, shaking her head. "Don't look so smug."

"I shall look as smug as I please. The woman who has filled my dreams and my every thought for months now finally admits she fancies me, and she wishes to wash my back. I'm cock of the walk, love, and don't think that's going to change anytime soon."

"Leo, you are the most ridiculous creature."

"I know, but you love me all the same."

Vi stiffened but he held her gaze.

"Give a fellow a bit of encouragement. You must love me, even if it's just a little bit," he coaxed, holding up finger and thumb and squinting at the tiny gap between. "That much?" he suggested.

Relenting, Vi laughed. "You really are impossible. Yes, I suppose I might love you that much," she said, showing him an even smaller amount between her own finger and thumb.

Leo nodded gravely. "I'll take it. Now, come and wash my back, if you please."

Vi took a deep breath, gathered the towel around her, and went back to kneel beside the tub.

"Good evening, Miss Spencer," he said, his tone formal as she settled beside the bath.

"Good evening, Mr Hunt," she replied in kind, though it was silly, but she was enjoying herself, enjoying his company and the realisation that she could be silly and playful with him because Leo could be silly and playful and would not think her odd or childish.

"Here," he said, handing her the soap. "I shall smell as sweet as a rose, though I might get some odd looks in the taproom," he added with a grin.

Vi took the soap, lathering it between her hands as she gazed at the expanse of broad back before her. He was tanned, she realised, and wondered at that.

"Where have you been with no shirt on?"

He glanced back at her and smiled. "I've a little sailing boat on the East Sussex coast. It can get dreadfully hot, so sometimes I strip off. Are you dreadfully shocked?" he teased.

"Dreadfully," Vi replied serenely, picturing him on the boat, hosting sails and the like with no difficulty at all. She smiled until she considered all the ways things could go wrong, and her heart pounded hectically. He might get caught in a storm, might fall overboard, might—*stop it*. He was sitting in a few inches of water in a tub in Cambridgeshire, he was not about to drown before her eyes.

"Everything all right back there?"

She glanced up, blue eyes meeting hers as she realised she was sitting with the soap in her hands, staring into space. Vi shook herself and nodded. "Yes, of course."

Hurriedly, she put her hands upon his back, but she did so without thinking, without giving herself time to prepare. She sucked in a breath at the feel of his warm flesh under her touch.

Leo seemed startled too, his breath catching as her palms glided over his wet skin. He moved, leaning forward, and Vi felt the shift of powerful muscles beneath her hands. Lord, but he was strong. Such a vigorous, strong body. Heat simmered beneath her skin as she fought to keep her breathing even and concentrate on washing his back. She followed the line of his spine down to the crease of his behind before losing her nerve and sliding her hand back up to his shoulders. Instead, she washed the back of his neck, aware of his damp hair curling and tickling her fingers. Wishing she could linger but aware every inch of his back had been thoroughly soaped, she scooped up the water and washed the bubbles away.

"There," she said, a trifle unsteadily. "All done."

He looked over his shoulder at her, their gazes locking. Vi melted under the heat of that look, unable to deny that she saw desire in his eyes, need. It gave her courage, knowing that he wanted her, that she was not alone in wanting to touch, to caress, to be held. So she leaned in, slowly, hoping she would not make a fool of herself as their lips drew closer and closer and…

There was a sharp knock on the door.

"Mr Huntington, sir? Beg pardon, I'm sorry to disturb you, but Reverend Harbottle is downstairs. He says he has news about something that might interest you."

Leo cursed but then his eyes widened as he heard who was waiting for them.

"Oh, Leo! It must be about Mau!" Vi said, regretting the interruption, but hoping it was good news.

"I'll be down directly," Leo called back, and stood up, water sluicing from his body as he rose like Neptune, all glistening skin and fascinating proportions.

Vi squeaked in surprise, but found she could not look away, not if her life depended on it. Heavens, but he was beautiful. Thankfully, Leo was too intent on getting dry and dressed to notice her open-mouthed gawking at him, and by the time he had pulled on his trousers, she was relatively in control of herself.

"Damned unfortunate interruption," he said ruefully, smiling at her. "But Mau—"

"Of course, you must go at once," Vi urged, knowing how worried he was about his cat. "I can't, for I have no clothes, so hurry back and tell me as soon as you can."

"I will," Leo promised, pulling on his shirt and fighting with it as the fabric clung to his damp skin.

"Not like that! Oh, do hold still," Vi scolded, hurrying over. With deft little tugs, she settled the shirt properly and reached for his waistcoat, helping him into it and doing up the buttons.

"This is nice," he said softly, gazing down at her.

Vi smiled but said nothing. It *was* nice, and the sort of intimate, domestic thing she could do for him if she were his wife, but it was best not to think about that. *Just one night*, she reminded herself. His coat came next and soon he was dressed decently, if not neatly, and hurried to the door.

"Won't be long," he promised her, and rushed out.

Vi nodded and then sat down on the bed. Her heart was still careering about in her chest in a peculiar fashion, and she took a few deep breaths to calm herself. *Just one night*, her mind repeated, and she wished she did not feel so very much like weeping.

<h1 style="text-align:center">Chapter 8</h1>

PS.

*Cara, I cannot ask this of Mama for she will
just sigh and go all dewy eyed and say how
wonderful it is, so please tell me truthfully,
what is it like to be married?*

**—Excerpt of a letter from the Hon'ble
Miss Violetta Spencer (cousin and
adopted sister to Lady Aisling, Lady
Cara and Conor Baxter – Viscount
Harleston) to The Right Hon'ble Cara De
Vere, Viscountess Latimer.**

**24th June 1850, The Queen's Head, Wrestlingworth, the
Bedfordshire, Cambridgeshire border.**

Leo took the stairs two at a time, apologising as he rounded
the corner and almost knocked down an indignant-looking rotund
man. Fate was having a laugh at his expense, he thought with a
sigh. Giving on one hand and taking on the other, for the
interruption had been dreadfully frustrating. Still, he felt more
optimistic about his relationship with Vi than he ever had before.
The realisation that she wanted him, and did not despise him half
so much as he feared, was immensely cheering. If the vicar had
good news about Mau, so much the better.

Upon seeing Jenny, he asked her if it might be possible to have Vi's gown ready for her tonight in case they had to go out again. Jenny looked dismayed until Leo held out more coin that she'd usually earn in a month, upon which she bobbed a curtsey and told him it was no bother at all. She directed him to a private parlour where he was told the reverend was awaiting him.

"Ah, Mr Huntington," the reverend said as Leo entered the room. "I do apologise for disturbing you, but in the circumstances, I thought it best to contact you at once."

"If you have news about Mau, I can only thank you, sir," Leo said, sitting down at the table across from the reverend.

"It's my pleasure, for I do think I may be of help," the reverend said with a grin, pouring himself a glass of port from the decanter on the table before pushing it towards Leo. "My sister always keeps the good stuff for me, the kindly soul. Do have a drop yourself. Warm the cockles of your heart, eh?" he added with a good-natured chuckle.

Leo accepted, wishing the reverend would get to the point, but he was such a nice old gentleman he didn't like to rush him.

"Now, then, after you left, I got to thinking about the kind of person who might do such a hare-brained thing as kidnap a cat," the reverend said, leaning across the table and lowering his voice as if he feared they'd be overheard by spies or ne'er-do-wells. "And it suddenly occurred to me that the Hatt brothers fitted the bill rather splendidly. So, I took myself on a little reconnaissance mission," he whispered, looking inordinately pleased with himself.

Leo stared at him. "Sir, that is terribly decent of you, but surely that was a little reckless. We don't know what these men are capable of."

The reverend grunted. "The Hatt brothers are capable of nothing but a bit of minor mischief, so I believed myself in no danger. They are a foolish pair, idle rather than wicked, but I'm afraid you are in the right all the same, for if I have not missed my guess, they were not the origin of this plot, only the means of carrying it out."

"You're certain they're the kidnappers?" Leo asked, his hopes for getting Mau back rising.

"Not certain, but they are the most likely pair to be involved in such a scheme, and when I went to their property—a ramshackle place down past Mud Pightle—my suspicion grew."

"How so?" Leo asked, taking a drink from the glass of port he'd been nursing, for the reverend had finished his and was pouring another.

"Well, it was all lit up, candles burning, which is most peculiar for the two never spend money on such luxuries, and there was an old curricle outside. A battered thing it is, nothing so fine and fancy as your tilbury, Mr Huntington, but still far above the Hatt brothers' touch. It seemed to me they had guests, so I dared to go a little closer and…"

The reverend paused for dramatic effect, clearly enjoying himself enormously.

"And?" Leo said, as it appeared what the reverend wished for him to say.

"*And* I heard raised voices, shouting," Harbottle said, sounding triumphant. "Whoever the villain that came up with the idea is, he's there at the house, and he's not a happy man."

"Well, neither am I," Leo said, getting to his feet. "Would you be able to give me directions to this Mud Pightle? I feel in need of an urgent conversation with the blackguard."

"I'll take you there myself, Mr Huntington," the reverend said, grinning and looking pleased as he gave Leo a critical look up and down. "I reckon a fellow like yourself ought to know how to 'handle one's fists,' eh?" he asked, such a hopeful glint in his eyes that Leo laughed at both his enthusiasm and the fact he knew such a cant expression

"As it happens, I do."

"Excellent," the reverend said, chortling merrily to himself and rubbing his hands together.

Leo opened his mouth to enquire if it was entirely godly to be hoping to see a proper turn up but closed it again. He liked the reverend and, if he was anticipating a good mill, Leo was only too keen to accommodate his wishes. The bastards who had taken Mau, or had come up with the dastardly scheme, or all three of them, were going to get a proper hiding if he had anything to do with it. The idea that someone had been watching him, perhaps watching him and Vi, as they'd been together when it happened, made him feel ill. How long had it been going on, with the devils plotting and waiting their chance to steal Mau away? Fury ran through his blood at the desire to take his revenge. Still, three against one was not such good odds.

"These Hatt brothers," he began, only for the reverend to shake his head.

"Not in your class, sir, I suspect. The taller one, Edgar, fancies himself as something of a pugilist, but I reckon you'll deal with him tidily enough. His younger brother, Burt, is a coward, simply put, and won't stand. The new fellow, however, I can't tell you." The reverend frowned. "I caught a glimpse of him through the window, and he looked as tall as Edgar, but more than that, I'm afraid I don't know."

Leo nodded. Well, provided none of them did anything idiotic like produce a pistol, he should be fine. However, he was not about to take Violetta into such a situation. He sighed with regret, not liking to leave her out of the adventure, for he suspected she would handle herself well in a tight spot, but the terror he felt at the idea of her getting hurt far outweighed any satisfaction he would gain from proving to her how brave and capable she really was. She would not like it though, he thought with regret, and just as he was getting into her good books, too.

"Would you wait for me, I shan't be above a moment, but I must tell Mis—my wife that I'm going out," he said, hurriedly covering up his slip. Lord, but he needed to be more careful.

"Of course, of course," the reverend said, settling back with the port. "I'm in no hurry and I rather doubt the Hatt brothers are going anywhere tonight."

Leo nodded and hurried back up the stairs, giving a sharp knock before entering. "It's me, love," he said, his breath catching as the sight before him burned itself into his eyeballs.

Vi was sitting at the dressing table, once again wearing the indecent nightgown. She was unpinning her hair, which fell down her back in a shimmering curtain of gold. Her hands were raised, searching for the last pins, and the upraised position pressed her breasts firmly against the thin cotton. The little nubs of her nipples were clearly defined, as was the gentle curve of her belly, and she turned and smiled at him, her expression eager.

"Is there news?" she asked him hopefully, and Leo opened his mouth to reply, but produced nothing but a strangled croak. He felt winded, his reasons for returning suddenly vanishing against the sudden, urgent desire to tumble her onto the bed and do the wickedest things he could think of. "Leo? What's wrong? You've gone all red."

Leo leaned back against the door and closed his eyes, giving a low groan.

"Leo! Whatever is the matter? Are you ill? Is something wrong? Is it Mau? Oh, for heaven's sake, why don't you—"

"Nothing is wrong," Leo said gruffly, opening his eyes to discover Vi in front of him—far too close—clutching at his lapels. "Lord above, Vi. Give a fellow a bit of warning, eh?"

"Warning? Whatever do you mean?"

"I mean, that if you're going to look like… that—" He gestured wildly to the indecent nightgown without actually looking at it. "—and take your hair down and smile at me in that… that provoking manner, then you've to expect me to… to…"

"To do what?" she asked, looking far too interested in the answer.

"To lose what's left of my sanity," Leo retorted, aggrieved. "Just cover yourself up, will you, or I'm never going to find the willpower to leave the room, and Mau is depending on me."

"Oh, Leo, is there news? Whyever didn't you say so?" she demanded crossly.

"Because you distracted me!" he shot back, irritated. "You'd try the patience and the best intentions of a saint, and I'm no saint, Vi."

Leo shook his head as he saw her arrange her face into something grave and repentant when he could see very well that she was pleased as punch by his words, the wicked girl.

"I beg your pardon, Leo," she said, obediently going to the bed and tugging the counterpane around herself. "Better?" she asked, but with such a glint in her eyes, Leo almost growled at her.

"No. But I suppose it will have to do. Now, Harbottle thinks he knows who has Mau. Two brothers, by the name of Hatt, apparently, though it seems a third party put them up to it. We're going there now to get Mau back, so just sit tight and—"

"What do you mean, sit tight?" Vi objected, glaring at him. "I'm coming with you."

"In that?" Leo asked, gesturing to the quilt she was wrapped in and relieved he could use her lack of clothing as an excuse. "I think not, love."

He prayed Jenny did not come up with the gown any time soon or he would be in the basket. If only he hadn't asked her to do it tonight. He hadn't been thinking past the fact that he wanted Vi with him at that point, never considering that it might not be safe for her.

"Then ask Jenny for it back," she said crossly. "I'll wear it as it is."

"No, love," Leo said, with genuine regret, for he hated leaving her behind. "I don't want you there. I'm sure it will be fine, but—"

"Oh my word, you think there will be a fight!" she exclaimed, getting to her feet and once more clutching at his lapels. If ever he got home again, his valet was going to have an apoplexy, and he could hardly blame the fellow. As she moved, the counterpane fell to the floor and Leo sighed. Fate was definitely laughing at him. "Leo, you don't know these men! They are obviously criminals, they may be armed and—"

"Calm down, love. These are small-time crooks. Opportunists not hardened criminals. Harbottle says one is certainly a coward, and the other brother will go down easy. It's only the organ grinder who might put up a fight, not the monkeys, so don't fret."

"Don't fret?" she repeated, her expression one of such fury he would have taken a step back if the door hadn't been behind him. "Leo Hunt, if you leave me here to worry whilst you get yourself involved in God knows what, I shall—"

Leo kissed her firmly to silence the words, his hand gripping the doorknob behind him. "I'm sorry, love, forgive me," he said, and let himself out, closing the door on her indignant face as her words became muffled.

"Leo! You are the most—"

"I know, Vi, I know," he muttered to himself as he hurried back down the stairs.

♡♣◇♠

"Oh!" Vi said in fury, vibrating with anger as she stared at the door that had just been shut in her face. She was trapped, quite unable to leave the room without her clothes and Leo was off getting himself into heaven alone knew what trouble without her.

"Idiot man," she raged, stomping up and down the bedroom. "Don't fret, love," she repeated, imitating his deep timbre as she stalked back and forth. "I'm a big, strong man and nothing can ever happen to me. *Idiot!*" she repeated, adding, *"Man!"* after that, for the two words seemed inextricably linked at this precise moment.

The soft knock at the door barely registered until a voice called through it.

"Ma'am?"

Vi paused in her rant and turned to the door, her heart leaping with hope. "Jenny?"

"Yes, Ma'am. I've your gown here. It's not as good as it might be, but—"

Jenny leapt about a foot in the air as Vi snatched the door open, grasped the girl's arm and hauled her inside.

"Quick!" she instructed, stripping the nightgown off and snatching the shift from the pile of clothing Jenny held. "Don't just stand there, help me get dressed before that stupid man goes and gets himself killed!"

"Killed, ma'am?" Jenny said in horror. "What man?"

"Mr Hunt—*ington,"* Vi said, shaking her head. "Oh, just wait until I get my hands on him. I'll wring his stupid neck, just see if I don't."

Jenny stared at her for a moment before letting out a long-suffering sigh.

"Men," she said in disgust. "They're all fools. Ma is always complaining about it for my father is a hothead. I walked out with a fellow for a short while until I discovered he was just the same. Well, I sent him packing. They go off half-cocked without thinking things through. Reckon they've got to go off and flatten someone to prove they're strong and capable when all that's needed is a bit of common sense."

"Exactly!" Vi said with feeling, recognising a kindred spirit as she wriggled into her corset. "And will they listen?"

"Nah. Leastways, my fellow never did," Jenny replied ruefully as she tugged at the strings. "But I wasn't going to spend my life like that. I knew it would be me that had to make things right again, patch up heads and torn clothes and make peace between him and whatever stupid beggar got him all riled up in the first place. No, thank you."

"Men!" Vi said, throwing up her hands in sympathy with this summary, though she'd never had an experience of that sort. Still, Jenny seemed to appreciate the solidarity.

"Can't live with them," Jenny said with a snort.

Can't live without them, Vi silently added. Oh, lord. If anything happened to Leo, she'd be wretched for the rest of her days, and he hadn't even made love to her!

Once she was decently attired, Vi ran for the door and then ground to a halt, realising she didn't have the faintest idea of where to go.

"Lud! How ever will I find him?" she exclaimed, before turning back to Jenny. "Do you know the Hatt brothers?"

"What on earth do you want with them two scoundrels?" Jenny asked, eyes wide.

"Nothing at all, but it's them that Leo… that is to say, Mr Hunt… *Huntington* has gone to see. They kidnapped his cat, you see and—"

"His cat?" Jenny looked sceptical, regarding Vi with less than her previous sympathy.

Vi sighed, realising she would have to tell the whole blasted tale again. "A very rare cat, valuable, the dreadful men have stolen it, hoping to hold it for ransom." She ran through the ludicrous story at record speed, with Jenny's eyes growing wider with every word.

"Mercy me," Jenny breathed. "I never would have thought Edgar and Burt had it in them."

"It seems they did not, there is some kind of criminal mastermind behind the plot," Vi said, hoping if she made it sound more exciting, Jenny would be more willing to help her.

"But what can you do, ma'am?" Jenny asked. "I don't say as how you've got a deal more sense than the menfolk, but if it comes to breaking heads, well, it might be dangerous."

"Nevertheless, Jenny, I am going. Please give me their direction."

Jenny sighed, recognising an immoveable object when she saw one. "Well, if you're determined, I reckon I'd best get Mick to come along too."

"Mick?" Vi repeated in confusion.

"They call him the mountain," Jenny said with a smile. "He's my brother. Not terribly bright, but he'll look after us."

"Us?"

Jenny grinned at her. "Don't think I'm going to let you have all the fun, do you? I'd pay good money to see Edgar Hatt get his comeuppance. Nasty bit of work, he is. Pinches my behind whenever he gets the chance. Besides, it ain't proper for a lady like you to be gallivanting about by herself at night. Your husband wouldn't like it, I reckon."

"True," Vi said with relief and smiled warmly at Jenny. "Thank you, Jenny. I will make sure to suitably recompense you for everything you've done for me."

"I ain't doing it for that, but much appreciated all the same," Jenny said. "Come on then, grab your bonnet. We'd best hurry if we're to catch them up before it's all over."

Chapter 9

Dear Cousin Felix,

I was wondering if you would have a word with Leo for me. I always thought he was a great gun, but he's being dreadfully unreasonable and won't let me join The Sons of Hades. I'm seven and ten years of age now, and no longer a child. Could you put in a word for me? Really, it is dreadfully unfair to treat me like a schoolboy when he's always been the one getting into such scrapes.

I'd be much obliged if you could make him see sense.

—Excerpt of a letter from The Lord Harry Adolphus (younger son of Their Graces, Robert and Prunella Adolphus, The Duke and Duchess of Bedwin) to Mr Felix Knight (son of Mr Gabriel and Lady Helena Knight)

24th June 1850, Mud Pightle, Wrestlingworth, the Bedfordshire, Cambridgeshire border.

The vicar took Leo up in his ancient dog cart, a small but sturdy pony trotting determinedly around the darkened lanes by the light of the carriage lamp that Leo held up. He was glad the vicar had suggested it, for Leo would not have enjoyed taking his tilbury and an unfamiliar horse around the tight bends on roads he didn't know in near darkness.

When they were almost in sight of the house, the vicar pulled the cart off the road and tied the pony, gesturing for Leo to follow him. As they grew closer to a building that looked more like a shack than a house, the reverend extinguished the light and Leo blinked in the sudden darkness until his eyes grew accustomed.

"He's still there," Harbottle murmured in satisfaction, nodding to the empty curricle. "Must have put the horses away. Reckon he's staying the night, then."

Leo nodded, frowning as he wondered how best to go about this. He could hardly get Harbottle involved for fear the old fellow would be hurt.

"Thank you, sir, for guiding me here, but there's no need to stay. I'm afraid I've kept you from your bed for long enough," he said quietly.

"Oh, want all the fun yourself, do you?" the fellow replied, sounding quite indignant. "I may not be in my prime, Mr Huntington, but I am not dead yet."

"I can see that, Reverend, but all the same—"

"I boxed a little in my youth," Harbottle went on. "I had quite a nifty right hook, if I do say so myself."

Leo looked at him sceptically, for the reverend looked built more for comfort than speed these days. "Reverend, I cannot in all conscience allow you—"

"You're allowing nothing, young man," Harbottle said with a snort, and before Leo could protest, he got to his feet and began creeping towards the building.

Cursing under his breath, Leo followed. Mud Pightle seemed aptly named and he could only be thankful that there had been no rain for the past weeks. As it was, deep ruts had dried in the soil, making walking across it a difficult endeavour in the dark. As they grew closer to the house, which seemed to be a haphazard assemblage of planks that stayed in place through more luck than judgement, dim light filtered through the filthy windows.

Leo froze, grabbing the vicar and hauling him flat against the side of the building as the creak of a door sounded.

"What on ear—"

Leo clapped his hand over the man's mouth before he could give them away.

"'Ere, Edgar, what was that?" demanded an anxious voice from around the side of the building.

"What was what? Bloody 'ell, Burt! You're afraid of your own shadow, you are. There's nowt out there but a fox."

"Didn't sound like no fox to me," Burt said sulkily.

"Just get out there and feed that blasted hell cat."

"I don't see why I have to go, just because he scratched you up so good and—"

"Burt!"

"I'm going, I'm going!" The door slammed shut and Burt stalked across the field, holding a lamp aloft and muttering under his breath as he headed towards a small shed that looked even more dilapidated than the house.

"You have ruined all my careful plans," said another voice from inside the building before Leo could decide to follow. It was by no means an educated accent, but he recognised the style of speaking as someone trying to mimic an upper-class accent. "I am a busy man, Edgar, and you have wasted a good deal of my time. I believe we need to have a little chat. It was a simple enough task I set, and you and your fool brother had to ruin it."

"It weren't our fault. How was we to know the fellow would chase us halfway across the country? We was only supposed to take the damned cat and bring him to you, but that weren't possible with the devil snapping at our heels. Cost us train fair, it did and bleedin' expensive that were too." Edgar's voice was indignant, a belligerent tone that carried clearly. The next man spoke more quietly, and Leo strained to hear the words.

"Nonetheless, your failure to lose him, and then the decision to abandon the hackney carriage I lent you, has caused me a good deal of trouble, not to mention expense. You may rest assured that expense will be taken from your share of the ransom."

"Bleedin' 'ell, we weren't getting much of a look in as it was, when we was takin' all the risk and—"

"And do you wish to argue with me, Edgar?" the voice was harder now, a dangerous edge to it.

Edgar fell silent.

The vicar shook Leo's arm, and he belatedly remembered he was half smothering the fellow. He removed his hand, and Harbottle gave a quiet crow of triumph.

"I told you!" he whispered. "Didn't I tell you?"

Leo nodded. "You did, sir, and I thank you," he said, wondering what to do. If he went in and dealt with the remaining two men and took them unawares, his odds might be better, but Burt could still escape with Mau. No, better to deal with Burt first and get Mau. He'd send the vicar back to the inn with him whilst he dealt with the other two villains.

"Stay here," he told the vicar. "I'll deal with Burt first and get Mau."

To his relief, the vicar nodded his agreement with no argument, so Leo set off in the direction Burt had taken.

There were no windows in the shed, and no openings other than the door Burt had gone through, but it was ill fitting and Leo looked through the gap. Burt stood looking at a metal cage, holding out what looked like a strip of rind from a slice of ham. He dangled it through the thin bars of the cage and dropped it in.

Leo's eyes settled on Mau with a rush of relief, seeing his feline friend look as hale and hearty as always, if not as content. Mau's tail gave a twitch that Leo knew well boded ill, and he stared at the piece of rind in disgust. His yellow eyes lifted to Burt, such a look of contempt burning there that Leo almost laughed.

"Well, it's all you're getting," Burt said, sounding nervous all the same. "So eat it or don't. You can starve if you prefer."

Mau hissed, and Burt yelped, taking a hasty step back.

"Well, it ain't my fault," Burt protested. "Weren't my idea to take you. Worst thing we ever done, if you ask me. I told Edgar it were a mistake, but he don't listen to me."

A low growl came from the cage, and Burt turned hurriedly to the door. "Ain't natural," he said, clearly shaken as he pulled it open. His face was a picture as he saw Leo standing there, and for a moment his mouth opened and closed like a fish. Leo grabbed him by the throat, covered his mouth with his free hand, and marched him back into the hut, kicking the door shut behind him.

"Good evening, Burt," he said conversationally. "I'm afraid you have got yourself into a bit of trouble. Mau there is a dear friend of mine, you see, and I want him back."

Burt made a strangled sound, but Leo was not yet ready to let him speak.

"If you are sensible and don't make a fuss, I'll tie you up nice and tight and there will be no need to cause you any er… harm," he said, giving the fellow an insincere smile that suggested he was very willing to cause him harm if he decided to give making a fuss a go. "Then you can tell your brother you fought back as hard as you like, if you can make him believe that."

Burt made muffled squeaking noises, his eyes growing wide.

Leo tightened his grip. "Are you going to behave, Burt, old man?"

Burt nodded vigorously.

Leo narrowed his eyes. "Don't try my patience. You'll get one chance."

Burt nodded again and Leo removed his hand from the fellow's mouth.

"Don't 'urt me, sir! It weren't my idea, I swear it. It were all Edgar's doing, 'im and that bleedin' snooty arseh—" Burt exclaimed the moment he could speak.

"Shut your mouth," Leo growled at him. "Sit down there," he added, pointing at the floor. Burt scrambled to comply, dropping to the dirt floor, and Leo looked around the shed, spying some coarse lengths of thin rope in a tangle in the corner. Snatching it up, he freed enough from the knot to secure Burt's ankles and wrists before untying the kerchief around the man's neck and using it as a gag. Only then did he turn back to Mau, opening the cage.

"All right, Mau?" he asked anxiously, praying there was no damage he could not see.

Mau stalked out of the cage, sent Burt a derisive glare, and then looked up at Leo.

"Miaow!"

As complaints went, it was eloquent, and Leo swept his cat up, hugging him tightly.

"I know, old man, I'm sorry. Truly, I am. I'll make it up to you, I promise. Chicken for dinner every night for a month, how's that?"

Mau made a grumbling sound but licked Leo's ear so he hoped he might be forgiven in time. Leo glanced at Burt to see his expression was one of horror behind the gag. He snorted. Poor Burt seemed to think Mau really was the devil's work. Perhaps he believed he was Leo's familiar. Setting Mau down on the floor, Leo turned back to the door.

"Right, Mau, we need to get out of here. Ready?"

Yellow eyes blinked at him in the lamplight, Mau's tail swishing expectantly.

Leo nodded. "Come along, then."

Leo extinguished the lamp, opened the door, and fastened it shut behind him before running back to where the vicar was waiting for him. Except he wasn't.

Leo looked around and cursed, wondering what the man was up to. He groaned inwardly as he heard voices from inside.

"Well, Reverend, what was you up to, sneaking about in the dark?"

Edgar's voice, Leo thought, hearing a tone similar to Burt's. *Damn and blast*. Why could the old fellow not just have kept still?

"Night Hoopooloos," the reverend replied placidly.

"Night whatapooloos?" Edgar repeated, baffled.

Leo listened, intrigued, as he wondered if the vicar had been as entirely taken in by their Egyptian Water Sphinx as they had believed.

"Hoopooloos," the vicar repeated. "A very rare bird, only sings at night and is almost never seen in this part of the world. Hails from Africa. A glorious thing, bright green and red, but the song… ah, the song is not to be missed. I tracked one all along the lane but lost it when I got close to your house. I think something frightened it. Such a shame. If I could prove it was here it would be quite a feather in my ornithological cap, if you will excuse the pun."

Leo shook his head. He had to hand it to Harbottle, he was cool under pressure.

"Well, there ain't no rare birds here," Edgar said firmly. "So I reckon I'll just be escorting you home."

"You may get Burt to do that," the faux upper-class voice cut in once more.

"Oh, no need to provide an escort," Harbottle said at once. "I'm quite capable of finding my own way—"

"Burt will escort you," the man said, his voice firm. "One wouldn't want you getting yourself lost or falling into a ditch. You might hurt yourself."

There was nothing resembling concern in the words, but the hint of menace was unmistakeable.

"Oh, well, if you insist," the vicar replied cheerfully, apparently not taking the fellow's meaning. "If we're lucky, we might hear the Hoopooloo again."

Leo shook his head. He wouldn't have long, but if he dealt with the man behind this scheme first while Edgar was finding Burt, he thought he could deal with the Hatt brothers without too much difficulty. The man coordinating this little scheme was clearly the dangerous one, and he needed to be taken out of the picture first.

Leo looked down at Mau, who had been winding himself in and out of Leo's ankles, purring contentedly.

"Stay here, Mau," he said quietly. "And if any of those men get near you again, run."

Mau gave him an affection nip on the calf through the fabric of his trousers, and Leo smiled before turning his attention back to the building. The door creaked open and swung shut and Leo watched Edgar cross the yard to the shed. Once he was out of sight, Leo ran around to the front door and kicked it open.

Harbottle jumped in his seat, and Leo looked from him to the man in the centre of the room, leaning against an ancient table. He pushed to his feet upon seeing Leo, his posture one that left Leo in no doubt there would be the turn-up the vicar had been hoping for.

"I know you," Leo said, frowning as he regarded the man. "Where do I know you from?"

"I couldn't say, Mr Hunt, and I doubt you'd remember in any case," the fellow replied with a sneer. "But it was good of you to come calling."

"Oh, you're welcome," Leo replied with a snort as the man gave him a considering look up and down. Where the hell had he seen him before? Leo wracked his brain but came up empty.

"You know, Mr Hunt. It occurs to me the ransom we can get for you will be a good deal fatter than the one I was going to ask for your cat. If you had only acted with a bit of sense, you'd have had your wretched pet back and I would have gained a couple of hundred quid you could easily do without. Where's the harm in that? But I see now I was thinking too small. That amount of money won't see me comfortably through all my days, now will it? But when I had the notion of ransoming the horrid creature, I had no idea his master would fall into my hands like a ripe plum."

Leo returned a grim smile. "Don't count your chickens, sir. I'm in no mood to be held hostage."

The man removed a pistol from his waistband and pointed it at Leo. "Is that so?" he asked with a grin.

Chapter 10

Dear Harry,

Leo is a great gun, but he's not half so daft as he makes out. You've got no chance before you're one and twenty. Believe me, I tried everything when I was your age. No dice. Just accept it, cuz. You may not like to hear it, but you've still got a deal of growing up to do. I didn't appreciate hearing that any more than you will now when I was in your position, but I can see the truth of it with hindsight. I'm really not a stick in the mud, as I hope you know, but you'll only cause yourself trouble if you keep on. Take it from one who knows.

—Excerpt of a letter from Mr Felix Knight (son of Mr Gabriel and Lady Helena Knight) to his cousin, The Lord Harry Adolphus (younger son of Their Graces, Robert and Prunella Adolphus, The Duke and Duchess of Bedwin).

24th June 1850, Mud Pightle, Wrestlingworth, the Bedfordshire-Cambridgeshire border.

"Is that it?" Vi asked, looking through the branches of a tree at the faint glow coming from the ramshackle building before them with a sense of foreboding. The foul stench of a midden close by drifted on the warm night air, making her wrinkle her nose in disgust.

"That's it," Jenny agreed. "And the fellas that live there ain't no cleaner nor tidier than the house, if you can call that pile of rotten wood a house. I always knew Edgar was no good, but I never thought he'd do something like this."

"Don't like it, Jen. You ought not be here." Mick's deep voice rumbled through the darkness, but Jenny just hushed him.

"Hold your tongue, Mick. We just need to make sure Mr Huntington gets his cat back and away safe, that's all."

"But Ma will be cross with me—" the big man protested.

As Jenny had indicated, her brother was built on gigantic proportions but was not the sharpest knife in the drawer. She had explained several times already why they were here and that they wanted to stop any trouble, not make it.

"Edgar pinched my arse twice last week," Jenny cut in, folding her arms over her skinny chest. It was curious how such a slight girl was related to a fellow the size of Mick, but Vi had seen the resemblance in their features when Jenny had introduced her at the inn.

Mick's face darkened with rage at this information, and Jenny nodded with satisfaction.

"Now, Mick, there's no need to break his head, but just help us make sure all goes as it should. You can leave Burt alone, he's harmless enough. It was only Edgar. You got that?"

Mick grunted, cracking his knuckles in a way that made Vi wince.

"I'll break his fingers," Mick growled furiously. "Then we'll see if he feels like pinching you again."

Jenny patted her brother's massive shoulder and made soothing noises, but did not seem to much mind this outcome. Vi shifted uncomfortably. Her eyes had adjusted to the darkness now and she could see a large shape to their left. It moved and let out a soft whicker.

Mick heard it too and gestured to Jenny. "That's Nipper, Harbottle's pony. They're here all right."

"Well, I told you they were, didn't I?" Jenny said, shaking her head.

"Yes, but now what?" Vi asked, and then sucked in a sharp breath as something warm and furry rubbed against her legs. Trying hard not to scream, she leapt back and then looked down to see large round eyes blinking up at her, glittering brightly in the darkness.

"Mau!" she exclaimed, falling to her knees and hugging the cat to her. "Oh, I'm so glad you're all right."

She ran her hands over the cat's head and sleek back, checking for injuries.

"Miaow!"

Vi stilled as Mau made a series of rather urgent sounds that ranged from sharp little miaows to quick barks to a plaintiff yowl that made the hairs on the back of her neck stand all on end.

"Bleedin' 'ell, it really is an Egyptian Water thingy," Jenny said in wonder, staring at Mau in astonishment. "I admit, I thought you might have made that bit up."

Vi let out a nervous laugh. "Mau is a very special cat," she replied, evading the need to lie any further.

"He ain't happy, whatever he is," Mick pointed out, regarding Mau, who was flicking his tail irritably.

"No. I think Leo and the vicar must be inside. He gets terribly upset if he can't be where Leo is," Vi explained, trying to calm Mau so he didn't draw attention to them.

"Well, what now?" Jenny asked, which was an excellent question.

Mick stood, rolling his huge shoulders. "Reckon I'll go have a word with Edgar," he said grimly, but before he could take a step or either woman could object and tell him to wait, the door to the building swung open and a man stepped out, hurrying towards a dilapidated shed some distance from the house.

"Mick, could you deal with that man? If you take him on his own, it might be easier and…" Vi didn't get to finish the sentence as Mick was already moving.

"It's Edgar," Jenny hissed, which explained why the sound of knuckles cracking accompanied Mick's soft footsteps as he followed the man in the darkness.

Vi nodded, almost feeling sorry for Edgar, as she turned back to the house to see a dark shadow moving to the front door. Whoever it was kicked the door open and strode inside.

"Leo!" Vi squeaked, and picked up her skirts, hurrying towards the building.

She did not know if Jenny followed her, and didn't blame the girl if she stayed put. There was no need for her to put herself in harm's way if she didn't have to. Hurrying to the side of the building, Vi muttered silent curses as brambles caught at her skirts. The side of the building was overgrown, and it was difficult to get close, but she ignored the prickle of thorns as she pressed herself against the wall and peered in through a grimy window.

"I know you. Where do I know you from?" Leo's voice reached her, but she could only see the edge of his sleeve. She wondered who the man was that Leo recognised. The Reverend Harbottle was sitting quietly in the corner of the room, but his eyes were alert as he watched the two men.

"You know, Mr Hunt. It occurs to me the ransom we can get for you will be a good deal fatter than the one I was going to ask for your cat. If you had only acted with a bit of sense, you'd have had your wretched pet back and I would have gained a couple of hundred quid you could easily do without. Where's the harm in that? But I see now I was thinking too small. That amount of money won't see me comfortably through all my days, now will it? But when I had the notion of ransoming the horrid creature, I had no idea his master would fall into my hands like a ripe plum."

There was a snort from Leo, who shifted a little, moving out of her eye line completely. "Don't count your chickens, sir. I'm in no mood to be held hostage."

"Is that so?"

Vi smothered a gasp, her hand covering her mouth as she saw another figure move to stand before the window, a pistol clearly visible in his hand.

A crash from the shed and a bellow of rage caught her attention, and the attention of those inside the building.

"Stay there," the man holding the pistol said, gesturing with it for Leo to move farther into the building.

He moved past the window to the door and Vi gasped as she too recognised the man, except she knew exactly who he was. That was Pembury, their new footman at Albany, the London house.

"Edgar! Burt!" the man shouted. "What the devil are you two idiots up to now?"

A wail sounded from the shed before the rickety building wobbled madly, then Mick smashed Edgar through a wall that disintegrated on impact, causing the entire structure to collapse in a heap. A smaller, stockier man belted away from the scene as fast as his short legs would carry him.

"Burt!" Edgar wailed, but Burt was moving with astonishing speed.

"Come back 'ere!" Mick bellowed at Edgar as he tried to crawl away on his hands and knees.

"'Elp!" Edgar shrieked, as Mick took hold of his ankles and began dragging him towards the woods. "Pembury, 'elp me!"

"Bloody hell," Pembury muttered in fury. "Right, a change of plan. Mr Hunt, if you would be so good as to come along, we are going to relocate."

"I don't think so," Leo said calmly. "I'm not going anywhere."

"Must I shoot you?" Pembury demanded, the question making Vi's stomach clench with terror. What was Leo doing, arguing with the man when he had a pistol?

"If you do, you won't get your ransom, now, will you?" Leo replied conversationally.

"Oh, I wasn't thinking of aiming for your heart," Pembury replied with a chuckle. "Perhaps I shall just ruin your chances for an heir."

"I doubt that thing is even loaded. It looks ancient," Leo said with a sneer of derision. "Is that the best you could do? Still, the state of the curricle outside answers that question, I suppose. I dread to think what kind of cattle were pulling it. Are they up to taking both our weights? Come to think of it, I'm not sure the curricle will make it over those ruts on the lane with both of us in it."

Leo, shut up! Vi shrieked mentally, wondering what he was playing at, for he seemed to be deliberately goading the man.

"The pistol is loaded," the man replied, though he sounded less sanguine now, and rather like he was gritting his teeth. "And once I have the ransom money, I'll be able to buy myself a new tilbury, or perhaps I'll just take yours."

"Oh, I shouldn't do that, sir," the vicar said cheerfully, apparently joining the conversation. "A tilbury takes a good deal of skill. Needs a bigger horse, you see, one with a bit of spirit. Not the kind of thing an amateur should attempt."

Good Lord! Vi thought in exasperation. Did they both *want* to get shot?

"Shut up, priest," Pembury said, swinging the pistol towards Harbottle.

"I am rather concerned about your immortal soul," Harbottle went on, apparently unperturbed by the gun pointing at his face. "You are not doing it a great deal of good, young man. Worldly goods are really not worth—"

"Shut up!"

Vi gasped as Pembury smacked Harbottle's face, yelling in fury.

There was a blur of movement and terror thrilled through Vi as she saw Leo force the gun in Pembury's hand up and shove him hard to the floor. Then she could see nothing more, but she heard the thuds and crashes that indicated a fight was in progress.

"Leo!" she cried, caring for nothing other than the fact Leo had put himself in harm's way and she could not stand by and do nothing.

Vi yanked her skirts from the brambles they were caught on and ran for the door, hesitating as she passed a wood pile. She gave the pile a cursory glance, then picked up a log about two feet in length and as thick as her forearm. If she was to give Leo the best chance possible, she ought to cause as big a scene as she could to put Pembury off balance. Holding the log in both hands overhead, she took a deep breath and then ran through the door, shouting something she hoped resembled a battle cry as loudly as her lungs would allow.

Pembury and Leo were still standing, wrestling over the gun, and both men jolted in shock, gaping in disbelief as Vi came thundering into the room, bellowing like a small but enraged warrior queen. To her relief, the shock must have slackened Pembury's grip on the pistol, for Leo rallied quicker. He smashed the man's wrist against the wall, and the gun fell with a clatter. Vi ran on, beating Pembury around the head and shoulders with the log until the man drew his arm back hard, elbowing Vi in the head.

Vi saw stars, pain exploding in her temples as the room went dark and her knees gave out beneath her.

All the breath left Leo's lungs as he saw Vi fall, her slender form collapsing in a tumble of pretty fabric on the filthy floor of the Hatts' disgusting dwelling. For a moment terror held him immobile, the need to go to her stronger than anything else, but Harbottle was there, leaning over Vi and patting her cheek.

"She's alive, just knocked out," Harbottle shouted, giving Leo's heart a reason to beat again as white-hot rage surged in his veins, erasing everything else but the desire to murder the man who had dared to hurt her.

The man Edgar had called Pembury had pushed clear of Leo during his distraction and the gun had been kicked under a moth-eaten armchair and out of sight during their scuffle. The two men circled each other now, fists raised. Pembury was a tall, well-built fellow, and the two of them evenly matched for weight. He was grim-faced, a look in his eyes that suggested he'd do whatever it took to get what he wanted, but Leo didn't care. He needed to get to Vi, to take her in his arms and see for himself that she was unharmed, and he could not do that until the man responsible had been dealt with to his satisfaction.

Pembury lunged but Leo dodged out of range and Pembury came on again, swinging wildly. To Leo's satisfaction, he saw the man had no actual skill, only a desire for violence and a willingness to use his fists. He stayed out of range, sizing him up as Pembury kept moving forward, overturning furniture as he went. Pembury swung again, a blow that might have broken Leo's jaw if it had connected. As it was, it only grazed his cheek but reminded him to keep his wits about him. Pembury swung once more and Leo dodged, following up with a hard right that snapped Pembury's head back.

"Oh, I say! Nicely done, sir!" Harbottle exclaimed.

Leo didn't look at the vicar, his eyes firmly fixed on Pembury, who wiped a trickle of blood from his mouth, but he was aware the vicar had dragged Vi to the corner of the room and laid her head on a cushion. Was she really all right? How hard had Pembury's elbow hit her?

"Look out, there!"

Leo cursed, realising he had been distracted and narrowly escaped a blow to the kidneys that might have doubled him up. This needed to be over so he could get to Vi. He delivered a right that Pembury evaded but followed up with a left that connected and a right to Pembury's midsection that made the man gasp and stagger backwards.

"One, two, *oh*, a peg, good, good! Pay away, now, Hunt, pay away!"

Leo registered the advice from Harbottle, who was standing to the side, fists raised, commentating on the match and bobbing and weaving as Leo did. The boxing speak, suggesting he finish the job with a series of rapid blows, seem an excellent idea to Leo, who was quite happy to do as he suggested. He bore down on Pembury, whose fists came up to protect his face and Leo delivered several punishing blows to his guts and kidney. As his fists lowered to protect his battered body, Leo drew back his right and hit him with all he had.

"A facer!" Harbottle cried in delight, watching as Pembury swayed and then crashed to the floor. "Floored! I say, Mr Hunt, you are a Broughtonian and no mistake. Well, done, well done indeed!"

Leo ignored the praise, caring nothing for the battered man at his feet or for Harbottle's admiration. He ran to Vi, falling to his knees beside her, and viewing the nasty lump rising on her forehead with anxiety.

"Vi? Vi, love?" he whispered, stroking her beautiful face as a fear held his heart in a vice.

Good God, this was why she didn't want to marry him, because he brought chaos and disaster in his wake. One full day in his company and look where it had got her, unconscious on the filthy floor of a disgusting hovel in the company of men who ought never be allowed within ten miles of her. He lifted her carefully, pulling her into his lap and cradling her head against his shoulder.

Vi groaned, her hand lifting to her bruised head.

"Darling!" Leo exclaimed. "Sweetheart, talk to me. Are you hurt?"

Vi blinked dazedly, struggling to focus. Finally, her gaze settled upon him, her eyes fixing upon his.

"Vi, darling, are you all right?"

A small frown tugged at her brows.

"All right?" she repeated faintly, before she gathered herself, her expression darkening. "All right?" she repeated, a different tone to her voice now that boded ill.

"Love?" Leo said, stroking her cheek gently.

Vi smacked it away. "No, I am not all right, Leo," she told him furiously. "How dare you! How dare you go off and leave me all by myself, coming here and getting yourself in God knows what trouble. He had a gun. *A gun!* Just like I told you he would, you great, ignorant, pig-headed, stupid, stupid, stupid, *man!"*

Leo stared at her, never having seen Vi roused to such heights of passionate fury before. But then her face crumpled, and she threw herself into his arms, hugging him tightly and sobbing hard.

"I'm sorry," Leo said, his voice unsteady with remorse. "Vi, I'm… I'm so very sorry."

"Shut up!" she told him.

So Leo shut up, pressing a handkerchief into her hand and just holding her until the sobs became uneven gulps and finally subsided.

"A good cry always makes them feel better, Mr Hunt, don't worry," Harbottle whispered confidentially, whilst he made a surprisingly neat job of tying Pembury up. "My dear wife would always feel much calmer once she had shouted at me and then had a good cry, God rest her beloved soul. It clears the air."

Leo nodded, hoping Harbottle was right, but miserably aware he'd likely messed up his last chance with Vi. Even if he'd had the nine lives he'd wished for, the events of the past day and night must have used up every one of them. She'd want nothing to do with him now, and he couldn't blame her for it either. If he couldn't keep her safe, what kind of husband would he make her? Perhaps she really was better off without him.

Then it occurred to him that Harbottle had called him Mr *Hunt*, not Mr Huntington.

Hell.

Chapter 11

Mr Knight,

I need some advice concerning a business venture, which I believe may interest you. I would be grateful if you could find the time to call on me at home next week to discuss the matter in more detail.

Might I request you arrive in the guise of a morning caller, however, and not a man of business? Whilst I have means of my own and no requirement for my father's permission, he would not approve of my scheme, and I prefer to keep the details from him. A mutual friend has vouched for your discretion and trustworthiness. I pray you do not let me down.

—Excerpt of a letter from The Lady Belinda Madox-Brown to Mr Felix Knight (son of Mr Gabriel and Lady Helena Knight).

25th June 1850, Mud Pightle, Wrestlingworth, the Bedfordshire-Cambridgeshire border.

Vi wiped her eyes and gave her nose a good blow, wishing she had not made quite such a scene, but really, seeing the man she loved held at gunpoint, and then being hit on the head, was rather provoking. In the circumstances, she did not think she had behaved so very unreasonably. *The man she loved.* The words repeated in her head with a sense of inevitability. Well, it wasn't like she could pretend otherwise, not any longer. She loved Leo Hunt, heaven help her, and she did not know what to do about it.

"Feeling better?" Leo asked cautiously, looking down at her.

There was concern in his eyes, and a look that suggested he believed she would pick up the log and attack him with it if he said the wrong thing. Sighing, Vi nodded.

"Yes, thank you. I can get up now."

Leo frowned, touching a gentle finger to her forehead, just beside the bruise. "How is your head?"

"Throbbing. But nothing a good night's sleep won't repair," she added in resignation, knowing she had lost her one and only chance to spend the night with Leo without becoming his wife.

He would never make love to her in this sorry state, and she really did not feel like it in any case. She was tired and dirty, and her head was pounding so hard she just wanted to sleep. In the morning, he would insist on taking her home, and in doing whatever was necessary to protect her reputation. She had no idea what damage had been done, but if there was the slightest hint of gossip, he would insist on marrying her, and Mama and Papa would agree. The thought of the scenes she must endure when she refused him was enough to depress her spirits thoroughly and make her feel utterly exhausted.

"Did Mick capture Burt and Edgar?" she asked, preferring to keep her mind from such dismaying topics for as long as possible.

"Is that the big fellow?" Reverend Harbottle asked, taking off his spectacles and rubbing them clean. "I believe he has Edgar in hand, yes. Burt, I think, may have absconded."

"No, he ain't."

Vi looked around at the familiar voice as Jenny walked in, pushing a wretched looking Burt ahead of her. One eye was swelling shut and he looked thoroughly miserable.

"Silly sod thought he'd try to pinch Mick's cart. I thought otherwise," Jenny said with a grin. "Not like he's got anywhere to go."

"I'll be transported," Burt said glumly, shaking his head.

"Nah, I don't reckon so," Jenny said briskly. "Can't speak for that disgusting brother of yours, but if you promise to behave yourself, me and Mick will speak up for you."

Burt's eyes went round. "You mean it, Jenny?"

"Maybe," Jenny shrugged. "Depends how helpful you are in sorting this mess out, eh?"

"I'll be helpful!" Burt exclaimed, immediately setting to, picking up furniture and tidying up.

Jenny met Vi's gaze before she turned to Leo. "Burt's harmless," she said quietly. "His brother has always bullied him, but there's no wickedness in him. If you think you could see your way to keeping him out of all this, sir? I know I have no right to ask it of you, but—"

"We shall certainly discuss it," Vi said, for Leo's face had darkened and he did not look like a man willing to give any quarter. "But perhaps in the morning. If Mick could help Mr Huntington and the reverend to get Pembury here and Edgar and Burt somewhere secure for the night?"

"There's the pub cellar, we can use that I reckon if Reverend Harbottle confirms the story to Mrs Caruthers. Leave it to me," Jenny said, and took herself out again, calling over her shoulder. "Burt, come and help me."

Burt put down the broken chair he'd been holding and hurried out after her.

"Help me up, Leo," Vi said, shifting on his lap.

Leo did so, but before she could take a step, he swung her up into his arms, making her gasp. "Leo, there's no need! I'm perfectly—"

"Hush," he said, his tone brooking no argument. "You are not taking a step or moving so much as an inch away from me. I want you where I can see you, where I know you are safe. The least I can do is get you back home in one piece."

There was a tone to his voice that she had not heard before, and Vi wondered at it.

"I'm quite all right, really."

"Oh, yes, just caught up in the middle of a fight in a disgusting hovel with criminals and guns and—"

"Oh, don't take a pet now," Vi said, shaking her head at him. "Pembury is our footman, for heaven's sake. He's obviously been planning this since that incident when Mau savaged him. That's unfortunate, but it's hardly your fault the man's a villain. You tried your best to keep me at the inn, didn't you? I was the one who came after you, you did not bring me along."

"No, but I wanted to, damn me for a scoundrel. I hated leaving you behind, and when I think of what might have happened—" Leo closed his mouth with a snap, but his voice had sounded a little odd, shaken.

"You did?" Vi asked in surprise. "You wanted me to come with you?"

"I always want you with me, Vi. Have you really not understood that yet?" he said in frustration. "The trouble is that you were right all along. You ought not to be in company with me. I… I'm a magnet for trouble, just as you always said I was."

Vi considered this as Leo carried her back to the dogcart and settled her on the seat. Mick and Burt had hauled a struggling Pembury into the back of Mick's cart between them, and Mick had carried Edgar, the man slung over one shoulder like a sack of coal, apparently still unconscious, which was probably just as well.

"Mau?"

Leo called anxiously and Vi smiled as a dark shape slid sinuously from the black shadow of the woods and wound itself in and out of Leo's ankles.

"Come on, Mau," Leo said, climbing in and patting his lap. Mau looked at the pony and cart with an expression that suggested such means of transport was beneath his touch but deigned to join them. When Harbottle got up too, it was a snug fit, but soon they were on their way back to the inn. Every rut in the road made Vi close her eyes against the throbbing in her head and she was more than relieved when they made it out of the wretched little lane and onto the main road.

"I'll drop you both back at the inn and then take myself off home, Mr Hunt," Harbottle said cheerfully. "Goodness, what an exciting evening it has been! I've not enjoyed myself so much in years."

"I'm glad we've entertained you, sir," Leo said, but Vi heard the concern in his voice as he glanced over at Harbottle. "Perhaps if you would be so good to receive me, sir, you might allow me to call on you in the morning. I believe there are… things we need to discuss."

Harbottle slanted a look at Leo before returning his attention to the road. "Perhaps, sir. Perhaps there are, at that."

Vi wondered what he meant by that but was too tired to consider it further. The sight of the inn ahead was a tremendous relief, and it took every scrap of energy remaining to climb down from the cart and make her way back to their room. Leo would have carried her, but she did not want to give any further cause for gossip. As it was, the reverend had to take some time placating his sister, Mrs Caruthers, and assuring her that all was well, that their cat would not cause havoc or make a mess in her best room, and her guests were perfectly respectable. He had a twinkle in his eyes as he bade them both a good night, however, that made Vi wonder.

Leo had asked Mrs Caruthers to fetch a doctor but Vi had persuaded him that the morning would be soon enough, and a good night's sleep was the best thing for her. Unhappy but resigned, Leo agreed, providing the doctor came first thing. This arranged, he helped her upstairs.

Leo unlocked the door and pushed it open but, before Vi could take a step, he picked her up and carried her inside. Mau shot in ahead of them, as keen as they were for his bed.

"Hush," Leo said, when she might have protested, so she hushed, and allowed him to strip off her bonnet and gloves, her gown and her corset, standing placidly as he made quick work of strings and buttons and fastenings.

Plenty of practise, she thought morosely, wishing tonight had been different. He had promised her more pleasure than she had ever dreamed of, and now it would be worse than before, knowing that he could have made her feel such wondrous things and she would never know. Unless she married him.

She *could* marry him.

The image of Pembury holding a gun on Leo flashed behind her eyes and she shuddered, her heart squeezing in her chest, such terror filling her as she considered what might have happened. Leo might have been killed. If anything happened to him, she did not know how she would survive it, but how much worse if he was her beloved husband, father of her children, rather than merely a very dear friend?

Leo didn't bother lighting the lamps, for which she was grateful. Instead, he moved her this way and that until she stood in her shift, guiding her to the bed and drawing back the blankets, helping her in and pulling the covers back up. She allowed it all placidly, too tired to protest his treating her like a child. In truth, it was rather soothing to be cared for, not to have to think, but to leave it all to him. She felt Mau jump onto the bed and curl up by her feet.

"Look after her, Mau," Leo said, stroking the cat's head before he moved away and sat down in the chair by the fireplace with a muffled groan.

Vi waited hopefully, but he didn't move.

"Leo?"

"Yes, love?"

"What are you doing?" she asked, peering into the darkness to see if she could make him out.

"I'll sleep in the chair, Vi. You need your rest, and I don't want to disturb you."

Vi swallowed, gathering her nerve. "B-But I don't want you to sleep in the chair."

There was a brief silence.

"What do you want?"

"Come to bed."

Vi listened intently, straining her ears for any sound of movement.

"If I come to bed, will you go to sleep?" he asked her, a slightly strained note in his voice.

"Yes."

"You promise?"

"Yes."

She relaxed as she heard him get to his feet and then the muffled sounds of him moving in the darkness, taking off his boots and undressing. Vi held her breath until she felt the mattress dip as Leo got in.

The moment he was settled she wriggled over to his side, cuddled against him.

"Vi… you promised," he said, the warning clear that he would leave if she tried anything.

"Just hold me, Leo," Vi asked, not having to try too hard to sound vulnerable and a bit pathetic. "Please?"

"All right, love. Come here."

He gathered her more securely and Vi lay her head on his chest, feeling the coarse hair tickling her cheek and hearing the reassuring thud of his heartbeat. Oh, that was better, much better. The warmth of his body enveloped her, easing away the stress of the past hours and Vi relaxed in his embrace, allowing herself to tumble into sleep, secure in his arms.

Leo lay still in the darkness, staring up at the ceiling. Vi's slender form was a delicious weight against him, her hair a tumble of curls over his chest. Tenderness and longing filled his heart, an ache of need and desire and regret so intense it felt like a knife lodged there.

She would never marry him now, and he could hardly blame her. How could he keep asking her to trust him, to allow him to prove how much he had changed after tonight's debacle? He should never have brought her with him in the first place, but how could he have left her behind when she wanted to come?

Her warm breath fluttered over his skin, and she shifted in her sleep, her hand straying from his chest to settle lower down over his belly. Leo closed his eyes, trying not to imagine her hand drifting lower still, touching him, wanting him.

She did want him. He knew that much, at least. But plenty of women had wanted him. He was blessed with a handsome face and form, which had meant he had never had to try to make people like him, or women desire him. Vi was different. He'd had to work for her good opinion, which was never given easily, if at all. If Vi had approved of something he'd said or done, it felt like it was worth something, like he was worth more than the sum of his parts.

For as long as he could remember, he'd been driven to do things: to travel, to seek adventure, to prove he was the fastest, the strongest, the best at whatever challenge was set before him. With Vi, that all seemed to go away. For all that they sparred and bickered and wound each other up, all he really wanted with Vi was to make her happy, to make them both happy, to find a way of living their lives together that would suit them. A home they could share, the opportunity to show Vi people and places she could not experience as an unmarried woman… perhaps children, if they were so blessed. But if it was just the two of them, he really didn't think he would mind, providing she did not. They could always adopt; she had been adopted, after all. It wasn't as if there weren't enough children in the world in need of a loving family.

All of that seemed moot now, however. The only thing he had needed to prove to her was that he was a good man, one she could rely upon, and he knew he had failed at that. Hopefully Harbottle would hold his tongue about their unmarried status. He was certainly the most unconventional reverend Leo had ever come across. Leo had half expected the man to tell his sister everything, and knew she would have turned them out without a moment's hesitation, but he had not done so. Perhaps he expected Leo to marry Vi, something he'd do in a heartbeat if only the reverend could talk her into it. He considered suggesting Harbottle speak to Vi, but then he rejected the idea. The thought of her needing a man of God to guilt her into accepting his proposal made him feel sick. If Vi wanted him, she would have him, if she did not… well, then she did not, and he would simply have to live with that.

It was not a happy thought.

Gloomy, his body sore from the fight and all on edge with unfulfilled desire as Vi's lovely frame pressed close to his. Leo sighed and resigned himself to a sleepless night.

Chapter 12

My Lady,

Thank you for your letter. An intriguing proposition, to be sure. Is it possible for you to give me a little more detail regarding the venture you wish to embark on so I might come fully prepared for our meeting?

Sadly, my appointments next week are all taken, however, I can call on Wednesday week, if this suits you.

Might I enquire who our mutual friend is?

I await your reply.

—Excerpt of a letter from Mr Felix Knight (son of Mr Gabriel and Lady Helena Knight) to The Lady Belinda Madox-Brown.

25th June 1850, The Queen's Head, Wrestlingworth, the Bedfordshire, Cambridgeshire border.

Leo looked down at the bed where Vi still slept peacefully and wondered if he would ever have the privilege of seeing her so again. Would he ever be so fortunate as to share a bed with her again, even if it was only to hold her in his arms? God, he hoped so, but he was afraid his legendary luck had finally run out.

"Stay," he told Mau firmly, giving his friend a rub under the chin that made the big cat purr contentedly.

He went out, closing the door quietly behind him.

"Good morning, Mr Huntington."

Leo turned, smiling at Jenny and pleased to see she was none the worse for last night's adventures.

"Good morning, Jenny. I'm glad to see you, I wanted to check you didn't get in any trouble last night."

"No, sir, though I thank you for the thought, but Reverend Harbottle made it all square with Mrs Caruthers. Though she didn't like it none, I can tell you," she added with a snort.

"I can imagine," Leo replied with a grimace. "Mrs Huntington is still sleeping, but I asked for a doctor—"

"Yes, sir, I know, begging your pardon. Dr Benson will be here at ten thirty. He attended a difficult birth last night and can't be here earlier than that, I'm afraid."

"Very well. In the meantime, would you take Mrs Huntington some breakfast? Something light. Boiled eggs, perhaps. I seem to remember that's what I was prescribed whenever I clouted my head," he added with a frown. "And some willow bark tea, she's bound to have the headache still this morning. If you could see your way clear to feeding Mau too, I'd appreciate it. A quick trip to the garden would likely be just as well, if you can manage it."

Leo fished in his pocket and handed Jenny a generous tip for her trouble.

"Very good, sir. Thank you. I'll see to it, don't worry. Shall I take Mrs Huntington's gown back for cleaning and pressing, too?"

Leo nodded his agreement. "Oh, but Jenny… give it back to her before I return at your peril, if the two of you are plotting any more madness together."

Jenny laughed. "Yes, sir, Mr Huntington."

With Vi and Mau taken care of for the moment, Leo hurried down the stairs and swallowed a cup of coffee as he waited for the grooms to put his horse to the tilbury. The moment they were ready, he left and arrived outside the reverend's house at precisely nine o'clock.

"Ah, Mr Hunt, I suspected I would see you bright and early this morning," Harbottle said as he opened the front door. "Excuse my state of undress, but I had rather a late night," he said with a quirk of his lips.

"Forgive me for the early call," Leo replied, a little stunned by the garish dressing gown the vicar wore. It was made of heavy saffron yellow satin, and richly embroidered in bright red, green and blue. It showed signs of wear now but was still an impressive garment for your average country vicar. Harbottle really was quite a character and Leo wondered if he had travelled in his youth, India perhaps. If things were different Leo thought he would enjoy chatting to the fellow. As it was, he needed to ensure Vi's reputation was safe.

"Have you had breakfast?"

"I had coffee," Leo replied, following Harbottle into a small dining room. The vicar paused on the way, sticking his head around what Leo guessed to be the kitchen door in order to call inside.

"Mrs Jenkins, I have a guest. Breakfast for two, if you please?"

"Very good, sir." A disembodied female voice replied to this instruction.

"My housekeeper, Mrs Jenkins. A wonderful cook. You'll be well fed," Harbottle assured Leo with a toothy grin as he patted his own belly. "I eat far better than I ought to," he added with a sigh.

"You're very kind, sir, but really there's no need. I do not wish to put you to any trouble—"

"Nonsense, nonsense, I'm just sitting here. Mrs Jenkins has all the work, but she enjoys feeding people so another mouth will please her no end. Now, do stop looking so anxious. I can imagine why you are here, but there is no need to fret. That is, providing you are intending to do the honourable thing by the young lady?"

Harbottle's kindly but intelligent eyes settled on Leo.

"I would marry her in a heartbeat, but… but the young lady is reluctant," Leo replied, and then hurried to clarify as he realised how that might sound. "Please, do not think, I mean, Miss— The young lady is of unimpeachable character and is only in this ridiculous fix because of me."

"Because of those men last night, you mean," Harbottle suggested.

Leo shrugged. "Yes, but I ought not to have involved her."

Harbottle laughed, his eyes crinkling at the corners. "From what I saw last night, your young lady is not the sort who likes being left out."

Leo's lips quirked. "She was mad as fire that I left her in her room, and no, she would not let me set her down whenever I tried to persuade her to turn back, but all the same—"

"All the same, she's a woman of sense, one with intelligence and fortitude from what I can see. Were you to ignore her wishes and impose your own will upon her?"

"No, but… but she could have been killed last night—" Leo protested, running a hand through his hair in frustration.

"But she was not, and neither were you. It's unlikely you will get yourselves in quite such a scrape again, I think. If I were you, I should stop fretting, enjoy the wonderful breakfast Mrs Jenkins provides you, and then tell the young lady you are desperately in love with her and need her to marry you or you will sink into despair."

Leo huffed with amusement. "Sadly, the last part is all too true, and I would do it without a second thought if I thought it would work."

"You think it would not?" The vicar looked at him curiously.

"I've had something of an adventurous life, Reverend. Vi thinks I'm a loose screw, not to be relied upon, that I'll get bored and set out on some mad adventure and forget about her, or take up a mistress, or get myself killed, any or all the above," he added gloomily.

"Is she right?"

"No!" Leo retorted at once. "No, certainly not."

"I have certainly heard of your exploits, Mr Hunt, and I confess, I have been a little surprised you survived your early years myself, at times."

"You… You have?" Leo said in dismay.

"Of course, anyone who reads the scandal sheets must know of Mr Hunt, and in more recent times, his magnificent cat, Mau."

Leo groaned and put his head in his hands. "You knew."

Harbottle nodded. "I did," he admitted somewhat smugly. "But I did not wish to spoil your adventure when you were having such fun."

"Fun?"

Leo stared at him in shock.

"Certainly. At least it seemed to me I was with two young people having a marvellous time despite their worries and who made an excellent team. You are well suited, I think."

Leo considered his words. It had been fun in parts, if he'd not been so worried about Mau, it would have been a good deal more enjoyable but… but Vi had enjoyed it too.

"Ah, Mrs Jenkins, a splendid feast as usual. You see, Mr Hunt, did I not tell you?"

"You did, sir," Leo replied, thanking the housekeeper as she came into the room and deposited an overflowing plate of eggs, bacon, sausages and fried potatoes and mushrooms before him. She gave the reverend a nod in response to his words and went out again.

The reverend snatched up his knife and fork eagerly before glancing back at Leo.

"If you would forgive an old man for his interference, would you mind me calling in on the young lady later this morning? I should like to see how she goes on and perhaps she might like to speak to me too," Harbottle suggested.

Leo frowned. He had thought of asking Harbottle to do just that, but….

"If she wishes to talk to you, certainly, but only if you give me your word you will do nothing to persuade her into accepting me for moral reasons, or… or for any other reason other than wanting to."

"Certainly, I shall, though are you certain there is no gossip. You are a well-known figure on the road, sir. If anyone has seen you, the lady's reputation—"

"Do *not,* whatever you do, raise that as a reason to marry me," Leo said, dropping his knife and fork in his anxiety. "Vi would run as far and fast as she could rather than do so in those circumstances."

Harbottle returned a rueful smile. "Ah, she is indeed a woman with spirit. In that case, I shall certainly not do so."

"Spirit? Ha!" Leo said with a bark of laughter. "She's the most obstinate, pigheaded, frustrating woman in the entire world."

"And you cannot live without her," Harbottle finished for him.

Leo stared down at his breakfast and sighed. "No," he agreed morosely, and prayed the vicar might succeed where he had failed.

Vi had not been in the best of humours when she'd awoken and found Leo had gone out without her. She'd had some lingering hope that she might have induced him to make love to her that morning, though a glance in the mirror on the dressing table had swiftly put paid to that notion. She'd looked a fright, her hair a tangle no self-respecting bird would deign to nest in, and the lump on her head, whilst not so pronounced, had turned some impressive shades that did little for her complexion.

The note Vi discovered on her pillow, explaining where he was going and why and how he could not bear to wake her when she'd had such a trying night, had mollified her somewhat. Finding he had arranged breakfast in bed, willow bark tea, and for her gown and Mau to be seen to, removed any lingering resentment at his going off on his own. At least she'd had time to make herself look something close to neat and tidy, even if lovely and desirable was now far out of reach and Jenny had helped her do something with her hair, which had helped somewhat.

Vi would have liked to have seen the Reverend Harbottle again too, for he seemed a nice man, even if he had led Leo into danger last night. But perhaps Leo would allow her to call in on him before he took her back home.

They *would* be going back home, she realised with a sigh of dismay. The adventure was over, and whilst she had no desire to ever endure the terrors of last night again, she had to confess that sharing all the trials and tribulations with Leo had been rather wonderful. She had enjoyed parts of it a great deal, she realised, looking back at the events of the previous day with a wistful sigh.

"Mrs Huntington?" Jenny called through the door.

"Yes, Jenny, come in."

"I brought your gown back, for the doctor will be here shortly, though Mr Huntington told me not to give it to you before he got back. I *think* he was joking," she added dubiously. "I'm afraid the hem is torn, but I tidied it up as best I could."

"You've done a splendid job. Thank you, Jenny, and thank you for everything you did last night. I'm so very grateful. You did wonders with my hair this morning, too. I confess, I thought it was beyond saving," Vi added, touching a hand to the elegant coiffure Jenny had created for her earlier with a smile.

Jenny blushed, pleased with such praise. "My pleasure, Mrs Huntington, and… well, if it ain't too cheeky to say so, if you should ever be needing a lady's maid… I mean, I know I'm not one, but I'm good with hair like you said, and with keeping clothes nice and properly pressed. I'm a quick learner, and I've a fair hand with a needle and thread too, and—"

Vi smiled as Jenny ran through all her talents. "Well, Jenny. If you are certain you don't mind leaving the village and your job here, I will certainly think about it. My own maid is due to be married in a few weeks, you see, and so—"

"Oh, Mrs Huntington! Do you really mean you'll take me on?" Jenny cried, and Vi saw the desire for this chance burning in the woman's eyes.

Vi considered this. She had not meant to make a snap decision, but Jenny had proven herself capable, brave, and resilient last night, and she thought she was someone in whom she could put her trust. Surely the girl deserved a chance. If Vi took her on now, Rachel would have a little time to train her up before she left to get married.

"I do," Vi said, nodding. She laughed as Jenny gave a little scream of delight and then gave Vi an impulsive hug before she remembered herself.

"I beg your pardon, Mrs Huntington. I… I'm just so happy for the opportunity."

Vi smiled, patting the girl's hand. She would have to explain she was Miss Spencer eventually and hope Jenny was not too shocked. "That's quite all right, but you might need to give Mrs Caruthers notice before you leave her employ. I shall leave you my address so you can follow on when she is able to let you go. Now, if you really want to impress me, hurry and get me dressed."

Vi sat at the table by the window in her room, sipping a cup of tea. The doctor had seen her and declared her fit and well. He was elderly, no nonsense man who told her frankly that he did not hold with ladies having fits of the vapours. In his opinion, there was little that could not be fixed with walks in the fresh air, looser corsets, and good food, but he warned her against overexerting herself. If she experienced any further headaches or dizziness, she was to seek medical help at once.

She had expected Leo back by now, and when she heard the knock at the door, her heart leapt, only to plummet again as she heard Jenny's voice.

"Reverend Harbottle is here, Mrs Huntington. Shall I show him in?"

"Yes, please do, Jenny," Vi called, getting to her feet. Why on earth had the vicar come to call? She hoped there was nothing wrong. Surely Leo could not have got himself into another scrape so quickly.

Jenny showed the reverend in and hurried out again instead of lingering, proving to Vi that the girl knew how to be discreet.

"Reverend, how lovely to see you again. I so hoped to thank you for everything you did for us last night."

"My pleasure, my pleasure," Harbottle said, spying Mau and going over to see him. "My, my, he is a handsome fellow, I must say. I've never seen a cat like him, even if he isn't an Egyptian Water Sphinx," he added, regarding Vi with a crooked smile.

"Oh," Vi said faintly, wondering what else he knew.

"I know the whole story, Miss Spencer," he said kindly, patting Vi's shoulder as she sank into the nearest chair. The implications of his words were obvious.

"I suppose Leo sent you here," she said bitterly. "To persuade me to do the right thing and marry him."

"Indeed, he did not," Harbottle said, shaking his head as he settled himself opposite her. "In fact, I was only allowed to visit you on the understanding that I do no such thing. He was very clear on that point. Said you would run as far and fast as you could if I so much as hinted at it."

Vi let out a breath. She should have had more faith in Leo. He knew by now that such tactics would not work, and he was neither foolish nor arrogant enough to try such a thing.

"Then why are you here?" Vi demanded, and then blushed a little at her lack of manners.

Harbottle shrugged, settling back into his seat. "For my own curiosity. I confess I am a little flummoxed."

"By what?" Vi said in confusion.

"By what would make a beautiful young woman refuse to marry a handsome young man she is quite obviously head over ears in love with?"

Vi blushed, looking away from Harbottle's sympathetic smile.

"You were very brave last night, rushing in like that. You put yourself in danger to save the man you loved. Quite admirable, Miss Spencer."

Vi shook her head, blinking back tears. She took a deep breath and spoke carefully so there could be no misunderstanding. "In the first place, Reverend, I am not a *young* woman. By society's standards, I am well and truly on the shelf, my best childbearing years behind me."

Harbottle shrugged. "If Mr Hunt does not care for this—"

"He has not thought it through," she said impatiently, staring out of the window, mortified by having to discuss such a thing.

"You think not? Is he mentally impaired in some way, then?"

"What? No, of course not!" Vi replied crossly before she rearranged her face. "I beg your pardon, but why would you say such a thing?"

"I did not," Harbottle replied calmly. "Mr Hunt seems to me to be an intelligent and capable man who knows his own mind. It is you who seems to think him incapable of making such a decision."

Vi coloured, shocked into silence.

"Mr Hunt told me he did not care a button if you never had children, so long as you were together. He said he would happily adopt children if you wished to but would be glad simply to share his life with you if you did not. You are adopted yourself, I believe, Miss Spencer?"

Vi nodded dumbly. There was a lump in her throat she could not swallow past, and her eyes burned.

"H-He said that?" she managed, wiping away a tear that fell despite her best efforts and blinking hard.

"He did," Harbottle replied, smiling kindly. "And I rather think you should give him the chance to tell you the same thing himself. But something tells me that this is not the real problem, is it, Miss Spencer? At least, it is not the only one."

Vi could not speak. Her chest rose and fell too quickly as she tried to keep her composure. The reverend seemed to have the strangest ability to see into her heart and she was not entirely sure she liked it.

"May I pour some tea?" he asked, spying the pot Vi had ordered, thinking Leo would be back by now. "I believe we could both do with a cup."

Vi nodded dumbly as the reverend got up, relieved to have a moment to gather her nerves. He prepared her a fresh cup and put it in her hands before seeing to his own. Settling down again, cup in hand, the reverend regarded her over the rim.

"Mr Hunt has been often in the scandal sheets, hasn't he? An entertaining young man, to be sure, if a little reckless. I confess that his exploits have given me a good deal of amusement over the years. I was delighted to have the chance to see him fight last night. I have heard much of Mr Anson's pugilistic talents, but I always understood Mr Hunt was quite clever with his fists too, as he proved in no uncertain terms."

Vi said nothing, for Leo's exploits had done nothing but give her sleepless nights and a terror of hearing he'd broken his silly neck. Last night's confrontation was not something she particularly wished to recall, yet the vision of Pembury holding a gun on him flashed behind her eyes once more and her stomach roiled.

"How did you come to be adopted, Miss Spencer?"

Vi looked up, startled from her thoughts by the sudden change in the conversation. "A-A carriage accident. I was six. My parents had gone out to visit friends, but… but my father took a corner too fast. There was something coming the other way." She shrugged, thinking that explanation enough.

Harbottle nodded. "A terrible shock for you as a young girl. Your parents were nice people, kind parents?"

"They were," Vi said, smiling. "My mother was very beautiful and my father… my father was wonderful, funny and clever. I was so proud of them both. I remember the feeling of being with them, of being safe, loved and secure. Then in a matter of moments, it all went away." Because her father had been reckless. She swallowed hard against a sudden wave of sadness. It had been so long since she had thought of them, of that time, that it took her by surprise.

"Your adopted parents are kind, however?"

Vi smiled, nodding. "They're wonderful."

he'll hurt himself, kill himself, worrying I'm too old, that… that I cannot compare to his mistresses, that I could not hold his attention."

"You seem to have his attention from where I'm sitting," Harbottle said with a smile.

"But can I keep it?" Vi demanded.

Harbottle shrugged. "I cannot tell you the future, but I can tell you that two people who love and respect each other and are willing to be honest and speak to each other from the heart, will never go far wrong."

Vi nodded, understanding that she was the one who had been keeping herself apart. Leo had tried to be open with her, tried to talk to her, but she had shut him out. That had been unfair and unkind.

"One other thing, Miss Spencer," the reverend said, leaning forward in his chair. "Why do you love Mr Hunt? I think that is something you need to consider, for the young man I just spent the morning with was dispirited and out of sorts, not at all the man I think he really is. He is determined to spend the rest of his days becoming a respectable, quiet and dull sort of fellow, for he believes that is the only way you will ever trust him and agree to be his wife. Perhaps you ought to think about that, and about what it is you really want."

With that, Harbottle got to his feet, holding his hand out to Vi. She stood and took his hand, and the vicar squeezed her fingers gently.

"Courage, Miss Spencer. Life is for living and loving, for making the most of the blessings the good lord has deigned to put before us. He wants us to be happy, my dear, but we have to meet him halfway and take advantage of those chances if we want to be all that we are capable of being. Don't let fear stand in the way of your dreams, for you will have a long time to regret the loss of them."

With that, he patted her hand, gave Mau another friendly stroke, and went out.

Vi watched the door close behind him and stood staring at it for a long moment, only roused when Mau got up and began rubbing himself about her legs. Vi got down on the floor, her back against the wall as Mau stepped delicately over the billowing fabric of her gown and settled down in her lap.

"Oh, Mau," she said, tears pricking at her eyes. "I've been the most stupid, stupid fool."

Mau pushed his nose under her hand, seeking another caress and purring sonorously.

"What should I do? I don't want Leo to be dull and respectable, I just don't want him to kill himself."

Large yellow eyes blinked up at her. Mau's placid gaze implied the answer was obvious, if only she thought about it.

"How do I prove to him I don't want him to change, not really?"

A knock at the door interrupted any answer Mau might have provided and Vi sighed.

"Yes?"

"It's Jenny, Mrs Huntingdon. There's a Lady Trevick downstairs asking for you. I told her you were occupied when you were talking to the reverend and put her in a private parlour, but now she's getting impatient so I said I would see if you were at home."

Mama! Lud!

"Well done, Jenny, thank you," Vi said, pushing Mau gently aside and scrambling to her feet. Thank heavens Jenny had given her time to think. "Tell her… Tell her I'll be down shortly."

"Very good, ma'am."

"Oh, Mau! If Mama is here, she knows all, and she'll tell me I must marry Leo. What if Leo thinks I'm doing it because I must, because Mama persuaded me? I don't want him to think that. I've put him through enough and he's... he's been so very kind, and loyal, too. Any other man would have given up on me when I was so rude and obstinate to him."

Mau sat down, regarding her thoughtfully, and then gave a loud and imperious miaow.

Vi looked at him. "What does that mean?" she demanded impatiently. "Oh, heavens, if only we'd had more time. I'm not ready for this adventure to end yet and—"

"*Miaow*!"

"Hush, Mau, I'm trying to think. Oh, what is it?"

"Miaooow!"

Vi stared at Mau, an idea forming in her head. "I'm not ready for this adventure to end," she repeated softly, before giving a squeal of delight and scooping the cat up, hugging him tightly. "Oh, you clever, clever puss. Well done!"

Vi found the note Leo had left her and turned it over. She took a small pencil from her reticule and wrote quickly, grinning to herself as she imagined Leo's face when he read it.

Gathering up the few items she had to her name in the circumstances, she looked about the room and then at the cat, who was sitting on the bed, watching her intently. "Well, Mau, come along, then. It's time to go. We'd better find out if Jenny wants to take up her position rather earlier than I expected."

Mau jumped down and walked elegantly to the door, tail aloft. Vi opened it and he darted out before turning and waiting for her, just as if he knew exactly what she was about.

Chapter 13

Dear Mr Knight,

Forgive me, but I prefer to discuss the matter in person.

In answer to your question, our mutual friend is Lady Catherine Kilbane.

I thank you for the appointment and shall look forward to our meeting on Wednesday next.

—Excerpt of a letter from The Lady Belinda Madox-Brown Mr Felix Knight (son of Mr Gabriel and Lady Helena Knight).

25th June 1850, The Queen's Head, Wrestlingworth, the Bedfordshire-Cambridgeshire border.

Leo stared into the pint of ale he'd ordered but had so far remained untouched as he sat in the taproom. He looked up as Reverend Harbottle appeared beside him, hardly daring to hope his talk with Vi had gone well. Yet the reverend was smiling at him, and not with a pitying expression, either.

"You spoke to her?" Leo asked, his heart beating too hard in his chest.

"I did," the reverend said, eyeing Leo's glass.

"Oh, would you like one?"

The reverend beamed and nodded. Leo caught the bartender's attention and ordered another.

"How did it go?" he demanded, striving for patience as Harbottle waited until his pint had been put before him, and then took a large swallow before he replied.

"Ah, just the thing to perk one up after a tiring night," he said, smacking his lips with approval.

"Sir," Leo said reproachfully.

Harbottle laughed softly and patted Leo's arm. "There, there, young man. I believe all will be well. Have faith."

Leo stared at him, stunned. "What do you mean? You… You think she'll have me?"

Harbottle's eyes were twinkling, but he merely shrugged. "That, I cannot say for certain, but I believe your chances have greatly improved."

"Leo!"

Leo started, almost spilling his pint as the familiar voice rang out across the taproom.

"Good heavens, I've been sitting in the parlour next door for close to an hour now. Have you been propping up the bar this entire time?" Lady Trevick demanded, sweeping into the room with a great rustling of emerald green silk and ribbons. The other men in the room gaped, mouths falling open at the impressive sight of the Countess of Trevick entering the male environs of the taproom.

"My lady," Leo said, surging to his feet. "I beg your pardon, I had no idea you were here."

"It's of no matter, though that man of yours, Norton, came back with me. He is outside too, champing at the bit. I wish to see my daughter," she said pointedly, giving the reverend a look of sudden interest. "Leo, have you something to tell me?" she asked, her eyes lighting up hopefully but unable to say more when they had an audience.

"Not yet," Leo said with regret, "but it seems the Reverend Harbottle here might have helped things along a little."

"Reverend Harbottle," Lady Trevick said, giving him a look of frank appraisal before holding out her hand to him. "If you have done so, I shall be in your debt."

Harbottle bowing over her hand. "My lady, how wonderful to make your acquaintance, and might I add that your lovely daughter is a credit to you. A delightful girl, and if I have done some good, that is all the reward I require."

"She is delightful, I agree. Stubborn as a mule, though," Lady Trevick said with a sigh. "But Leo, where is she? That young woman told me she would be down directly and I'm still waiting."

Leo frowned, shaking his head. "I'll go up and see. I can't think what's keeping her."

He hurried up the stairs to their room, knocking briefly before entering.

"Vi, love, your mama is—" he stopped as he realised he was talking to an empty room. Vi and Mau were gone. A cold sensation, akin to being doused with icy water, rushed over him. Had she run away from him? But why take Mau?

Leo scanned the room and suddenly saw the note on the mantelpiece over the fire. Frowning, he unfolded it, reading with astonishment.

Mr Hunt,

If you ever wish to see your cat again – come and get him. Be warned, the ransom is one you will pay for many years to come, for you will be forced to marry a woman long past her prime, but one who has loved you since she was a girl. If this is truly what you desire, you had best find her <u>and bring the means of performing a</u>

marriage. *There is no time to waste. Be warned, I do not want a dull, well-behaved man of impeccable good sense, but the adventurous, fun-loving, wicked fellow I have needed for so many years.*

If you wish to find me, you must cast your mind back to a day, long, long ago, and a girl with braids who followed you where she ought not and got a scolding from her maid when she returned soaked to the bone.

Don't let me down.

Vi x

Leo let a bark of startled laughter and sat down heavily on the bed, hardly daring to believe his eyes. She had kidnapped Mau!

Before Leo had time to get his befuddled brain around this astonishing information, Lady Trevick came bustling in, with the reverend close behind her.

"Leo, really, I am tired of waiting about when I've been in that carriage since early this morning and… and where is Vi?"

"You'd best read this," Leo said, grinning broadly as he handed the note to Lady Trevick. The countess took the note and read quickly, her face brightening as the words registered.

"*Oh!* That's my girl!" Kitty cried in delight, running to Leo and hugging him tightly. "Well, what are you still doing here? Go after her!"

"I… I will, but the means of performing a marriage. How am I to—"

"Leave that to me," Kitty said firmly. "I shall fly to Doctors' Commons and demand a special licence. Reverend, I don't suppose you would care to accompany me? I'm sure things would go easier with you to help things along. If we hurry, we might catch the midday train to town and then we shall be back here in time for supper."

"I should be delighted to, Lady Trevick," Harbottle said at once, clearly thrilled by the possibility of further excitement to come.

"Wonderful! Now, don't you worry about a thing, Leo. Just you bring her back here and then the reverend here will marry you and everything will be perfect!" Kitty said, clapping her hands together in delight.

"That sounds wonderful, ma'am," Leo said, smiling. "And I think I remember the place she is speaking of, but how—" He fell silent as he considered the question. "Oh, no."

"What—?" Kitty began, but Leo ran for the door, not waiting to listen.

He took the stairs two at a time, rushing out to the stable yard and getting the attention of the nearest groom.

"Where's my tilbury?" he demanded, realising at once it was not parked in the corner of the yard where it had spent the night.

"Mrs Huntington took it, sir," the groom said, his face paling as he realised he might have made an error. "I beg your pardon, but she said you told her to, and she seemed competent with the ribbons, so—"

"Dash it!" Leo muttered, running a hand through his hair in frustration. Vi was a capable whip, but she had never driven a tilbury before, and certainly not with such a strong horse in harness. Plus, the horse would be fresh and excitable after its rest. He only hoped she did not come to any harm.

"Sir! Sir!"

Leo turned to see Norton hurrying back into the yard. "It's gone, sir!" Norton said in dismay. "The tilbury is gone."

"Wh-Whatever is the matter?" Kitty asked breathlessly, as she and the reverend arrived beside him.

"My *wife* has taken my tilbury," Leo said crossly. "So how the devil she expects me to follow her—"

"Faint heart, Mr Hunt, faint heart," Harbottle said jovially. "I'm afraid you'll have to carry on to a bigger place to find a carriage and horses for hire. Tadlow is a sleepy place, but as I am going on a little journey with your delightful mama-in-law, I should be happy to lend you Nipper and my dog cart." Harbottle gestured to where the fat little pony was chewing contentedly on the hay provided for it and Leo stifled a groan.

"You're… You're not thinking of going about the countryside in… in *that*?" Norton said in absolute horror.

"I am," Leo said firmly. "But settle your feathers, Norton, I will not ask you to come along with me."

Norton managed to look at once indignant and relieved at this information, which Leo quite understood. He'd look utterly ridiculous tooling about the countryside in that getup, but… but Vi had set him a challenge and he was damned if he would back out of it. His goal was in sight, and no matter what he had to do, he would win her.

"Thank you, sir. I appreciate it." Leo said to Harbottle before turning back to his soon-to-be mother-in-law and colouring a little, as he was forced to admit to being low on funds. "Do you think you could lend me some money, Kitty? I only expected to take Vi on a jaunt around Hyde Park and I'm running short."

Kitty nodded and rifled in her reticule, pulling out a startling wad of notes. "I thought I might need to bribe people," she told him confidentially.

Leo laughed and moved to kiss her cheek. "You are a marvel, my lady, and no mistake."

"Yes, I am," Kitty said nonchalantly. "But never mind turning me up sweet, tell me where you will go?"

Leo turned back to smile at Kitty as the groom hurried to fetch the ponderous Nipper and put him up to the cart. "The seaside," he said, and his heart lifted at the realisation he was going to find his wife.

♡♧◇♤

"He's a bit feisty, Mrs Huntington," Jenny said anxiously, as the bay horse danced in the traces, shying at a stray bit of paper that blew across the road in front of them.

"He's fresh yet, Jenny," Vi said, trying her best to sound confident, when in truth she was wondering what on earth she had been thinking. Driving her little gig with a well-mannered mare up ahead was nothing compared to dealing with Diablo, as she had mentally named the spirited gelding. It was taking every ounce of her skill and attention to keep him under control. Still, he was indeed fresh yet, and now they were out on the open road, he ought to calm down as the miles flew past.

"Jenny," Vi said, knowing she needed to confess everything before she dragged her too far from home. If Jenny was scandalised and wished to have nothing to do with Vi, things could get very bad indeed. She knew she ought to have told the young woman everything before she had left, but there had been no time, and then controlling the horse had been all she could concentrate on. It was only now that she'd had time to think straight.

"Yes, Mrs Huntington?"

"Jenny, there is something I need to tell you, but before I do, I need you to understand that Lady Trevick is the Countess of Trevick, and my mama."

"Your mama!" Jenny repeated, eyes wide.

Vi nodded, hoping this might help, though she did not think Jenny was entirely motivated by ambition, she could not blame the girl for wanting to better her circumstances. "Yes, and… and she wants very much for me to marry Mr Leo Hunt."

Jenny frowned. "But you're already married to… *Oh!*"

Vi blushed scarlet, avoiding Jenny's eyes. "Before you say anything, I wish you to know that Mr Hunt is a perfect gentleman and has done and would do nothing ill-becoming to a man of honour. When Mau was kidnapped, I was with him, you see, and I would not let him put me down, but I did not expect things to go so far."

"And now you are ruined?" Jenny guessed.

Vi bristled at the words, never having believed her worth had anything to do with her virginity or her reputation. "If anyone discovers I spent the night in a room with him, certainly, though I do not know that it is the case."

"But you don't wish to marry him?" Jenny asked sceptically, clearly thinking Vi was queer in her attic if she did not snap up a man as beautiful as Leo.

Vi glanced at Jenny before she answered. "I thought I did not, but… but I do, Jenny. The thing is, I've berated him for years for being reckless and foolhardy, for taking nothing seriously and spending too much of his life having fun, but I've come to realise those are some of the things I love best about him. I don't want him to change, but I don't want him to marry me for any reason other than that he wishes to. And I don't want him to believe I married him because I had to. Does that make any sense at all?" Vi asked desperately.

"Yes, Mrs—I mean, miss. Yes, it does, and it sounds ever so romantic. But if that's the case, why are we running away from him and from your mama? Why don't you go home and get married?"

"Because I want an adventure with Leo. I want him to see that I'm brave enough to take him as he is, that he does not need to change a hair. So I kidnapped Mau," she explained.

Mau, hearing his name, raised his head, blinked sleepily, and then settled back to his nap across both women's laps.

"Well, I suppose that makes sense," Jenny said doubtfully, but she seemed content to go along with it, which was all Vi cared about. "So, where are we going now?"

"To the seaside," Vi told her, daring to take her eyes off the horse for a moment longer to study Jenny. "Are you terribly shocked?"

"Oh, terribly, yes," Jenny agreed amiably. "It never occurred to me I would ever have the chance to work for such a dashing and exciting woman. I think it's going to be wonderful. I'm having a marvellous time."

Vi laughed, startled and rather delighted to hear herself described in such terms, words she would never have ascribed to herself in a million years until the past twenty-four hours, but suddenly she rather thought they fit. She could be dashing and exciting when the mood took her, and a good deal braver than she had ever imagined.

25th June 1850, on the road to Newmarket, Suffolk.

Leo had not been sorry to hand Nipper over at the first large coaching inn he'd come to. The pony had been a game little fellow and gone far better than Leo had expected, but in contrast to what he was used to, it was like driving an amiable slug around.

Leaving funds and instructions that Nipper was to be well rested and then returned to the Reverend Harbottle in Tadlow, Leo lost no time in securing the inn's best cattle. There was no carriage to hire, but he persuaded the local squire's son to part with his curricle. It looked as old as Leo himself, but the lad clearly sensed he had him over a barrel, and demanded an exorbitant sum that would see him furnished with something far smarter in the days to come. In truth, Leo would have paid double just to be on the road again, and it was with relief that he guided the horses out onto the road.

Though the horses were good goers, his progress was hindered by the need to stop and check at the passing inns for signs that Vi had been there. His confidence waned as he made his way through Cambridge, for there were too many places to check, and he wondered if perhaps he was wrong. He had been so certain he knew where she was going but what if he'd made a mistake? By the time he got to Newmarket he was worried sick in case he'd made an error of judgement, but as he got out of the curricle, tipping the grooms generously to make sure to put the best animals they had in the traces, a young woman ran across the yard towards him.

"Beg pardon, are you Mr Leo Hunt, sir?" she asked him politely.

Leo looked at her clean white apron and guessed she was an upstairs maid in the respectable establishment he'd stopped at.

"I am. Can I help you?"

"Yes, sir, for your wife left a note for you." She handed it to him, bobbed a quick curtsey, and hurried away before Leo could ask her anything further.

Relieved beyond measure to discover he was on the right track, Leo tore the sealed note open.

Leo,

Jenny turned her ankle at the last change, and though she has been terribly brave, she's in a deal of pain. I have taken a private parlour here and paid a girl to look out for you. I have told them I am Mrs Hunt. Please come inside. It is not at all the adventure I had hoped for, but I need your help.

Your Vi. X

Leo's heart gave an erratic thump as he read the words *I need your help*. Never in all his life had he believed he would hear those words from Vi, who would rather die than admit she needed

"Sometimes we lose wonderful things, wonderful people, but our lives would be so much the poorer if they had not been in it at all," the reverend said, watching her closely.

Vi looked up at him and saw the sympathy in his eyes.

"My wife died, Miss Spencer. She was…" He paused, smiling as his eyes grew misty. "She was the greatest joy of my life, my love, my soulmate, and I miss her every day."

"Oh, I'm so terribly sorry."

"So am I. But how much sorrier I would be if I had not married her? We had ten wonderful, magical years. Not nearly enough, but she left me a daughter who is the image of her and brings me great joy. I have a grandson now too, who is a delightful little chap. All these things would have been missing from my life if I had allowed the fear of losing them to stop me from living."

Vi stared at him for a moment and then burst into tears.

Harbottle got up and pressed a neatly folded handkerchief into her hands. "I came prepared for once," he told her with a smile. "You have a good cry. Don't mind me. I'm quite used to it. Do it myself now and then when I'm feeling blue devilled."

Vi did as he suggested, quite unable to stop, for the tears kept coming as though some dam had burst, the emotions surging through her in an unstoppable torrent. When she finally subsided, Harbottle smiled at her.

"I do not think Mr Hunt is still the reckless young man we have both read so much about. There comes a time in every man's life when he realises he needs to grow up, that he wants something more than the company of his friends, and the things that excited him for so many years suddenly become devoid of interest. It takes some men longer than others, but as I said, Mr Hunt knows his own mind. The only question is, Miss Spencer, do *you*?"

Vi swallowed, taking in his words carefully, thinking them over. "I've spent so many years worrying about him, worrying anything from him, let alone wanted anything. Yet she had signed it *your Vi.*

With his heart feeling lighter than it ever had before, Leo told the grooms to hold off on the horses and hurried inside. He found someone to help him and lost no time in following their instructions to the parlour. He knocked and, upon hearing a familiar soft voice answer and bid him to come in, pushed open the door.

"Vi!"

"Oh, Leo!" Vi rushed from her seat and ran to him, taking him quite by surprise by hugging him tightly. "I'm so glad you're here."

Leo looked down at her, finding a foolish smile curving over his mouth. "Are you really, Vi?"

She blushed, suddenly shy as she looked away from him, but she nodded. "I really am. We're in a bit of a fix, Leo, for I've no luggage, save for what Jenny brought, and the landlady was not very kind. I was terribly embarrassed by the way she spoke to me. I believe she thinks we are no better than we ought to be. I persuaded her to allow us to take tea in a private parlour and to send for a doctor to treat Jenny's ankle but paying for it all used every penny I had left."

"Never mind, love. I'll deal with that." He squeezed her hands. "Are you all right, Jenny?" he asked the girl, who was looking a little woebegone, her ankle propped up on a stool with a cushion atop it.

Mau sat on the empty chair beside her, an alert look in his eyes, his nose twitching at all the interesting smells that had drifted in when Leo opened the door.

Jenny brightened at his enquiry, returning a game smile. "I'll mend, sir. Only I'm so s-sorry to spoil Miss Spencer's splendid plan. It was ever so r-romantic, too," she said, snivelling and wiping eyes that looked to have already done a fair bit of weeping.

"Now, now, Jenny, none of that," Vi said severely. "I told you, it's not your fault in the least. These things happen. Now Leo is here, all will be well. You'll see."

Leo felt a foot taller than usual at Vi's certainty. She had never given him the slightest reason to believe she thought him capable of anything but causing chaos, but now here she was, saying he would make everything right for them.

"Leave it to me, love," he told her, kissing the back of her hand and holding her gaze as she blushed prettily, looking like an innocent girl. His heart gave an uneven thump. She was going to marry him. She'd said so. He had it in black and white, and he would not give her any reason to back out.

Leaving Vi to comfort Jenny, he went out and asked to speak with the landlady at once. The woman arrived, looking somewhat harassed. She was a skinny creature with a stern face and lines around her mouth that suggested she scowled more than she smiled. Judging at once that a charm offensive would not cut any ice with the formidable dame, Leo kept his tone crisp.

"Are you the landlady?"

"I am, sir. My husband, Mr Rogers, and I run this establishment."

"Then perhaps you would inform me why my wife and my maid have been treated with less than cordial attention," he asked coldly. "We were due to meet my mother-in-law, Lady Trevick in Tadlow. Our luggage is already en route to The Queen's Head, but Mrs Hunt was forced to stop here as her maid has turned her ankle. It is sheer luck that I stopped here myself to change horses, and now I discover that you have had the temerity to put her quite out of countenance."

The lady paled in the face of his annoyance, more so when she realised the Countess of Trevick was the lady's mama.

"I-I beg your pardon, sir. I did not know, only it looked a little strange, the two of them alone in the tilbury with no luggage and that great big horse—not the sort of thing you usually see ladies driving, you must admit—and with that peculiar cat too!"

"The cat is mine," Leo replied dryly. "And my wife is a capable whipster. Now, if you believe propriety has been served, I need two rooms, one for myself and my wife and one for her maid. I understand a doctor is on the way?"

"Yes, sir, indeed, sir," Mrs Rogers said hurriedly. "I will see to it all at once."

"Excellent," Leo said, pressing a more than generous sum into the woman's hand. "Put that towards our account. In the meantime, where might we go to furnish ourselves with what we will need to spend a night here?"

"Mrs Fanshaw is the closest modiste. Just two streets away. She's very well regarded in these parts," Mrs Rogers said, eager now to please. "And the apothecary carries soap and brushes and the like. He's only a few doors up from her establishment."

"Very good. Please have someone help my wife's maid to her room once it's ready and see she has everything she needs. There is a small valise in my curricle, which I will require as well. I will escort my wife to Mrs Fanshaw."

"Yes, sir, at once, sir."

Leo nodded and watched the woman hurry off, content that she would take good care of Jenny now.

"Everything is arranged," Leo told the two women upon his return. He felt a surge of pleasure at the warmth in Vi's expression.

"I knew you would make it all right," she told him with a sigh. "I cannot tell you how glad I am you are here."

"No more than I am," he replied softly, and then cleared his throat, aware that Jenny was watching the exchange with obvious delight. "Mrs Rogers will treat you kindly now, Jenny, and if she does not, you be sure to tell me. A room is being prepared for you and you may order tea or a meal or whatever you wish. Someone will come to help you up when all is prepared for you. In the meantime, if you will excuse us, I am going to take my wife here on a little shopping trip."

"Yes, Mr Hunt," Jenny said, looking a good deal happier than she had earlier.

"I will check on you when I get back, Jenny," Vi assured her, but Jenny only grinned and shook her head, a twinkle in her eyes.

"There's no need, Mis—Mrs Hunt, I'm sure you'll have other things to think about and I reckon I'll be well looked after now, like Mr Hunt said."

Vi blushed and sent Jenny a reproving look but gathered up her bonnet and gloves. Once she was properly attired, Leo led her out of the parlour and onto the busy main street.

Newmarket was a bustling place, and Leo was only glad there were no large race meets or the likelihood of bumping into people he knew would be exceedingly high. As it was, he kept his eyes open, hoping to avoid anyone who might recognise them.

"I suppose you know every tavern and club in the neighbourhood," Vi remarked as they walked.

Leo glanced down at her, ready to be given a scolding, but there was no censure in her eyes, and her lips quirked a little in amusement.

"I suppose I do," he replied ruefully. "But all that will stop now, Vi, I—"

To his surprise, she ground to a halt, so suddenly a man walking behind them muttered an oath as he ploughed into Leo's back before hurrying past.

"No!" Her tone was so imperious he could only gaze at her in consternation.

"No?" he repeated cautiously.

"Did you not read my note?" she demanded, glaring up at him.

"Of course I did," he replied, indignant. "I not only read it, I intend to have it mounted and framed so I have proof."

"Well, then, why—"

Leo tugged at her arm. "We can't discuss this in the middle of the street, love. Everyone will look and I'm too well known in these parts to pass unnoticed for long."

They walked on in silence for a moment and Leo smiled as he looked down at her. "I'm glad you don't want me to change, love, but the truth is, I already have. I'm not the madcap fool I was. I'm not pretending I'm capable of being entirely sensible all day and every day, but I don't want to be rushing about the countryside causing mayhem any longer. I want a home with you, Vi, and if I do go rushing about on an adventure, I want you to come along and join in with it."

She glanced up at him, her eyes rather too bright. "You really mean that?" she asked, her voice a little unsteady.

"I do," he told her, covering the hand on his arm with his own. "Most sincerely."

Vi blinked hard and nodded. "Th-That's good, then."

Leo smiled and then looked up as he saw the elegant green painted shop front that proclaimed *Mrs Fanshaw, Modiste*. "Here we are, love. Now then, before we go in, I should like to remind you that you are Mrs Hunt, and that your husband wishes to dote upon and spoil you, and if he enjoy colours that are brighter than what you usually wear, and fashions that you secretly love but fear are too young for you, I beg you will not be foolish but will hold your tongue and listen to the voice of reason."

"You mean to bully me, then?" she asked, one blonde eyebrow raised in polite enquiry.

"No, you wretched creature, I mean to show you how young and lovely you really are. Now go inside before you vex me into saying something that causes a row."

"Yes, Leo," she said demurely, batting her eyelashes at in him in a provocative manner that made him laugh.

175

Chapter 14

Dear Cat,

I have received a letter from Lady Belinda Madox-Brown commanding me to attend her regarding a business matter, the details of which I am not to know unless I appear. Yet I am to arrive in the guise of a morning caller, so her father, the earl, does not know what I'm about. Apparently, you have vouched for my trustworthiness and discretion. What the devil have you got me into, you wretched creature?

The Earl of Keston is not a man I wish to make an enemy of. He's a wicked old devil who likes to control everyone and everything. If I come a cropper, I shall murder you, and so you may tell that husband of yours, too.

—Excerpt of a letter from Mr Felix Knight (son of Mr Gabriel and Lady Helena Knight) to The Most Hon'ble Catherine 'Cat' St Just, Lady Kilbane (daughter of The Most Hon'ble Lucian and Matilda Montagu, the Marquess and Marchioness of Montagu).

25th June 1850, Mrs Fanshaw's Modiste Shop, Newmarket, Suffolk.

Leo was enjoying himself enormously, Vi thought with a sigh. Having already put her to the blush by choosing a variety of undergarments and nightwear which Vi considered nigh on indecent, he was now compounding matters with his ideas on appropriate gowns.

"It's red," she replied, stating the obvious. It was also daringly low cut and clung to her curves in a way that made her look like someone she hardly recognised. Good lord, she might be his mistress in this getup!

"It is."

Vi turned away from the looking glass, unable to read the strange note to his voice. It became clear as she met his eyes. *Oh.* Vi swallowed, turning back to the looking glass and surreptitiously studying Leo in the reflection. He looked… hungry, she thought, with an odd sensation uncoiling low in her belly. Heat rushed over her skin, and she felt suddenly breathless. *Goodness.*

"Well, Mrs Hunt, will you take the red gown? I know it's a rather daring choice, but—"

"Yes!" Vi said before the woman had the chance to persuade her. Her voice seemed alarmingly high and squeaky and so she cleared her throat and said a little more calmly, "Yes, I will take it."

She glanced nervously back at Leo. He was smiling at her, but it was a somewhat alarming, predatory smile that did not help her with the sudden lack of air in the room.

"If you would help me, Mrs Fanshaw, I believe I have enough gowns now."

And I believe my corset is laced too tightly, she added silently, hurrying from the room to change her gown.

Leo chuckled to himself as Vi fled. She was such a darling. Bold and brave enough to tell him he was an idiot and put him in his place, he had only to look at her without disguising the desire in his eyes, and she turned into a blushing schoolgirl. It was quite delightful. Not that he wished for her to be made uncomfortable, or afraid, certainly not that, but he did not believe it had been fear in her eyes. She *had* ordered the red gown.

He congratulated himself on having bribed Mrs Fanshaw an extraordinary amount to change whatever orders she had made for other clients to fit Vi. There were going to be a few annoyed ladies who would have to wait a little longer for their orders, but it had been worth it. He'd have paid five times as much just to see Vi in that red gown, never mind the other things he'd bought for her. Happily, the redoubtable Norton had brought Leo's own belongings back from town with him, so he needed nothing himself.

Sitting back in the comfortable chair provided for husbands or protectors, Leo sipped the surprisingly decent glass of brandy. No wonder Mrs Fanshaw was popular. She was not only clever with her designs, but she made every effort to make the male visitors to her shop welcome. The latest racing journals lay in neat piles on the table, alongside scandal sheets and a tray bearing pastries and sandwiches.

Leo ignored the journals, more interested in considering Vi. God, to see her in that gown only confirmed everything he had known and yet underestimated, for she had taken his breath away. She had been hiding her light under a bushel. Oh, she had always dressed beautifully—elegant and with style—but she was not as bold as she might be. Her choices always trod the line of what she deemed proper for a woman 'past her prime' as she insisted on believing herself. What tosh. He had never seen Vi look more beautiful. As a young woman she had been pretty indeed, lovely in fact, but now, with a little more maturity and her figure a touch fuller, she was stunning.

He took another sip of the brandy, his thoughts drifting to the lovely bits of nothing he had insisted she buy as nightwear. Leo grinned, aware he had shocked her but entirely unrepentant about it. In his opinion, it was time Vi woke up and realised just what kind of woman she was. Somehow, despite being loved and cosseted by Kitty, who was a woman of fiery passions herself, Vi had come to see herself as something less than she was. Leo intended to change that view entirely, and he was going to thoroughly enjoy himself in the process.

The time passed pleasantly enough, though he was getting impatient to see Vi again when a rustle of expensive fabric made him look up. He almost gasped when he saw the vision before him.

There she stood, the woman he was to make his wife. His heart gave an uneven thud and for a moment, his legendary charm deserted him. He could only gape. The walking dress was a spectacular deep yellow gold. He had known it was perfect for her the moment he'd seen it and asked Mrs Fanshaw to persuade Vi into it. The gown hugged her figure perfectly, and Mrs Fanshaw had paired it with delicate yellow kid half boots and gloves and a charming bonnet framed with yellow silk roses. "Good God," Leo finally managed, which was a mistake.

Vi's face fell. "I told Mrs Fanshaw it was too much," she said in dismay. The glow that had been visible in her eyes just moments before faded at once. "It's too dashing, too—"

"Shut up, you darling idiot," Leo said, pushing to his feet and crossing the space between them. He took Vi's hands in his, raising each in turn and kissing her knuckles. "Though I admit it was not my most eloquent comment, that *was* a compliment, love. You look splendid, glorious—" He paused, moving away a step to give her a slow, lingering look up and down. "Edible," he added in a low, provocative voice.

She blushed scarlet but he could tell she was pleased all the same.

"You really like it, you don't think—"

"I do not," he said firmly. "I *do* think you are the most ravishing creature I have ever seen, and I have never been prouder of anyone or anything."

"Thank you, Leo," she said, meeting his eyes properly now, happiness shining there. Leo suddenly felt quite winded. He had put that look in her eyes. *Him!* How extraordinary! He was going to make her happier still before the night was over, though he rather suspected that would shock her a good deal, too. It was all in a good cause, he told himself, squashing any concerns about propriety. Kitty would certainly give him her blessing and they would be married as soon as they returned to Tadlow… though he had not yet asked Vi properly. That needed dealing with in style. Vi deserved the best of everything when she had missed out on such a lot of fun by keeping herself out of society.

"Ready to return to the inn?" he asked. "I'd love to show you off about the town, but I think we'd best keep a low profile for now."

"Indeed, they might mistake me for your mistress," she said mischievously.

Vi looked up at him and flashed a wicked smile, once again making him feel like he'd been hit in the head with a heavy blunt object. How had he spent so many years without realising this woman was the one he'd needed all along? God, what a fool he'd been. The idea that he might never have woken up, might never have come to his senses, struck him square in the chest, making him feel breathless and rather ill. He stopped in his tracks and turned to Vi, who stared up at him in alarm.

"Leo? Whatever is the matter? You've turned the ghastliest shade. You're white as a milk pudding."

"I love you," he said urgently, holding her fingers too tightly. "You do know that, don't you, Vi?"

Vi gazed at him as if he'd lost his mind, and then glanced around her at the passersby, who were staring at them with interest. "Leo, are you quite well?" she murmured under her breath.

"Perfectly well," he said impatiently. "Just listen to me, will you? I love you, Violetta Spencer. I think perhaps I always have, I… I was just too stupid to realise it. But I've stopped being stupid, Vi. I'm going to be everything you need, whether that's a sensible, reliable husband or a fun-loving fool who will take you on madcap adventures. Do you understand?"

Her face softened, her eyes suddenly bright and sparkling. "I understand, Leo and… and I love you too, though I think this is the most inappropriate setting for such a declaration, you ridiculous man."

Leo beamed at her, not caring a damn for who saw or heard. He would quite happily have shouted that he loved Violetta Spencer to anyone within earshot, but didn't like to push his luck. They weren't married yet.

He guided her back to The Rutland Arms, feeling a swell of pride as he noted all the admiring glances she drew. Mrs Rogers came rushing up to them as soon as they entered.

"Mr Hunt, Mrs Hunt, your room is all ready for you. If you would come this way."

She let them up the stairs and along to a large, handsome chamber resplendent with a massive fourposter bed with elegant green velvet curtains. The lamps had been lit, for the day had become grey and stormy, threatening rain and the room was cast with a cosy, golden glow.

"It's our best room," she said proudly. "I had the fire lit too, for it was a little chilly and, with the weather turning, I thought the evening might be somewhat cool."

"Thank you, Mrs Rogers," Leo said with an approving nod. "My wife and I will dine in our room tonight."

"How is Jenny?" Vi asked before he could make any further arrangements.

"Miss Clark has seen the doctor, and it's only a sprain, though she is to rest it for a few days. She has ordered dinner, which I shall take up to her myself presently," she said, at which Vi smiled.

"Wonderful. I'm so glad she's all right."

Leo walked Mrs Rogers to the door before she could continue talking. In an undertone, he instructed her to bring a bottle of champagne with their dinner.

"In half an hour, sir?"

He nodded, and Mrs Rogers took herself off. Relieved to have got rid of the woman, Leo turned back to Vi. She'd gone to stare out of the window, undoing her bonnet as she looked outside.

"I think that was lightning," she said, as a low rumble sounded in the distance. "Goodness, but we were lucky with the weather today. I dread to think what it might have been like keeping that fiend in check in a thunderstorm."

"But you managed him?" he asked, watching her laid the bonnet aside and began tugging at her gloves.

"I did," she said with obvious pride.

Never had he taken such pleasure in watching a woman in such a way. She wasn't even taking off any interesting items, only gloves! Yet desire stirred all the same and he rather wished he could have put off dinner, but Vi must be famished and Leo did not want his lovemaking interrupted because she was faint from hunger.

"When shall we be married?" She blurted the question out so hurriedly he did not think she had intended to say it at all. The colour that crested her cheeks confirmed his suspicions.

"As soon as we return to Tadlow. Your mama rushed off to get a special licence with Reverend Harbottle. I suspect they've had a wonderful day together; they're both as tricky as each other."

Vi laughed, though he detected a note of anxiety in the sound. "Oh, indeed. Reverend Harbottle is a wonderful man, and rather wise, I think."

"I think so too," Leo said with a smile as he crossed the room to her. "I'm afraid I have something to tell you, though, Violetta."

Her smile dimmed at the use of her full name, and the serious tone of her voice.

"Oh?"

"Mm-hmm," he said, pulling her into his arms.

"What is it, Leo? You don't h-have a lovechild somewhere, do you? I mean, it would make no difference to me if you had, I suppose. I know these things happen, it's not uncommon, and I would not judge you harshly, well, so long as you've made provision—which I know you would do, for even though you are sometimes reckless, I know you are not irresponsible with anyone else's life, only your own, and—"

"Devil take you, Vi!" Leo said in consternation. He gave her a little shake. "I've got no children. Good Lord, woman, the things you say."

"Oh, thank heavens," she said, letting out a breath.

"I thought you said it would make no difference," he remarked dryly.

"Well, it wouldn't, but I cannot pretend I liked the idea."

Leo shook his head and laughed. "Fair," he agreed, pulling her more firmly against him. "Any other questions?"

She hesitated for a moment before she spoke again. "I won't share you with a mistress, so if you still have one—"

"You're very hard on a fellow's self-esteem, love. I broke things off before I began courting you, and I will never put you in such a position. Next?"

She gave a sigh and shook her head. "That's all."

Leo snorted, gazing down at her.

"What did you wish to tell me, then? It isn't anything dreadful, is it?" she asked nervously.

It was the hardest thing to keep his face grave, but he returned a soulful expression, saying regretfully, "Well, it is rather dreadful, I'm afraid."

"Oh, dear," she said, before taking a deep breath. "Go on then, I'm ready."

"I am afraid," he said, bending to whisper the words in her ear. "I am afraid, Miss Spencer, you will not be a virgin on your wedding night."

"I-I won't?" she stammered, and it was almost impossible to keep his countenance when he saw the delight in her eyes. Struggling not to laugh, he shook his head.

"You have got yourself entangled with a rather desperate fellow, you poor little innocent, and I fully intend to debauch you and take your virtue. You will be quite thoroughly ruined by morning."

"I w-will?" she stammered, sounding quite breathless now.

"You will," he agreed solemnly.

"Oh, Leo!" she exclaimed, throwing her arms around his neck. "How wonderful. Thank you!"

Leo burst out laughing, hugging her tightly. "Wicked, wicked girl. I always knew it. The quiet ones are the worst," he told her confidentially.

"Are they?" she asked, gazing up at him with such love and trust in her eyes it was no longer difficult to pretend to be serious.

"And the very best," he whispered, and lowered his mouth to hers, kissing her softly. He cradled her cheek, stroking the silken skin with his thumb as she melted into his embrace. "Vi," he whispered.

"Yes?" she managed, in between his kisses.

But there was nothing to say, nothing to tell her that couldn't be spoken with the press of his lips to hers. The kiss went on, lingering, tender, an expression of love and hope for the future and of the promises he would keep.

The inevitable knock at the door sounded.

"Oh, drat the woman," Vi said crossly.

Leo chuckled and gave her one last kiss. "Don't worry, Vi. Nothing will interrupt us once dinner is out of the way."

"Well, hurry up and let them in, then," she said, giving him a little push.

Leo grinned at her and did as she suggested. "Yes, ma'am," he said, as eager as she was for the meal to be over.

Dinner was an exercise in torture, as far as Vi was concerned. Beside herself with a combination of excitement and anxiety, she ate little and tasted less. Leo seemed equally distracted, his gaze drifting to her mouth on several occasions and remaining there. When she had licked a small drop of cream from the corner of her lips, the look in his eyes had been both wonderful and daunting. She could not help but wonder what she had got herself into. Well, she'd find out soon enough now.

Though it was exactly what she had wanted, she still could not quite believe he would make love to her before they were wed, and half expected him to prevaricate and change his mind. If he did, she was going to kill him, she decided.

Finally, the meal was done, and Leo went away to have a quiet drink in the taproom to give her some privacy to prepare herself. Without Jenny to help it was a little difficult, but the new gown and corset unfastened in the front which made a great difference. In the corner of the room, Vi had made a little nest for Mau, who had thankfully curled up and gone to sleep after finishing much of the dinner to which the two of them had not been able to do justice. The soft sound of his snoring reassured her, for the idea of having an audience for the coming night, even if it was only a cat, was most disconcerting.

Vi poured warm water from the jug she had ordered and washed herself, pleased with the delicately scented soap she had found at the apothecary's shop. It smelled of vanilla, sweet and enticing, and she hoped the scent would linger on her skin. Choosing what to wear was difficult, as the little slips of nothing Leo had chosen were all lovely. Mrs Fanshaw had confided that they were French, sent over from Paris. Vi could well believe it, for she had seen nothing of the sort in any of the shops in London she'd visited before.

Whilst the nightgown fell to the floor, it was made of a delicate silk that clung lovingly to her body, almost sheer, revealing more than it covered, the fabric cools against her skin. Around the bust, which seemed moulded to her breasts, it was embellished with lace that curved over her décolletage. Vi unpinned her long blonde hair and brushed it out, letting it fall in a sleek cascade down her back. She stood, looking at herself in the small hand mirror, holding it up and angling it this way and that.

Colour rose to her cheeks as she saw the dark shadows of her nipples pressing against the silk and her breath caught as she imagined Leo looking upon her. What would he do? Her imagination provided the answer as she gazed at her reflection, feeling wicked and desirable in a way she had never known before, making her heart thud in her chest so hard she did not hear his soft knock, nor the opening of the door. It was only as she allowed the mirror to travel back up her body that she saw him, her breath catching at his expression, which was everything she had imagined and more. Raw desire burned there, his blue eyes dark with need.

Violetta turned, the mirror still in her hand as Leo's gaze raked over her.

"You like it?" she ventured, knowing very well that he did. The answer was so obvious that a smug smile played at her lips.

Leo let out an uneven huff of laughter. "God, Vi. If this is what I'm going to be treated to every night, I'm going to be putty in your hands. You can have anything you want, do anything you want, I don't care. I'll give you anything, only for heaven's sake, come here."

She laughed, setting the mirror down and running into his embrace, throwing her arms about his neck as he kissed her, hard and deep and with no reservations. This time he did not hold back, his hands sliding down her back to her waist, pulling her firmly against him. Vi's breath hitched as she felt the press of his arousal against her belly and then his hands fell lower still, grasping her bottom. She gasped, but he stole her breath, deepening the kiss and taking more. Vi could do nothing but hold on, tangling her hands in his hair and following where he led.

Finally, he broke the kiss and Vi let out an unsteady breath, her chest rising and falling rapidly. "H-Heavens," she managed.

Leo flashed her a wicked grin that made her heart feel light and insubstantial, as though happiness weighed less than air and it would simply float off into the sky.

"So beautiful," he whispered, nipping at her ear. "If you only knew how I have longed for this, dreamed of it, you would realise how much power you have always had over me. I ought not tell you, I think, for you might abuse it."

"I never would," she replied reproachfully, though the idea that she could was tantalising. Did he really desire her so very much? It seemed unlikely and yet here was the proof of it, visible in the dark hunger burning in his eyes, in the proud jut of his arousal that seemed to beg for her attention.

Too curious to pretend maidenly shyness, Vi's hand covered the rigid line visible beneath his impeccably tailored trousers and Leo sucked in a sharp breath. She snatched her hand away, startled by his reaction before she realised he had not wanted her to stop. Of course, Kitty had given her some rather indelicate advice in the past and now it came back to her, and she felt eager to put it into practise. Cautiously, she returned her hand and gently squeezed.

Leo groaned, resting his head atop hers, his eyes closed.

"You like that," she said, feeling rather pleased with herself.

He snorted and nodded his head. Biting her lip, Vi dared to unbutton the fall of his trousers and slide her hand inside, searching for entry beneath his smallclothes. Leo's hands fell to help her, but she batted them aside.

"Hurry," he said urgently, the rough edge to his voice giving her a little thrill of excitement.

Finally, she found the access she needed, and her hand touched his flesh, blazing hot and so very hard, the skin finer than anything she had ever known. He made a strangled sound as she closed her hand around him and stroked.

"I've died," he murmured. "Died and gone to heaven."

Violetta smothered a laugh against his chest, uncertain it was the moment for laughter but then she glanced up and saw the mischievous glint in his passion-dark eyes and she laughed out loud, delighted by him, and by this, which was not at all what she had expected.

"I love you," he told her. "I love to hear you laugh, even if you are laughing at me, and I want to make love to you so much I feel I shall run mad."

"I'm not stopping you," she pointed out, firming her grip on the hard length of his arousal. His breath caught, and he bent his head, kissing her ferociously, devouring her like a man starved. Leo's arms pulled her hard against him until she was aware of every button on his clothing, every curve of muscle and line of bone, and then, just as suddenly, he released her.

"Take it off," he commanded, the need in his voice making her react at once.

She let go her hold on him, her hands flying to the tiny pearl buttons at the lowest point of her neckline. Somehow her shaking fingers got them undone and she shimmied the silken nightgown down to her hips, but he could not wait, tugging at the fine fabric, yanking it down her body until he could gaze upon her nakedness.

Vi shivered under the heat of his gaze, her skin prickling, nipples tightening into hard little buds as his eyes took in every detail.

"Perfection," he whispered, before his head lowered, his mouth closing over her nipple and sending darts of pure delight charging through her body. The tugging of his mouth seemed to tug at another, secret part of her that had never before experienced such a tumult of sensation.

"Oh, L-Leo," she stammered.

He raised his head in enquiry but Vi caught hold of his hair and guided him back, not wanting him to stop. A soft huff of laughter fluttered over her skin, but he did as she asked of him, lavishing attention on her breasts until her entire body was alive and tingling with anticipation. Finally, he raised his head, gazing at her as though he would eat her in one bite.

Finding it suddenly hard to stand, Vi took a few shaky steps backwards and felt the mattress behind her. Bracing herself against it, she leaned back, her breath catching as Leo fell to his knees before her.

"This is how you ought to be viewed," he told her, staring up the length of her body, his eyes vivid with desire, the black of his pupils swamping all but an electric flash of blue around the edges as his gaze settled upon the place between her thighs. "A goddess, ready to be worshipped."

Vi gave an unsteady laugh. "Don't be s-silly," she scolded him, but her words died as she registered the look in his eyes.

"A goddess," he told her firmly, a tone to his voice that would brook no argument. "And I your willing supplicant, come to worship at your altar."

He pressed his mouth against the darker gold triangle of curls between her thighs, pressing a kiss there, their eyes still locked.

Vi felt the blush rush from her toes, up her body, her cheeks scarlet, and yet there was power in it too, despite her embarrassment. He really meant it, she realised, meant to worship her, to hold her above all others and love her as he loved no one else.

Her breath hitched as his mouth drifted lower, the kiss pressing in a place that made a soft exclamation escape her lips. His tongue darted out, licking softly, and Vi melted into a puddle, her legs giving out as she collapsed back onto the mattress.

"Like that, do you?" he asked, getting to his feet and sounding very pleased with himself.

"It's the wickedest thing I ever… ever… good heavens, Leo."

Leo stood over her, grinning now. It seemed positively indecent that he should stand there fully dressed, gazing down on her nakedness, yet Vi realised in that moment that she liked it. She liked the way Leo looked at her, liked to see the desire in his eyes, relished the fact that he wanted her badly, so very badly.

"Answer the question, love," he pressed her, amusement lurking in his dark gaze.

"Yes, Leo," she whispered, smiling up at him. "I like it, I like it all, and I love you very, very much."

Chapter 15

Dear Felix,

Oh dear. I am sorry, my friend. I swear I did not know when she asked me about you what she had in mind. Do be careful. She's a lovely girl, but very single-minded and her father is everything you said of him and more. He rules his household with a rod of iron, but he will not crush Belinda, no matter his tyrannical ways. She defies him at every turn and delights in besting him. I do fear you may be the means of her next battle. Have your wits about you, Felix, but she's a beautiful creature, so perhaps you will not mind so much. What a way to go.

—Excerpt of a letter from The Most Hon'ble Catherine 'Cat' St Just, Lady Kilbane (daughter of The Most Hon'ble Lucian and Matilda Montagu, the Marquess and Marchioness of Montagu) to Mr Felix Knight (son of Mr Gabriel and Lady Helena Knight).

25th June 1850, The Rutland Arms, Newmarket, Suffolk.

Leo gazed down at Vi, his breath sawing in and out of his lungs like he'd been running for his life. He couldn't help it, he was strung tight with desire, every part of him vibrating with need for the woman who was returning his gaze so boldly. She was no shrinking violet, but he'd always known that. For all that she had behaved like the perfect young lady he had known, at heart, there was someone fiercer, wilder, and far more exciting beneath that prim exterior, and here she was, laid out for him like a gift from some beneficent god. He sent up a silent prayer of thanks, knowing he must have been on his last life, his last chance to win her, but he'd done it, she was his, and he would never let her regret that decision.

The taste of her still lingered on his tongue and he hungered for more.

"Move back, love," he told her, not taking his eyes from hers as she scrambled backwards, settling herself against the pillows. Leo shed his coat, tore impatiently at his cravat and cast it aside, and then undid his waistcoat buttons with such a lack of care it was a wonder they didn't scatter to the four corners of the room. He had no patience for the rest and climbed onto the bed, his hands sliding around her ankles as he pushed her legs wide. Vi stared at him in shock and then relaxed, settling back on the pillows once more, gazing at him placidly.

"Good girl," he said with a grin, and held her gaze.

Never taking his eyes from hers, he leaned in and pressed a kiss against her thigh. Vi's breath caught, the sound delighting him and heightening his own anticipation further. He trailed his tongue a little higher, teasing the crease that ran beside the little triangle of the golden thatch of curls.

His bold beloved pressed her hips towards him, wanton with desire, her eyes pleading for him to stop teasing her. Leo smiled against her skin, captivated by her. Any fears he might have harboured that Vi would be afraid and need coaxing went up in smoke in the heat that flamed between them.

He rewarded her boldness by parting those springy little curls and sweeping his tongue over the delicate flesh beneath. Vi clutched at the sheets, moaning and throwing her head back as he repeated the move. Leo was lost in her then, entirely caught, heart, body and soul. The sounds she made, the soft pleading noises, were so enticing that his own body reacted alarmingly, and he knew he could not keep this up for much longer or he would lose his mind.

Somehow, he reined in his own desires as she shattered beneath his mouth, crying out with one hand clutching at his hair. Though he wished to linger, he could not, and began stripping off his shirt, the movements so obviously frantic that he heard Vi laughing, but he did not mind that.

By the time he was naked, he was at the edge of sanity. He fell upon her, taking her mouth hungrily, as if he would die without it. His hands weren't as gentle as he'd meant to be, but the sweet temptress beneath him didn't seem to mind.

"Vi, Vi, oh God, you'll kill me," he murmured desperately as she reached for him, her hand closing around his aching shaft once more. She stroked, sending pleasure surging through him and the thought of letting her continue touching him so was tantalising, but this night was for her, for her pleasure, and he would let nothing distract him from that, not even Vi herself, not when he had fought so hard to be here. "Stop," he told her, reluctantly drawing her hand away.

She stared at him curiously. "But you liked it."

"I did," he agreed with a choked laugh. "And I always will, so any other time, please go ahead. Right at this moment, however, I need to be inside you. Right now, Vi. I can't wait any longer."

"Oh," she said, apparently pleased by this explanation. She settled beneath him, opening her legs in invitation and Leo groaned.

"You're marvellous, you do know that?" he told her desperately. "Truly, truly magnificent, and—"

"You've already seduced me, Leo," she said, laughing as her hands glided down his back and settled on his behind. "You've got your way. I'm all yours."

"Yes," he murmured, finding his place between her thighs. "Yes, yes, yes, thank you God, oh, God, Oh…"

He groaned, the sound deep in his chest as he pushed inside the welcoming heat of her body. Unable to hold back, he thrust deep, and then belatedly cursed himself for a brute, but Vi only sighed, clinging to him. Reassured he had not hurt her or caused her any distress, Leo moved inside her, his entire being suffused with the most encompassing pleasure he had ever experienced. Overwhelmed by his senses, he discovered all his desires set before him. The scent of her, delectable as vanilla, filled his nose, the sounds of her pleasure delighting him as the taste of her, tart and sweet at once, lingered on his tongue. His hands could not get enough of her silken skin, of the soft roundness of her lovely body, and to look into her eyes was to know that he was loved, that he would love this woman for the rest of his days. Yet she continued to surprise him, to delight him, and when she came beneath him, suddenly and with sheer abandon, he thought his heart would burst with the wonder of it, of her. As her body tightened around him, pulling him in deeper, her arms and legs holding him to her as if she would never let him go, he could not hold back. He shattered, crying out and giving her all that he was, this night, and for all the nights to come.

Leo stared down at Vi, grinning stupidly. He felt like the cat who'd got the cream and no mistake, but then Vi looked pretty pleased with herself too.

"Well," she said, gazing up at the ceiling. "It's a wonder anyone ever goes out."

Leo burst out laughing, feeling so ridiculously happy he was almost giddy with it.

"It's not like that with everyone," he assured her, reaching out and stroking her cheek. "You and I, together we're special, Vi. We fit. We always have, it's just it took us a little while to recognise that."

She turned towards him, smiling. "Yes, that's it. You're my missing puzzle piece."

Leo shook his head, smirking. "No, love, you're *my* missing puzzle piece."

Vi sat up, clutching the covers to her breasts and scowling. "No, Leo, that's wrong. You're the missing piece because—"

Leo kissed her, pressing her back against the pillows. Once she was silent, he released her, gazing down at her curiously.

"*That* is a most unfair method of winning an argument," she told him severely.

"I know, love," he told her, unrepentant.

"I suppose you will use it whenever you don't get your own way," she said, pursing her lips.

"I certainly will," he agreed, nodding gravely.

"Good," she replied, before snuggling against him.

Leo laughed, holding her tight. "Your mama will be in alt."

"Oh, don't," Vi said, burying her face against his chest. "She'll be quite unbearable now, winking and telling me how she told me so."

"Well, she did," Leo pointed out. "Kitty has always known I'm perfect."

"I'm not sure perfect is a description she has ever given, Leo," Vi said dryly.

"I'm certain she has told you I am perfect for you, though," he retorted.

"Perhaps," she admitted, conceding the point.

"Shall we go back to Tadlow tomorrow?" he asked, nuzzling into her hair and breathing in the scent of her.

"Must we?" she asked with a sigh.

"Must? No, I suppose not, but don't you want to get married?" he asked, suddenly struck with a dart of anxiety.

She turned in his arms, gazing up at him. "Of course I do," she said, reaching up to stroke his cheek. "But I'm rather enjoying being wanton and debauched. I've never been ruined before and—"

"I should hope not!" Leo said with a snort.

"*And*," she continued, "I don't know if I want to be all respectable and well-behaved just yet."

"Fine by me," Leo replied, leering at her.

"Idiot," Vi said, pushing him away and squealing when he tried to stick his tongue in her ear.

He laughed and settled her back against his chest once more, promising to behave, for now. "We don't have to go back just yet, I suppose, but we must have a care, love. We must not risk your reputation any more than we already have."

"Well, if we don't leave the room, that ought not be a problem," she murmured, tangling her fingers in the hair on his chest, her attention diverted by the sight of his nipples.

Leo watched, his body reacting as she circled the small, pink disc with her finger and then gave the tiny nub a little squeeze. Leo jolted, surprised himself by his reaction.

"Oh," she said, gazing up at him. "Is it the same for you?"

"Why don't you try it and see," he managed, his voice hoarse.

She grinned at him, ducking her head and Leo's breath caught as she drew his nipple into her mouth and sucked.

Leo groaned and closed his eyes. "We're staying," he said desperately. "As long as you want, love. We'll never leave if you don't wish to…"

Vi laughed softly against his skin and carried on, giving him reasons not to change his mind.

♡ ♧ ♢ ♤

"I suppose we really must go," Vi said with a sigh, regarding the large four-poster with a wistful expression.

Leo stood behind her, his arms crossed around her waist, holding her against his chest. He nuzzled her neck and nipped at her ear.

"We really must," he agreed, though he saw no reason to make her *wish* to leave.

They had stayed for two more nights, unable to tear themselves away from each other, or from the bed. Every meal had been taken in their room and they had been grateful Jenny's ankle was on the mend so she could take over care of Mau, who was rather disgruntled by the lack of attention. They must make a great fuss over him to ensure he did not resent Vi's sudden presence in Leo's life.

Vi turned in his arms, coiling her arms around his neck and gazing up at him.

"Thank you," she said, and he heard the sincerity behind the words, gratitude of a depth he did not understand.

Leo frowned at her. "What for?"

"For never giving up, for knowing who I am, who I *can* be, even if I was too afraid to be her for a while."

Leo's heart contracted at the words, and he held her close. "Never thank me for that, love, for my actions were entirely selfish. I can't live without you, you see."

"I could not live without you, Leo, that is the reason I was so afraid, you know that, don't you? I cannot love you this deeply and lose you, I… I should go mad and—"

"Hush," he told her, holding her tighter still. "I'm going nowhere, and I'll take no silly risks, you have my word."

The tension left her with his reassurance, and he looked down, lifting her chin so he could kiss her. "Vi?"

"Yes?"

He had thought of and discarded a dozen different ways to ask her the question he had longed to ask for such a long time, but in the end, it was simple now. She would not want some grand gesture or convoluted expression of undying love, she knew she had his heart in the palm of her hand already. So, he simply got to one knee, holding her hands in his, knowing everything he felt must be written clearly upon his face.

"Violetta Spencer, my darling girl, my dearest friend and most vexing adversary, I love you, I shall love you alone, forsaking all others, for the rest of my days. Please marry me, love, and I shall do my utmost not to annoy you beyond reason, and to make you as happy as it is possible for two people to be together."

She laughed, tears sparkling in her eyes as one drop fell, sliding down her cheek.

"Oh, Leo, you are the most wonderful, most ridiculous man, as if you needed to ask. Of course I shall marry you. I cannot think of anything I wish to do more. Well…" she added, glancing at the bed.

Leo gave a bark of laughter and got to his feet, hauling her against him and kissing her soundly. "My beloved, you are a wicked, wicked woman," he said in delight, turning her around and giving her behind a sound smack that made her exclaim and glare at him in the most enticing manner.

Yes, marrying Vi would be an adventure all of its own, he thought with a grin.

Chapter 16

Dearest Belinda,

I am most deeply vexed by you, my friend. Now I understand why you were so interested in Mr Knight. Fool that I was, I suspected you had a tendre for him, or at least that you meant to pretend one to incense your father. Now I see it was more diabolical even than that. Have a care, Belle. Felix is a dear friend, and I will not see him sacrificed at your altar simply to best your father. I hope your intentions are honourable, if they are, however, you may count on my support, only let me in on the secret!

—Excerpt of a letter from The Most Hon'ble Catherine 'Cat' St Just, Lady Kilbane (daughter of The Most Hon'ble Lucian and Matilda Montagu, the Marquess and Marchioness of Montagu) to The Lady Belinda Madox-Brown.

28th June 1850, The Rutland Arms, Newmarket, Suffolk.

Leo guided Vi down the stairs and left her with Jenny whilst he paid the reckoning. Mau came with him, draped over his shoulder and vocal in his disapproval at having been left in Jenny's care for several days.

"I'm sorry, old man, but some things are private," Leo told the cat in an undertone.

Mau stared at him, yellow eyes unblinking, tail swishing irritably.

"I said I'm sorry," Leo told him with a sigh, reaching up to stroke his head.

Mau batted at his hand with his paw.

Leo stopped, giving Mau a stern look. "Now, none of that. It's not like you don't adore Vi yourself… or is that the problem? Jealous, are you?"

Mau butted his head against Leo's cheek, a deep rumbling purr emanating from him. Leo laughed, and then looked around, suddenly aware of people staring at him. He cleared his throat and hurried to the front desk, where Mrs Rogers was waiting. She gave Mau an uneasy glance before looking at Leo.

"I never saw a cat like that one, sir. Does he always go with you? Seems more like a dog, don't he?"

Mau miaowed, such a sound of disapproval that Leo had to smother a laugh at Mrs Rogers' look of absolute horror. "He's an Egyptian Water Sphinx," Leo said, struggling to keep a straight face.

"Is he now?" Mrs Rogers said, apparently impressed.

Leo paid the bill, leaving a generous tip in the hopes Mrs Rogers would accept Mau without protest if ever they stayed here again.

Leo returned to escort Vi and Jenny out into the yard and helped Vi into the tilbury before assisting Jenny to sit up on the back where Norton usually resided. He'd bought a travelling case to transport all Vi's new dresses and the other items they'd purchased for their stay, and the ostlers were strapping it on with his own valise. Mau leapt down from his shoulder, sniffing around the tilbury's wheels with interest.

"Mind the horse, Mau," Leo warned him, for whilst most horses did not mind Mau's presence, occasionally one would object. Mau looked up for a moment before carrying on his inspection of the carriage. Knowing Mau was more than capable of looking out for himself, Leo went to check the horse was hitched to his satisfaction and shared a few words with the ostlers. He was just thanking them and handing over a tip when he heard a furious growling noise, followed by a bark.

"Oh, the devil," he muttered, turning to see a large man who looked like the very image of a country squire, had entered the yard with two hunting dogs at his heels.

Naturally, the dogs had spotted Mau and thought to hunt him. They bayed and barked excitedly, tails wagging with the thrill of the chase. Except Mau did not run from dogs, he faced them down.

"Get your dogs under control, sir, before they get hurt," Leo shouted at the man as he hurried to intervene.

The squire looked surprised and then rather annoyed. "It's only a cat. Dogs chase cats, it's in their nature."

"The cat is mine, sir, and it is not in his nature to be chased. Your dogs risk—"

Before Leo could finish the sentence, Mau swiped out, claws extended towards the closest dog, who yelped and retreated, whimpering and hiding behind the squire. The second dog, having not learned a lesson from his comrade, surged forward, barking and snarling. Mau leapt, claws digging into the creature's back. The dog took off like a rocket, with Mau clinging on like a small furry jockey.

"Leo!" Vi cried in alarm.

"I know, love," Leo replied, rushing after the dog. The frantic animal had unfortunately entered the inn, almost knocking an elderly man flying as he burst through the door ahead of him.

"Sorry, sir," Leo shouted to the old man, trying not to do the same as he ran past the fellow, the indignant squire at his heels. He halted in the foyer, for the dog had disappeared, but it did not take long to discover its whereabouts. A howl rent the air, followed by feminine screams and male shouts of annoyance.

Muttering curses, Leo took off towards the disturbance, barrelling into the dining room, where many patrons were still enjoying a late breakfast. A crash met his ears as Mau leapt from one table to the next, plates and teacups smashing to the floor as he went. The dog barked, believing he was in pursuit when Leo had no doubt Mau was only leading him a merry dance. The dog knocked a table over, china exploding on the tiled floor beneath and upturned a chair as women screamed and ran from the room. A large lady in her middle years swooned dramatically, caught by her husband, who was far finer of build and not up to the task. The two of them tumbled to the floor with a billow of deep purple satin as the lady's vast skirts enveloped them. Mau leapt over them and the man gave a shout of alarm as the dog followed.

"Mau!" Leo shouted, certain that his wicked cat was enjoying himself enormously and was not about to stop the fun. "Mau, you devil, stop it at once."

Mau leapt from the table onto a large, handsome oak dresser and regarded Leo from his lofty position, yellow eyes gleaming.

"Oh!" Mrs Rogers shrieked, upon coming in upon the chaotic scene. She spied Mau on top of the dresser and wailed. "No! No, not my best china, oh, n—"

Leo watched the scene unfold as though trapped in some horrible dream where he was frozen to the spot, unable to do anything. He leapt, hoping to grab the stupid dog as it jumped onto the table, thinking itself agile enough to follow Mau up to the dresser's top. Instead, it skidded across the tabletop, pushing the table over as it jumped inelegantly, and landed on the base of the dresser, before attempting to use the shelves as a ladder to scramble up to get Mau. China crashed down on all sides, the dog's claws scratching the polished oak as it tried to find purchase enough to climb.

Mrs Rogers screamed, threatening criminal proceedings, lawyers, and God alone knew what else as the squire belatedly caught up to them, puffing and red in the face. The squire hauled his dog down from the dresser and carried him out of the room, also shouting threats of suing Leo and his demon-possessed cat. Mau, the provoking creature, sat placidly on top of the dresser and washed his paw.

"Mau!" Leo growled in an undertone.

Mau paused his washing and looked down at him, his expression imperious as he surveyed the devastation in the room with mild surprise.

"Here, Mau," Leo said, struggling to keep his tone calm.

He needed to defuse this situation as quickly as possible, and he dared not leave Mau loose to cause more chaos. Leo knew, however, that there was more at stake than Mrs Roger's threats to sue him. He and Mau were well known, and it would not take long for the story to get about, nor the news that Mr Leo Hunt and *his wife* had been staying at the inn. He needed to get Vi out of here and a ring on her finger with as much haste as possible. That she might be embarrassed, or her reputation tarnished because of him, made Leo feel rather sick.

Mau finished washing his paw before he deigned to move. Then he leapt sinuously down and wound himself in and out of Leo's ankles, purring. Leo bent and scooped him up, holding on tight. Mau butted his head at Leo's chest, seeking caresses.

"You must be joking," Leo told him frankly. "I am not speaking to you. That was very badly done and I'm exceedingly vexed."

"He's mad!" Mrs Rogers wailed, pressing a large handkerchief to her face as her staff hurried to comfort her. "He talks to the thing like it understands."

One of the serving girls putting a glass of brandy into the woman's hand and guided her to a chair. "I think it does!" Mrs Rogers cried, clutching at the girl's hand in agitation, before taking a large swallow of the brandy.

Leo hurried out to the tilbury where Vi had captured the second dog, bless her, and was instructing one of the ostlers to lock it in a stall until the squire came back for it.

"Leo!" she exclaimed alarm, hurrying over to him. "Whatever happened? People ran from the inn screaming."

"Not now, love," he said tersely. "I need to make reparations and pray no one wishes to sue me as they are threatening to do."

"Oh no," Vi said in dismay. "This is bad, isn't it?"

Leo did not wish to upset her, so he said nothing, only handed Mau into her arms. "Do not let him out of your sight," he replied, his voice firm.

Vi nodded, and Leo hurried back inside to deal with the squire and Mrs Rogers.

Ten minutes later and Leo's pockets were empty of all the money Kitty had given him and he had left his address, so any expenses that the amount did not cover could be paid at a later date. He did not doubt Mrs Roger's china was going to turn out to be some rare variety of porcelain that was nigh on priceless, but he did not care about that. What he could not stop was the gossip.

He was quiet as he drove the tilbury out of the yard and back onto the road. Thankfully, the weather had improved a good deal, and it was a mild day. Glimpses of blue even showed behind the clouds.

Vi reached over and rested her hand on his.

"Don't worry, Leo," she said with a smile. "It will be fine. We'll be married before the end of the day."

"What if anyone looks into the business and discovers we were not wed during our stay there," he asked her frankly.

Vi shrugged. "What if they do? My friends and family will not care a button and, if anyone else minds, they can stop speaking to me with my blessing. I do not care to know such judgemental fools."

Leo could only smile at the superior tone in her voice. He looked at Mau, who had decided it was safer to sleep in Vi's lap for the time being. The two of them were better matched than they knew.

"I'm glad to hear it, love, but I prefer you are caused no embarrassment. I promised I should never bring you trouble, and we've had nothing but."

"I know," Vi said, her lips trembling. There was a tone to her voice that he could not quite read. Was she going to cry, or was she trying to keep her temper?

"What is it?" he asked, frowning.

Vi shook her head and bit her lip.

"No, Vi, out with it. If you're angry with me, I beg you will say so," he demanded, for she had every right to be furious with him.

She turned her wide blue eyes on him. "A-Angry?" she stammered, then burst out laughing. "Oh—! Oh, Leo, you precious fool. I'm n-not angry. This… This is the most fun I've ever had in m-my entire life!"

Leo stared at her, disbelieving for a moment, then he let out a breath of relief and shook his head. "Darling, I would kiss you if I could," he told her frankly, but there were carriages coming in the other direction and he did not wish to heap more scandal down upon them.

He ought not to have been surprised, however, when Vi reached up a hand, catching him around the back of the neck and pulling him down to her. She kissed him soundly, her lovely eyes glittering with mischief and happiness when she finally released him.

His heart gave a series of uneven beats in his chest as he realised how fortunate he was, just how kind the fates had been. It might be his last life, but it was going to be the very best of them all.

Chapter 17

Dearest Cat,

Good heavens, love, don't take a pet. I won't eat him! From all I hear, Felix Knight is a big boy and well able to look after himself. My intentions, as you put them, are entirely honourable, well mostly anyway. I cannot tell you my plans yet, dear friend, but you will discover them in time.

The next time you see your brother, do apologise for me on my father's behalf. I have told him again and again that Ashburton and I will not suit but he refuses to heed me. It was most embarrassing the way he threw the two of us at each other yet again last week.

—Excerpt of a letter from The Lady Belinda Madox-Brown to The Most Hon'ble Catherine 'Cat' St Just, Lady Kilbane (daughter of The Most Hon'ble Lucian and Matilda Montagu, the Marquess and Marchioness of Montagu).

28th June 1850, The Queen's Head, Wrestlingworth, the Bedfordshire, Cambridgeshire border.

Leo threw the reins to the waiting ostler before jumping down from the Tilbury and going around to help Vi. Mau stepped off her lap before she got up, stretching luxuriously before following them inside. Jenny hurried after them and took Mau with her up to their rooms to unpack the case.

"Violetta!"

They looked up once inside to see Kitty hurrying down the stairs towards them, alight with excitement. She glanced from one to the other.

"I have a private parlour, come at once," she said, taking Vi by the hand and towing her bodily along.

Vi cast Leo a look of amused resignation as he followed behind her.

"Norton, have tea and sandwiches brought. Oh, and some cake too," Kitty said, apparently having commandeered Leo's servant in his absence.

Norton disappeared, exchanging a rueful glance with Leo as he went. Kitty sat down and eagerly patted the seat to her right. "Well?" she demanded. "Why were you away so long?"

Leo glanced at Vi, who promptly turned scarlet. Kitty squealed with delight and leaned over, hugging Vi tightly before hurrying to Leo and kissing his cheek.

"Well done!" she said gleefully.

Vi made a choked sound. "Mama!" she reproached Kitty. "You are not supposed to be so delighted when a fellow ruins your daughter."

"Oh, pish!" Kitty said, waving this away. "The two of you are made for each other. I've always known it, even if you did not. Besides, Reverend Harbottle has the special licence and is standing ready. What a dear he is. We had the most delightful time on the journey to town."

"I can imagine," Vi said wryly.

"Kitty, is he at the vicarage now?" Leo asked. "We must be married at once. I'm afraid there was a scene as we left. Mau caused rather a stir and is still in disgrace. I fear the scandal sheets will be full of it."

"How exciting, I cannot wait to hear all about it, but I can do better than that. Reverend Harbottle is already at the church. Papa is here, darling," she said, turning to Vi. "And he and the reverend are getting on famously. Papa has gone to look at the church with him. Apparently, there is an incised slab just inside the door, which he believes may be a memorial to one of Papa's ancestors. Medieval, I think he said," Kitty added vaguely.

"Then do you think we can be married today?" Leo asked.

Kitty beamed and nodded at him. "I am certain you can. What's more, you even have a best man."

Leo frowned, looking confused. "What do you mean?"

"Larkin is here. He was so intrigued by your letter that he followed me down here. He's in the taproom, I think."

Leo snorted. "Of course he is." He got up and took Vi's hand, kissing her fingers. "If you'll excuse me, I'll leave you to your tea and sandwiches. I'll be with Larkin until you are ready to go to the church."

Vi nodded, smiling up into Leo's face. "I won't be long," she assured him.

Kitty gave her a critical once over. "Indeed, that is a splendid gown, Vi. I have never seen you look more beautiful."

Leo could not resist a smug grin as he left the room, for it was one of the gowns he had chosen for her.

As he made his way along to the taproom, he was not entirely surprised to hear laughter and the sounds of merriment. Leo stepped through the door and discovered Larkin at one of the tables, a pint of ale at his elbow, a cigar in his mouth and cards in his hand. He had evidently got up a game with some of the locals. To Leo's relief, he noticed Larkin was only playing for small stakes, for he was an excellent player and could easily trounce the entire village if the mood took him.

"Leo!" Larkin leapt to his feet, embracing Leo warmly and clapping him on the shoulder. "You devil! I came all the way down here to see what you were about, only to find you gone. Happily, Kitty was here, so she explained all," he added, waggling his eyebrows.

"Sorry to have missed you," Leo replied, shaking his head with amusement as shouts of disapproval and impatient mutterings came from the other players. "It seems you have not been too bored."

"Yes, yes, I'm coming," Larkin said, sitting back down. "I'm never bored, Leo. Want a hand?"

Leo shook his head. "No, but I need you, so hurry up and finish that, would you?"

Larkin grinned. "Anything for you, old man."

Leo sighed and ordered himself a pint and something to eat and waited for his friend to finish his game.

Half an hour later, the two men were sat in a quiet corner making their way through a large pile of ham and pickle sandwiches.

"So, she finally gave in," Larkin said, regarding Leo with a smile. "Congratulations. I'm happy for you. It's about time."

Leo nodded, watching his friend closely. Larkin had gone off the rails for a while, drinking far too much and spending half his time hanging around with people who were as likely to murder him as buy him a drink, and the other half working all hours like a maniac. More recently, he seemed in good spirits, still working and playing hard, but drinking less and laughing more. Larkin had always been rather more romantic and sensitive than the rest of them and had been badly hurt by the woman he'd fallen in love with, who had been less than honest with him. Leo hoped he had put that behind him and was ready to move on, but he felt there was much Larkin wasn't saying.

"Thank you, though I'm praying the debacle in Newmarket doesn't come back to haunt us," he said with a sigh. "If anyone asks, we were married before we left and were on our honeymoon."

"Of course. You may rely on me to put things straight," Larkin said, nodding gravely. "She's a lovely woman, Leo. You'll be happy, I'm certain of it."

"So am I," Leo replied. "But what of you, Larkin? What are you up to these days?"

"Oh, this and that, here and there," Larkin said with a laugh. "I've just finished a marvellous painting. Best thing I've done in an age. Going to submit it for the Academy exhibition," he added, and Leo got the impression he was keen to change the subject.

"That's good. You've not been seen in society for a long time, though. Are you—"

"Another?" Larkin said, getting up and holding his empty glass aloft.

Leo sighed, nodding. Larkin clearly did not wish to talk, and he was not about to force the issue. All he wanted from this day was to marry Vi and make her his wife. He only hoped she would be ready soon.

Vi regarded the mirror Jenny held up, turning this way and that to admire her hair. It had been rather squashed by her bonnet and the journey and Jenny had redone it for the occasion.

"Oh, Jenny, it looks splendid, thank you."

"You're welcome." Jenny beamed. "I was going to go to the garden and pinch some rosebuds, but then I thought we'd best not draw attention to the fact you're not already married."

Vi laughed and nodded. "A lovely thought, Jenny, but yes, you are quite correct. However, I feel far more like a bride with my hair done so prettily."

"You look wonderful," Jenny said, smoothing out the fabric of Vi's gown.

It was the golden yellow walking dress that Leo had liked so much, and such a sunny colour it made Vi feel happy simply wearing it. Whenever she remembered his words, when he'd first seen her wearing it, she could not keep the smile from her face.

"I have something else for you, though."

Vi turned back to Jenny, who grinned and revealed a small posy of white roses. "I'll keep them hidden until we get to the church, but you can't get married with no flowers."

"Oh, how sweet of you! Thank you, Jenny," Vi said gratefully. "I'm so pleased to have you as my maid."

"Not half so pleased as I am," Jenny replied with a snort. "Now then, we'd best get going or that man of yours will think you've done a runner."

Vi laughed, happier than she could ever remember being, as she made her way down the stairs. Kitty was waiting for her, beaming happily.

"So beautiful, my darling daughter," Kitty said, taking her hands and blinking rapidly.

"Mama! Don't cry. It's not supposed to be a special occasion, remember?" Vi said, glancing around to see if any of the other guests had noticed.

"Sorry, sorry, yes, I know. I shall save my tears for the church," Kitty said at once, instantly repentant. "I sent word to

Papa and Harbottle to stay at the church so all should be ready," she added in an undertone.

Vi nodded, suddenly nervous, as she realised she really would be Mrs Hunt in a very short time. She drew in a breath, feeling her heart thud. Kitty gave her a sceptical look.

"You're not changing your mind?"

Vi laughed and shook her head. "Indeed, I am not. Just a little nervous."

Kitty snorted. "I don't know why, for you've done the bit most brides fret over."

"Mama!" Vi murmured, blushing rosily.

Kitty smirked. "Come along. Leo and Larkin are already there. I sent them ahead half an hour ago, for Larkin appeared a deal too cosy in the taproom. We might never have winkled him out otherwise."

Vi nodded, relieved to know Leo was already at the church. She followed her mama out to the waiting carriage and sat down beside her.

By the time they got to the church, Vi's nerves had fled. Mama was right after all, she reflected with amusement. What was there to be nervous about? She was marrying the man she had loved all her life, safe in the knowledge that he would not be the reckless fool she had feared him to be, and yet neither would he be dull or chafe at restrictions she felt she must place on him. Instead, they would have fun and many adventures, and they would have them together, and whilst she still feared he might regret not having children if she failed to produce them, she did not believe he would ever hold it against her or love her less.

When they arrived at the church, Vi found her father waiting for her.

"Luke, isn't she beautiful?" Kitty said, hurrying down from the carriage with a rustle of flamboyant blue silk as she ran to embrace her husband. Papa kissed his wife firmly, his arm going around her waist and squeezing before he looked up at Vi.

"Indeed, she is, Kitty. More beautiful than I ever remember seeing before. It must be because she is happy. You *are* happy, love?" he asked Vi, releasing Kitty and holding out his arms to her.

Vi ran to him, and he embraced her warmly. This man had been a father to her from the moment she lost her own and, whilst he was a quiet soul, he had been a strong and steadfast presence in her life, one to be relied upon.

"I am, Papa," she told him sincerely. "I am so very happy."

"Then let us go in and witness the beginning of your new life," he said, holding out his arm. "Kitty, you had best go ahead, love. I shall bring her in on my arm."

Kitty gave a squeal of excitement and then hesitated, turning to Jenny, who was dithering by the carriage. "Well, come along, my dear. Norton is inside too. You don't want to miss it, do you?"

"Oh! No, my lady," Jenny said with a gasp, and hurried after Kitty as fast as she could.

Vi laughed and turned back to look up at her father. "I'm so happy you are here," she said sincerely. "Only I now realise how sad Leo must be not to have his own parents here," she added with a frown.

"They are here," he told her with a smile. "Your mama sent for them when she returned to town. They arrived half an hour ago. We also asked them if they wished for Bella to be here too, but they said we would never keep it quiet if Bainbridge was anywhere in the vicinity."

"No, indeed!" Vi said, laughing, and so she was still as she walked into the church.

She met Leo's gaze and saw his eyes twinkling with amusement and knew that their lives would be full of laughter if he had anything to do with it.

They stood before the Reverend Harbottle, who beamed down at them, his expression one of delight as he regarded them both.

"Dearly beloved," he began, sounding as if he truly meant it.

The service was short and sweet and once more they had Kitty to thank, for she'd had the forethought to provide a gold ring for the occasion. Vi almost cried when she realised it was her own mother's ring and had to abandon the ceremony for a moment to hug Kitty for the wonderful thought.

Then it was time to sign the register. Leo signed first, then Violetta signed her name for the last time as a single lady. She paused as she looked down to where the Reverend Harbottle had filled in the date of their marriage on the certificate.

"I'm sorry, it's rather messy," he said with apparent regret. "The pen splotched, and it looks for all the world like it says the twenty-fourth and not the twenty-eighth, does it not?"

He gave her such a look of innocence that Vi gave a bark of laughter.

Leo stepped forward and took the man's hand, shaking it warmly. "Thank you, reverend, I shall never cease to be grateful to you."

Harbottle grinned wider still, looking exceptionally pleased with himself. "I cannot tell you how happy I am to have been of help. I believe my wife will be proud of me this day, for she was a romantic soul. I'm sure she is looking down upon us and smiling."

"I'm very certain she is," Leo said. "And as for the roof you're needing, get it done and send me the bill."

Harbottle's mouth fell open, and he gaped at Leo. "B-But Mr Hunt, I… I hope you do not believe that I… for one moment did any of this in the hopes o-of—"

"No, reverend, I certainly do not," Leo said, patting his shoulder. "Which is why I shall be pleased to help you in any way I can. You need only ask."

The reverend sighed, shaking his head in wonder. "And my god will supply every need of yours according to his riches in glory in Christ Jesus," he said serenely.

Leo was about to turn back to Vi and escort his new wife from the church when Harbottle spoke again.

"I don't suppose you're looking for a country house, are you?"

Leo looked to Vi, who answered for him. "Here?"

Harbottle nodded. "One reason the church is in such a state of disrepair is that it sits on private land. It belonged to a noble family, but the last heir never married and there was no one to take it on when he died. The house is hidden behind the trees, but it has been abandoned for over a decade. It's a beautiful place, a very fine house and just the sort of place newlyweds might like to raise a family," he added hopefully.

Leo laughed. "Then we shall certainly take a look at it, sir. Thank you."

"Thank you, Mr Hunt, Mrs Hunt, and I wish you many, many years of joy to come, wherever that may be."

Whilst he knew Vi regretted they could not all celebrate together, Leo was not entirely sorry to wave their parents and Larkin away, back off to town. He'd been more than happy to see his parents in the church and grateful to Kitty for organising it, for his mother would have been devastated not to have been present when he finally shook off his bachelor status. As the eldest of his peers, she had despaired of him. At least he was free of her nagging him to find a wife. He knew too that Kitty was itching to organise some grand party to celebrate their nuptials soon.

He stood with Vi in the churchyard, her hand on his arm as their parents' carriages turned a corner and disappeared. He looked down at her, finding her smiling up at him. She looked happy.

Pride glowed inside him as he realised he had done that. *He* had made her happy, made her smile.

"I like it here," he said, looking up and regarding the small churchyard.

The birds were singing, and the sun beat down warmly on his face. The church was not a fine one by any means, with nothing much to recommend it save its age and its vicar. Yet the place had a warm, friendly air about it, and they were close to Cambridge, with all its commerce and links to the city.

Vi nodded. "I do too," she said thoughtfully. "Leo, might we just take a quick look at the house before we return to the hotel?"

Leo laughed, having half expected as much. He was eager to give his wife a proper wedding night despite having spent the past three days in bed with her, but he too was curious to see the house of which Harbottle had spoken. The vicar had shown them a private path that led from the church to the house, for the gates to the main driveway were locked.

"Just quickly," Vi added, apparently reading his mind as her cheeks turned pink.

Leo bent and kissed her cheek. "Anything for you, love, but don't be shocked if I ravish you among the ruins if you take too long."

He leered at her, and she gave a little shriek and hurried along the path ahead of him. Leo laughed and then turned back to see Norton and Jenny standing side by side and grinning inanely. Leo smiled at them.

"We're going to see the house Harbottle told us about. You two go back to the inn We'll be along in a while," he said, and hurried after Vi.

"Don't do anything I wouldn't, sir," Norton called after him, cheeky blighter. Leo snorted, hearing their soft laughter follow him along the path.

Chapter 18

Dearest Leo,

I had a letter from Mama this morning. Congratulations, brother dear! I am in alt and so happy you finally won your lady. Bainbridge is crowing, naturally, for he puts it all down to his advice. I warn you if you have a son, he fully expects it to be named in his honour.

I beg you will come and see us as soon as you may. I promise we shall give you a private wing and keep our brats from your hair for at least half the time you are here. I so long to spend some time with my new sister. I know Vi, of course, but not as well as I should like, and I would love to get to know her better. Much love to you both, Leo, if you are half as happy as I am with my darling Bainbridge, you will have a wonderful life indeed.

—Excerpt of a letter from The Most Hon'ble Arabella Grenville, The Marchioness of Bainbridge, to her brother, Mr Leo Hunt. (children of Alice and Nathaniel Hunt).

28th June 1850, Fairhaven, Tadlow, Cambridgeshire.

"Mind, darling," Leo said, lifting a branch from the overgrown path so Vi could duck under it. Thankfully, the warm weather had dried the ground since the downpour, or the long grass would have soaked them. As it was, it made the going somewhat tricky with Vi's voluminous skirts. Still, she was determined to see the house, so see it they would.

Eventually, the path ended at a gate and Leo forced it open, wincing as the hinges shrieked in complaint.

"Oh, Leo!"

Leo looked up at Vi's exclamation, following her gaze towards the building in the middle distance.

The house glowed in the sunlight, the mellow golden stone warm and the many windows glinting. It was a Jacobean style manor house and Leo only had to glance at Vi to know she had fallen irrevocably in love. He could not blame her, for whilst he saw the roof was in a state of disrepair and there was ivy scrambling up the walls in all directions, the setting was idyllic and the house so romantically beautiful it would have been a crime to turn his back on it.

He turned to stare at Vi, who was standing with her hands pressed to her heart, her eyes alight with a look of such excitement that his own heart gave a hard thud in sympathy.

"Well, love, what do you think?" he asked, already knowing the answer.

She turned to him, her lovely face full of hope. "I never saw anything so lovely in all my days," she breathed.

"It's a good deal smaller than Trevick Castle," he pointed out in amusement.

"Oh, fiddle. As if I care for that. Trevick is splendid but I don't have the slightest desire for such an enormous property."

"I am relieved to hear it," Leo said amiably, earning himself a look of exasperation from Vi.

"Don't tease, Leo. You know I do not care a button for such grand properties, only… only I *do* love this house. I—" Vi bit her lip, her expression becoming serious. "I suppose it would take a vast sum of money to restore it, though."

"Oh, vast indeed," Leo said, trying his best not to smile.

Vi nodded sadly. "It would be a great investment, not only of money but of time."

"It would," he agreed.

She sighed, and then gave a squeal as Leo swept her up into his arms. "Darling idiot," he said fondly. "Did you never think to enquire as to your husband's finances?"

"Of course not," she said indignantly. "My dowry is a generous one, I know, so I did not fear for our future, but I married you because… because I love you, Leo. Not for any other reason."

Leo's face softened, and he set her carefully down before pulling her into his embrace. "I love you too, Vi, and if this house is what you want, then you shall have it." He put a finger to her mouth to silence any protests. "For your information, love, I'm the major shareholder in the Sons of Hades, which is actually becoming a profitable club at last. Surprising as we only began it as a lark. More importantly, I also have a hand in Hunter's," he added, naming the famously exclusive club his father had run for decades.

"Oh," Vi said, her eyes widening. "I knew about your club, naturally, but I suppose I never stopped to consider you had a hand in Hunter's. It's profitable then, your share?"

Leo laughed and kissed her nose. "Obscenely," he said, with no little pride. "And I shall throw a good deal of it at this house and make it the home of your dreams, if that would please you, Vi?"

"It would please me greatly to live in this beautiful place with you, Leo, so long as it pleases you too."

"It does," he said solemnly. "And so do you. Come along, wife. Let us explore a little closer."

They spent a good hour investigating the grounds and peering in through dirty windows. To Leo's relief, the house seemed solid and in much better repair than he'd feared at first glance. No doubt there were disasters enough waiting to be unearthed, but he did not think it would take too long to bring it back to its former glory.

"Oh, Leo, look! Come here!"

Leo had been trying to make out if the plaster was falling off the ceiling in what appeared to be a formal salon, but he turned to see Vi disappearing through a small door in a walled part of the garden. Smiling, he followed her.

The intoxicating scent of roses enveloped him as he entered, and Leo gasped when he discovered what Vi had seen. It was a small square garden, intimate, with climbing roses scrambling madly up walls and over arches. A large fountain sat in the centre, dry and filled with debris now, but he could imagine the sound of the water falling, the sun sparkling upon it. There were benches on three sides around the fountain, but on the fourth was a small patch of green.

"It's a chamomile lawn," Vi said, bending to touch her hands to the little white flowers, rubbing them gently and raising her fingers to her nose to inhale the sweet, green scent. "A bit overgrown, but it's still here."

Leo walked over and shrugged off his coat, laying it on the springy green surface and sitting down. He held out his hand to her. "Join me?"

Vi did as he asked, settling herself on his coat.

"I can almost see the fountain, hear the water falling," she said with a sigh, echoing his earlier thoughts.

Leo nodded. "It's beautiful," he said, turning to look at her. "I want to live here with you, Vi."

The smile that dawned upon her beautiful face was as lovely as a sunrise and filled his heart with such emotion he wondered how his chest could contain it. Thank God she was his and thank the Reverend Harbottle for doing whatever he had done to change her mind. Leo could not imagine his life without her in it now, or what he might have done if she had not married him.

"Yes, please," she said softly.

Leo reached for her and pulled her into his arms. "I want everything, Vi. I want it all. Now, and for every day to follow. I want to make you happy, to live here with you, to take you abroad and to places you've never been, places that will shock and surprise you and change the way you think about the world. I want every day, every hour, every moment with you, love."

Vi blinked, her eyes rather too bright. "Is that all?" she said, sounding somewhat breathless.

"No," Leo said gravely, easing her down to lie upon his coat. He stared down at her, happiness a warm weight in his chest. "Not even close," he whispered, before pressing his lips to hers.

She reached up, arms coiling around his neck while he kissed her tenderly and then with growing passion as his hands slid over her slender curves. She was pliant beneath him, all eager willingness and Leo thought his heart might burst with an intoxicating mixture of love and desire. His hand closed over her breast and squeezed, but suddenly Vi shoved at him.

Startled, Leo moved back at once, wondering what he'd done wrong, only to find Vi pushing him down. Watching, open-mouthed, Leo regarded his new wife with fascinated awe as she hitched up her skirts and petticoats, giving him a splendid view of her stocking clad legs, before she climbed over him, straddling his hips.

"Vi!" he croaked, certain he meant to say something other than that but whatever it had been disappeared from his brain as she settled her weight upon him. His arousal twitched in anticipation as the warmth of her pressed firmly against him.

She shifted back, and he regretted the loss of contact until he saw her elegant fingers undoing the buttons on his trousers.

"Oh God," he murmured, before adding silently, *thank you, thank you, thank you God.*

Leo watched the intent expression on his wife's face as she released him from the confines of his trousers and small clothes and stroked. He swallowed a groan, throwing an arm over his eyes and praying for deliverance as she tortured him with slow, decadent strokes from her slender hands. When she finally moved back into place, easing him inside her body, where he was welcomed into her lush, feminine heat, Leo was ready to lose his mind.

"Love you," he managed, his voice hoarse with a combination of desperation and adoration as he thrust into her.

Vi's soft laughter tickled his ear as she bent down to kiss him. "Love you too," she whispered, and they spent a good deal of time proving the words to each other, as the scent of the chamomile lawn and the rich perfume of the roses blended on the warm air of a perfect summer's afternoon.

Epilogue

Three years later…

Dearest Aunt Matilda,

Thank you so much for the gifts you sent for our new arrival. I do hope you will come and visit us soon. The house is finally finished and whilst it has been a labour of love, we are more than content with the results. I do not believe Vi will ever "finish" the garden, which she has become enamoured of, but the results are quite spectacular, and it is a place I never tire of spending time in.

Bella and Bainbridge and their horde are coming to stay with us, arriving today and so Mau and I are spending the last blissful moments of peace in my study before all hell lets loose.

—Excerpt of a letter from Mr Leo Hunt (son of Alice and Nathaniel Hunt) to his aunt, The Most Hon'ble Matilda Barrington, The Marchioness of Montagu).

5th August 1853, Fairhaven House, Tadlow, Cambridgeshire.

"Well, he's a handsome fellow," Bainbridge said, gazing down at the tiny babe in his arms. "Takes after Vi, obviously."

"Obviously," Leo said wryly.

"May I hold the baby, Father?"

Bainbridge looked down at his son and heir, Aurelius, the Earl of Clivedon. He was eight years old now, with the same deep auburn hair as his father and a light scatter of freckles over his nose. Leo frowned, a little anxious to see his infant son passed into the boy's hands. Bainbridge noticed and gave a soft laugh.

"Don't fret, Papa. Aurelius here has had plenty of practice with babies."

Leo snorted. Well, that was true enough. Bainbridge and Bella's seventh child, Winnie, was only three months old. So, he watched as Bainbridge carefully handed Charles Nathaniel Hunt into Aurelius's arms. He and Vi had named the child after both their fathers, but Charlie seemed to be the name he would answer to among the family.

"Oh, Leo, it's such a beautiful house! I love everything you've both done to it, though I know Vi must have chosen most of the furnishings, for she has such exquisite taste."

Leo and Bainbridge looked up as Bella came into the room with Vi, followed by a trail of children and nursemaids. Leo laughed softly at the sight. Only two of the eight were his and Vi's: twin girls called Beatrice and Evelyn.

"I have excellent taste," he replied indignantly.

"In gowns for your wife, I grant you. Furnishings, not so much," Bella replied firmly.

Leo sighed and his eyes met Vi's as she came into the room. His heart still lightened at the sight of her. He smiled, seeing the expression reflected at him as his wife carried little Bea into his waiting arms. His daughter looked ruffled and sleepy, having just woken from a nap. She wrapped her chubby arms around Leo's neck and clung tightly, resting her head on his shoulder. Leo kissed the silken blonde curls atop her head and cuddled the child to him. Kissing his cheek, Vi went to take an equally bleary Evelyn from her nurse and sit down with her.

Bainbridge walked over to Leo, regarding him holding his daughter.

"It's terrifying, isn't it?"" Bainbridge mused, gently reaching out a large hand to stroke the girl's hair. "They're so precious, so fragile and so very loved, and they look to us for everything, to keep them safe. Then they go out and fall down and out of trees and catch disgusting diseases and do everything they can to scare us half to death. Yet we'd not change it for the world."

Leo smiled. Whilst he had always regarded Bainbridge as an amiable lunatic, there was no denying he'd been a surprisingly wonderful father and a devoted husband to Bella.

"That about sums it up," Leo agreed.

Bainbridge nodded and then looked down as one of his daughters tugged at his hand. Rayne had red hair a shade lighter than her mother's but looked set to be every bit as lovely.

"Papa," she said urgently. "Ava!"

Apparently, this was enough to have Bainbridge on alert. "Where?"

Rayne pointed and Leo looked across the room to see five-year-old Ava climbing up the bookshelves. She'd attained quite a height already and Leo's heart jolted with anxiety. Bainbridge said not a word, only moved. He was astonishingly quick for such a large man, but Leo suspected he'd had a good deal of practice. A moment later, he had crossed the room and plucked the child from the shelves. He set her down on the floor, bending down low until he could look her in the eyes.

"No!" he said succinctly, wagging a finger at her.

Ava put a finger in her mouth and sucked, looking back at the shelves wistfully. "Up there." She took the finger from her mouth and pointed.

Bainbridge shook his head, scowling and attempting to look formidable. Strange, for he *was* formidable if you were an adult; small children, however, could wrap him about their fingers.

"No, Ava," he repeated.

Ava pouted. "Want to go up!" she said forcefully.

Bainbridge sighed and got to his knees. "If you go up there," he said carefully. "You will fall down here, with a bump, and you will cry, and then Papa will cry because you are hurt."

Ava considered this. She patted her father's shoulder gently. "Don't cry, Papa," she said, and walked away from the shelves, no doubt to find some other way of turning her father's hair grey.

Bainbridge got to his feet and went to rejoin Leo. The noise in the room was becoming quite deafening and Leo wondered at his son still sleeping peacefully in Aurelius's arms. The boy's twin sister, Marie-Ann, had come to sit beside him and reached over, stroking Charlie's downy head.

"Nicely done," Leo said with a smile.

Bainbridge snorted. "That one gives me nightmares. We're a nursemaid short because of that little devil. I'm thinking of locking her up until she's forty. I dread to think what kind of young woman she'll be when— *Ava!* Ava, don't do that!"

Leo jumped and Bea clung to him tighter as Bainbridge's voice bellowed across the room.

"Excuse me," Bainbridge said with a sigh and hurried off.

Bella came to stand next to him and leaned in to kiss her niece. Bea smiled at her auntie but did not let go of Leo's neck.

"Fatherhood suits you," his sister told him with approval. "I've never seen you look so well."

Leo snorted. "I can't think why, I've not slept in weeks! Vi refuses to let the nursemaids see to the babies at night."

"I never could, either. Well, until we had the second set of twins," Bella admitted. "I had to give in then or I'd never have survived. But you do look well, Leo. Yes, tired, I can see that, but you're happy, settled."

Leo nodded at his sister. "I am, Bella. I'm happier than any fellow has the right to be, I think. I'm a lucky dog."

"You've every right to be happy, brother dear," Bella said affectionately, leaning into him. "But you *are* a lucky dog. I hope you remember to say such things to your wife at regular intervals. We need to hear such things often, especially in the months after having a baby."

"I know that," Leo said in exasperation. "Honestly, Bella, you and Bainbridge think I'm a complete fool."

Bella laughed at that, shaking her head. "We think nothing of the sort, but I became used to fretting over you when you were forever out doing reckless things, and it is a hard habit to break."

Leo frowned, never having considered that his sister had been as worried for him as his mother and Vi had been. He looked down at Bea in his arms, at Evelyn cuddled with her mother, and at his baby son, sleeping peacefully. What if they grew up and indulged in mad curricle races and leaping off cliffs into the sea, and boxing matches? Whilst it was unlikely his daughters might do such rash things, his son might well hear of his father's exploits and decide to follow suit. Leo felt the colour leave his face in a rush.

Bella chuckled, a soft sound, part amusement, part pity. He turned to see her watching him with interest. "I think the penny has finally dropped," she said with a smile, patting his arm. "My work here is done."

Leo let out a shaky breath as Vi got to her feet now Evelyn had woken up and gone to play with her cousins. "What's wrong?" she asked him in concern.

"It's just occurred to me how much worry I caused my parents and sister, and you," he added, staring across at Charlie. "What if our son decides to be as stupidly reckless as I was?"

Vi shrugged, sliding her hand through his arm. "Then you will teach him the difference between skill and recklessness, and we shall love him and worry over him and guide him the best we can. If he is anything like his father, he will learn the lessons life has to give and be a wonderful man of whom we will both be very proud."

Leo smiled ruefully and leaned over to kiss Vi.

"I think, for all my exploits and ridiculous adventures, you are the bravest of the two of us, for you loved me despite the pain I caused you."

"Not pain, never that," Vi said softly. "Only fear. And I was not brave enough, Leo, not until you reminded me of the girl I really was."

"The girl I love," he murmured, gazing at her and wondering if anyone would notice if he escaped with his wife for a couple of hours and left the children with his sister and Bainbridge and the army of nursemaids.

"*Miaow!*"

Leo looked down to see a large pair of yellow eyes glaring at him accusingly.

"Oh, Mau, darling. What happened to you?" Vi exclaimed, scooping the cat up into her arms and untying the dozens of colourful ribbons that had been tied about his middle.

"Ava," Leo guessed with a sigh.

"Poor darling," Vi crooned.

The big cat preened and purred loudly as she stroked his head.

"Perhaps Mau needs to be taken somewhere quiet—*for a lie down,*" Leo suggested nonchalantly.

Vi shrugged. "I expect he just wants to go out and—*oh,*" she said, suddenly understanding as she noticed the frantic waggling of Leo's eyebrows. "Oh, yes. Yes, I'm sure all this noise is too much for him," she said gravely.

"Bea, darling, do you want to play with Evelyn and Leona?" Leo asked his daughter.

Bea nodded and wriggled so Leo put her down, watching as she toddled over to examine the building blocks with which her sister and cousin were playing.

"Quick, while they're distracted," Leo hissed, taking Vi's hand and dragging her from the room.

"That's a dirty trick!" Bainbridge called after them. "Wish I'd thought of it," he grumbled as Leo closed the door on the chaos.

Vi laughed and set Mau down. The cat trotted away towards the front door. Leo pulled Vi into his arms and kissed her.

"Time for our afternoon nap," he told her firmly.

"Do we take naps?" Vi asked, laughing as he towed her towards the stairs.

"We do now. I cannot think why I never thought of it before. But we'd best hurry, or the two of us might really fall asleep."

Vi gave a snort and ran up the stairs ahead of him, her skirts held high, giving him a glimpse of her lovely ankles. Leo grinned, suddenly not nearly so tired as he had been, and set off in pursuit. Life with Vi was everything he'd known it would be, and so much more. He really was a lucky dog… or perhaps, he amended with a snort, the luckiest cat with nine lives.

independence is something she will not consider. Having tasted success writing under a false name in The Lady's Weekly Review, her alter ego is attaining notoriety and fame, and Prue rather likes it.

A Duty that must be endured

Robert Adolphus, The Duke of Bedwin, is in no hurry to marry, he's done it once and repeating that disaster is the last thing he desires. Yet, an heir is a necessary evil for a duke and one he cannot shirk. A dark reputation precedes him though, his first wife may have died young, but the scandals the beautiful, vivacious and spiteful creature supplied the ton have not. A wife must be found. A wife who is neither beautiful or vivacious but sweet and dull, and certain to stay out of trouble.

Dared to do something drastic

The sudden interest of a certain dastardly duke is as bewildering as it is unwelcome. She'll not throw her ambitions aside to marry a scoundrel just as her plans for self-sufficiency and freedom are coming to fruition. Surely showing the man she's not actually the meek little wallflower he is looking for should be enough to put paid to his intentions? When Prue is dared by her friends to do something drastic, it seems the perfect opportunity to kill two birds.

However, Prue cannot help being intrigued by the rogue who has inspired so many of her romances. Ordinarily, he plays the part of handsome rake, set on destroying her plucky heroine. But is he really the villain of the piece this time, or could he be the hero?

Finding out will be dangerous, but it just might inspire her greatest story yet.

To Dare a Duke

From the author of the bestselling Girls Who Dare Series – An exciting new series featuring the children of the Girls Who Dare...

The stories of the **Peculiar Ladies Book Club** and their hatful of dares has become legend among their children. When the hat is rediscovered, dusty and forlorn, the remaining dares spark a series of events that will echo through all the families... and their **Daring Daughters**

Dare to be Wicked
Daring Daughters Book One

Two daring daughters ...

Lady Elizabeth and Lady Charlotte are the daughters of the Duke and Duchess of Bedwin. Raised by an unconventional mother and an indulgent, if overprotective father, they both strain against the rigid morality of the era.

The fashionable image of a meek, weak young lady, prone to swooning at the least provocation, is one that makes them seethe with frustration.

Their handsome childhood friend ...

Cassius Cadogen, Viscount Oakley, is the only child of the Earl and Countess St Clair. Beloved and indulged, he is popular, gloriously handsome, and a talented artist.

Returning from two years of study in France, his friendship with both sisters becomes strained as jealousy raises its head. A situation not helped by the two mysterious Frenchmen who have accompanied him home.

And simmering sibling rivalry ...

Passion, art, and secrets prove to be a combustible combination, and someone will undoubtedly get burned.

Dare to be Wicked

Also check out Emma's regency romance series, Rogues &
Gentlemen. Available now!

The Rogue
Rogues & Gentlemen Book 1

The notorious Rogue that began it all.

Set in Cornwall, 1815. Wild, untamed and isolated.

Lawlessness is the order of the day and smuggling is rife.

Henrietta always felt most at home in the wilds of the outdoors
but even she had no idea how the mysterious and untamed would
sweep her away in a moment.

Bewitched by his wicked blue eyes

Henrietta Morton knows to look the other way when the free
trading 'gentlemen' are at work.
Yet when a notorious pirate bursts into her local village shop, she

239

can avert her eyes no more. Bewitched by his wicked blue eyes, a moment of insanity follows as Henrietta hides the handsome fugitive from the Militia.

Her reward is a kiss, lingering and unforgettable.

In his haste to flee, the handsome pirate drops a letter, a letter that lays bare a tale of betrayal. When Henrietta's father gives her hand in marriage to a wealthy and villainous nobleman in return for the payment of his debts, she becomes desperate.

Blackmailing a pirate may be her only hope for freedom.

**** **Warning**: This book contains the most notorious rogue of all of Cornwall and, on occasion, is highly likely to include some mild sweating or descriptive sex scenes. ****

Free to read on *Kindle Unlimited*: The Rogue

Interested in a Regency Romance with a twist?

A Dog in a Doublet
The Regency Romance Mysteries Book 2

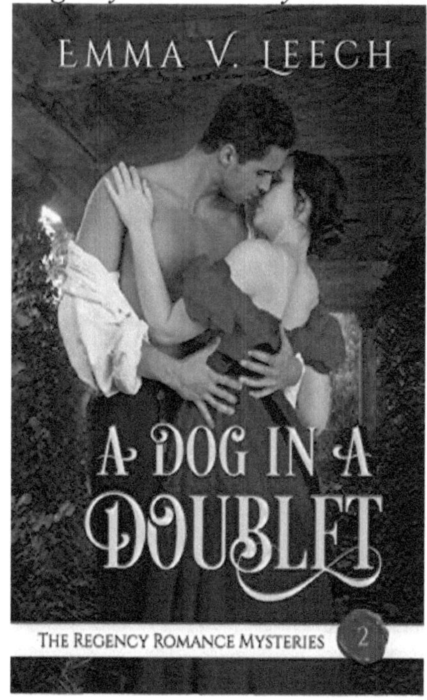

A man with a past

Harry Browning was a motherless guttersnipe, and the morning he came across the elderly Alexander Preston, The Viscount Stamford, clinging to a sheer rock face he didn't believe in fate. But the fates have plans for Harry whether he believes or not, and he's not entirely sure he likes them.

As a reward for his bravery, and in an unusual moment of charity, miserly Lord Stamford takes him on. He is taught to read, to manage the vast and crumbling estate, and to behave like a gentleman, but Harry knows that is something he will never truly be

Already running from a dark past, his future is becoming increasingly complex as he finds himself caught in a tangled web of jealousy and revenge.

A feisty young maiden

Temptation, in the form of the lovely Miss Clarinda Bow, is a constant threat to his peace of mind, enticing him to be something he isn't. But when the old man dies his will makes a surprising demand, and the fates might just give Harry the chance to have everything he ever desired, including Clara, if only he dares.

And as those close to the Preston family begin to die, Harry may not have any choice.

Order your copy here. A Dog in a Doublet

Lose yourself in Emma's paranormal world with The French Vampire Legend series….

The Key to Erebus
The French Vampire Legend Book 1

The truth can kill you.

Taken away as a small child, from a life where vampires, the Fae, and other mythical creatures are real and treacherous, the beautiful young witch, Jéhenne Corbeaux is totally unprepared when she returns to rural France to live with her eccentric Grandmother.

Thrown headlong into a world she knows nothing about she seeks to learn the truth about herself, uncovering secrets more shocking than anything she could ever have imagined and finding that she is by no means powerless to protect the ones she loves.

Despite her Gran's dire warnings, she is inexorably drawn to the dark and terrifying figure of Corvus, an ancient vampire and master of the vast Albinus family.

Jéhenne is about to find her answers and discover that, not only is Corvus far more dangerous than she could ever imagine, but that he holds much more than the key to her heart …

Now available at your favourite retailer.

The Key to Erebus

Check out Emma's exciting fantasy series with hailed by Kirkus Reviews as "An enchanting fantasy with a likable heroine, romantic intrigue, and clever narrative flourishes."

The Dark Prince
The French Fae Legend Book 1

Two Fae Princes
One Human Woman
And a world ready to tear them all apart

Laen Braed is Prince of the Dark fae, with a temper and reputation to match his black eyes, and a heart that despises the human race. When he is sent back through the forbidden gates between realms to retrieve an ancient fae artifact, he returns home with far more than he bargained for.

Corin Albrecht, the most powerful Elven Prince ever born. His golden eyes are rumoured to be a gift from the gods, and destiny is calling him. With a love for the human world that runs deep, his friendship with Laen is being torn apart by his prejudices.

Océane DeBeauvoir is an artist and bookbinder who has always relied on her lively imagination to get her through an unhappy and uneventful life. A jewelled dagger put on display at a nearby museum hits the headlines with speculation of another race, the Fae. But the discovery also inspires Océane to create an extraordinary piece of art that cannot be confined to the pages of a book.

With two powerful men vying for her attention and their friendship stretched to the breaking point, the only question that remains...who is truly The Dark Prince.

The man of your dreams is coming...or is it your nightmares he visits? Find out in Book One of The French Fae Legend.

Available now to read at your favourite retailer

The Dark Prince

Want more Emma?

If you enjoyed this book, please support this indie author and take a moment to leave a few words in a review. *Thank you!*

To be kept informed of special offers and free deals (which I do regularly) follow me on *https://www.bookbub.com/authors/emma-v-leech*

To find out more and to get news and sneak peeks of the first chapter of upcoming works, go to my website and sign up for the newsletter.
http://www.emmavleech.com/

Or follow me here......

http://viewauthor.at/EmmaVLeechAmazon